Kelley Armstrong lives in rural Ontario with her husband, three children and far too many pets. She is the author of the supernatural 'Women of the Otherworld' series and a new crime series involving a female assassin. *The Summoning* is the first book in her young adult trilogy, 'The Darkest Power'.

Also by Kelley Armstrong

the Summoning

KELLEY ARMSTRONG

sphere

SPHERE

First published in Great Britain in 2008 by Sphere

A CIP catalogue record for this book
is available from the British Library.

ISBN 978-1-84149-710-5

Printed and bound in Great Britain by
Clays Ltd, St Ives

Sphere
An imprint of
Little, Brown Book Group
100 Victoria Embankment
London EC4Y 0DY

An Hachette Livre UK Company
www.hachettelivre.co.uk

www.littlebrown.co.uk

the Summoning

twelve years earlier . . .

MOMMY FORGOT TO WARN the new babysitter about the basement.

Chloe teetered on the top step, chubby hands reaching up to clutch both railings, her arms shaking so much she could barely hang on. Her legs shook, too, the Scooby Doo heads on her slippers bobbing. Even her breath shook, puffing like she'd been running.

"Chloe?" Emily's muffled voice drifted up from the dark basement. "Your mom said the Coke's in the cold cellar, but I can't find it. Can you come down and help me?"

Mommy said she'd told Emily about the basement. Chloe was sure of it. She closed her eyes and thought hard. Before Mommy and Daddy left for the party, she'd been playing in the TV room. Mommy had called, and Chloe had run into the front hall where Mommy had scooped her up in a hug, laughing when Chloe's doll poked her eye.

"I see you're playing with Princess—I mean, *Pirate* Jasmine. Has she rescued poor Aladdin from the evil genie yet?"

Chloe shook her head, then whispered, "Did you tell Emily about the basement?"

"I most certainly did. No basements for Miss Chloe. That door stays closed." When Daddy came around the corner, Mommy said, "We really need to talk about moving, Steve."

"Say the word and the sign goes up." Daddy ruffled Chloe's hair. "Be good for Emily, kiddo."

And then they were gone.

"Chloe, I know you can hear me," Emily yelled.

Chloe peeled her fingers from the railing and stuck them in her ears.

"Chloe!"

"I c-can't go in the basement," Chloe called. "I-I'm not allowed."

"Well, I'm in charge and I say you are. You're a big girl."

Chloe made her feet move down one step. The back of her throat hurt and everything looked fuzzy, like she was going to cry.

"Chloe Saunders, you have five seconds or I'll drag you down here and lock the door."

Chloe raced down the steps so fast her feet tangled and

she tumbled into a heap on the landing. She lay there, ankle throbbing, tears burning her eyes as she peered into the basement, with its creaks and smells and shadows. And Mrs. Hobb.

There'd been others, before Mrs. Hobb scared them away. Like old Mrs. Miller, who'd play peek-a-boo with Chloe and call her Mary. And Mr. Drake, who'd ask weird questions, like whether anyone lived on the moon yet, and most times Chloe didn't know the answer, but he'd still smile and tell her she was a good girl.

She used to like coming downstairs and talking to the people. All she had to do was not look behind the furnace, where a man hung from the ceiling, his face all purple and puffy. He never said anything, but seeing him always made Chloe's tummy hurt.

"Chloe?" Emily's muffled voice called. "Are you coming?"

Mommy would say "Think about the good parts, not the bad." So as Chloe walked down the last three steps, she remembered Mrs. Miller and Mr. Drake and she didn't think about Mrs. Hobb at all . . . or not very much.

At the bottom, she squinted into the near darkness. Just the night lights were on, the ones Mommy had put everywhere when Chloe started saying she didn't want to go downstairs and Mommy thought she was afraid of the dark, which she was, a little, but only because the dark meant Mrs. Hobb could sneak up on her.

Chloe could see the cold cellar door, though, so she kept her eyes on that and walked as fast as she could. When something moved, she forgot about not looking, but it was only the hanging man, and all she could see was his hand peeking from behind the furnace as he swayed.

She ran to the cold cellar door and yanked it open. Inside, it was pitch black.

"Chloe?" Emily called from the darkness.

Chloe clenched her fists. Now Emily was being *really* mean. Hiding on her—

Footsteps pattered overhead. Mommy? Home already?

"Come on, Chloe. You aren't afraid of the dark, are you?" Emily laughed. "I guess you're still a little baby after all."

Chloe scowled. Emily didn't know anything. Just a stupid, mean girl. Chloe would get her Coke, then run upstairs and tell Mommy, and Emily would never babysit her again.

She leaned into the tiny room, trying to remember where Mommy kept the Coke. That was it on the shelf, wasn't it? She darted over and stood on her tiptoes. Her fingers closed around a cool metal can.

"Chloe? Chloe!" It was Emily's voice, but far away, shrill. Footsteps pounded across the floor overhead. "Chloe, where are you?"

Chloe dropped the can. It hit the concrete with a crack, then rolled against her foot, hissing and spitting, soda pooling around her slippers.

"Chloe, Chloe, where are you?" mimicked a voice behind her, like Emily's, but not quite.

Chloe turned slowly.

In the doorway stood an old woman in a pink housecoat, her eyes and teeth glittering in the dark. Mrs. Hobb. Chloe wanted to squeeze her eyes shut, but she didn't dare because it only made her madder, made everything worse.

Mrs. Hobb's skin rippled and squirmed. Then it went black and shiny, crackling like twigs in a campfire. Big chunks fell off, plopping onto the floor. Her hair sizzled and burned away. And then there was nothing left but a skull dotted with scraps of blackened flesh. The jaws opened, the teeth still glittering.

"Welcome back, Chloe."

one

I BOLTED UP IN BED, one hand clutching my pendant, the other wrapped in my sheets. I struggled to recapture wisps of the dream already fluttering away. Something about a basement . . . a little girl . . . me? I couldn't remember ever having a basement—we'd always lived in condo apartments.

A little girl in a basement, something scary . . . weren't basements always scary? I shivered just thinking about them, dark and damp and empty. But this one hadn't been empty. There'd been . . . I couldn't remember what. A man behind a furnace . . . ?

A bang at my bedroom door made me jump.

"Chloe!" Annette shrieked. "Why hasn't your alarm gone off? I'm the housekeeper, not your nanny. If you're late again, I'm calling your father."

As threats went, this wasn't exactly the stuff of nightmares. Even if Annette managed to get hold of my dad in Berlin, he'd just pretend to listen, eyes on his BlackBerry, attention riveted to something more important, like the weather forecast. He'd murmur a vague "Yes, I'll see to it when I get back" and forget all about me the moment he hung up.

I turned on my radio, cranked it up, and crawled out of bed.

A half hour later, I was in my bathroom, getting ready for school.

I pulled the sides of my hair back in clips, glanced in the mirror, and shuddered. The style made me look twelve years old . . . and I didn't need any help. I'd just turned fifteen and servers still handed me the kiddie menu in restaurants. I couldn't blame them. I was five foot nothing with curves that only showed if I wore tight jeans and a tighter T-shirt.

Aunt Lauren swore I'd shoot up—and out—when I finally got my period. By this point, I figured it was "if," not "when." Most of my friends had gotten theirs at twelve, eleven even. I tried not to think about it too much, but of course I did. I worried that there was something wrong with me, felt like a freak every time my friends talked about their periods, prayed they didn't find out I hadn't gotten mine. Aunt Lauren said I was fine, and she was a doctor, so I guess she'd know. But it still bugged me. A lot.

"Chloe!" The door shuddered under Annette's meaty fist.

"I'm on the toilet," I shouted back. "Can I get some privacy maybe?"

I tried just one clip at the back of my head, holding the sides up. Not bad. When I turned my head for a side view, the clip slid from my baby-fine hair.

I never should have gotten it cut. But I'd been sick of having long, straight, little-girl hair. I'd decided on a shoulder-length, wispy style. On the model it looked great. On me? Not so much.

I eyed the unopened hair color tube. Kari swore red streaks would be perfect in my strawberry blond hair. I couldn't help thinking I'd look like a candy cane. Still, it might make me look older . . .

"I'm picking up the phone, Chloe," Annette yelled.

I grabbed the tube of dye, stuffed it in my backpack, and threw open the door.

I took the stairs, as always. The building might change, but my routine never did. The day I'd started kindergarten, my mother held my hand, my Sailor Moon backpack over her other arm as we'd stood at the top of the landing.

"Get ready, Chloe," she'd said. "One, two, three—"

And we were off, racing down the stairs until we reached the bottom, panting and giggling, the floor swaying and sliding under our unsteady feet, all the fears over my first school day gone.

We'd run down the stairs together every morning all through kindergarten and half of first grade and then . . . well, then there wasn't anyone to run down the stairs with anymore.

I paused at the bottom, touching the necklace under my T-shirt, then shook off the memories, hoisted my backpack, and walked from the stairwell.

After my mom died, we'd moved around Buffalo a lot. My dad flipped luxury apartments, meaning he bought them in buildings in the final stages of construction, then sold them when the work was complete. Since he was away on business most of the time, putting down roots wasn't important. Not for him, anyway.

This morning, the stairs hadn't been such a bright idea. My stomach was already fluttering with nerves over my Spanish midterm. I'd screwed up the last test—gone to a weekend sleepover at Beth's when I should have been studying—and barely passed. Spanish had never been my best subject, but if I didn't pull it up to a C, Dad might actually notice and start wondering whether an art school had been such a smart choice.

Milos was waiting for me in his cab at the curb. He'd been driving me for two years now, through two moves and three schools. As I got in, he adjusted the visor on my side. The morning sun still hit my eyes, but I didn't tell him that.

My stomach relaxed as I rubbed my fingers over the familiar rip in the armrest and inhaled chemical pine from the air freshener twisting above the vent.

"I saw a movie last night," he said as he slid the cab across three lanes. "One of the kind you like."

"A thriller?"

"No." He frowned, lips moving as if testing out word choices. "An action-adventure. You know, lots of guns, things blowing up. A real shoot-'em-down movie."

I hated correcting Milos's English, but he insisted on it. "You mean, a shoot-'em-up movie."

He cocked one dark brow. "When you shoot a man, which way does he fall? Up?"

I laughed, and we talked about movies for a while. My favorite subject.

When Milos had to take a call from his dispatcher, I glanced out the side window. A long-haired boy darted from behind a cluster of businessmen. He carried an old-fashioned plastic lunch box with a superhero on it. I was so busy trying to figure out which superhero it was, I didn't notice where the boy was headed until he leaped off the curb, landing between us and the next car.

"Milos!" I screamed. "Watch—"

The last word was ripped from my lungs as I slammed against my shoulder belt. The driver behind us, and the one behind him, laid on their horns, a chain reaction of protest.

"What?" Milos said. "Chloe? What's wrong?"

I looked over the hood of the car and saw . . . nothing. Just an empty lane in front and traffic veering to our left, drivers flashing Milos the finger as they passed.

"Th-th-th—" I clenched my fists, as if that could somehow force the word out. *If you get jammed, take another route*, my speech therapist always said. "I thought I saw some-wha-wha—"

Speak slowly. Consider your words first.

"I'm sorry. I thought I saw someone jump in front of us."

Milos eased the taxi forward. "That happens to me sometimes, especially if I'm turning my head. I think I see someone, but there's no one there."

I nodded. My stomach hurt again.

TWO

BETWEEN THE DREAM I couldn't remember and the boy I couldn't have seen, I was spooked. Until I got at least one question out of my head, focusing on my Spanish test was out of the question. So I called Aunt Lauren. When I got her voice mail, I said I'd phone back at lunch. I was halfway to my friend Kari's locker when my aunt called back.

"Did I ever live in a house with a basement?" I asked.

"And good morning to you, too."

"Sorry. I had this dream and it's bugging me." I told her what bits I could recall.

"Ah, that would have been the old house in Allentown. You were just a tyke. I'm not surprised you don't remember."

"Thanks. It was—"

"Bugging you, I can tell. Must have been a doozy of a nightmare."

"Something about a monster living in the basement. Very cliché. I'm ashamed of myself."

"Monster? What—?"

The PA system on her end cut her off, a tinny voice saying, "Dr. Fellows, please report to station 3B."

"That'd be your cue," I said.

"It can wait. Is everything okay, Chloe? You sound off."

"No, just . . . my imagination's in overdrive today. I freaked Milos out this morning, thinking I saw a boy run in front of the cab."

"What?"

"There wasn't a boy. Not outside my head, anyway." I saw Kari at her locker and waved. "The bell's going to ring so—"

"I'm picking you up after school. High tea at the Crowne. We'll talk."

The line went dead before I could argue. I shook my head and ran to catch up with Kari.

School. Not much to say about it. People think art schools must be different, all that creative energy simmering, classes full of happy kids, even the Goths as close to happy as their tortured souls will allow. They figure art schools must have less peer pressure and bullying. After all, most kids there are the ones who *get* bullied in other schools.

It's true that stuff like that isn't bad at A. R. Gurney High, but when you put kids together, no matter how similar they seem, lines are drawn. Cliques form. Instead of jocks and geeks and nobodies, you get artists and musicians and actors.

As a theater arts student, I was lumped in with the actors, where talent seemed to count less than looks, poise, and verbal ability. I didn't turn heads, and I scored a fat zero on the last two. On a popularity scale, I ranked a perfectly mediocre five. The kind of girl nobody thinks a whole lot about.

But I'd always dreamed of being in art school, and it *was* as cool as I'd imagined. Better yet, my father had promised that I could stay until I graduated, no matter how many times we moved. That meant for the first time in my life, I wasn't the "new girl." I'd started at A. R. Gurney as a freshman, like everyone else. Just like a normal kid. Finally.

That day, though, I didn't feel normal. I spent the morning thinking about that boy on the street. There were plenty of logical explanations. I'd been staring at his lunch box, so I'd misjudged where he'd been running. He'd jumped into a waiting car at the curb. Or swerved at the last second and vanished into the crowd.

That made perfect sense. So why did it still bug me?

"Oh, come on," Miranda said as I rooted through my locker at lunchtime. "He's right there. Ask him if he's going to the dance. How tough can that be?"

"Leave her alone," Beth said. She reached over my shoulder, grabbed my bright yellow lunch bag from the top shelf, and dangled it. "Don't know how you can miss this, Chloe. It's practically neon."

"She needs a stepladder to see that high," Kari said.

I banged her with my hip, and she bounced away, laughing.

Beth rolled her eyes. "Come on, people, or we'll never get a table."

We made it as far as Brent's locker before Miranda elbowed me. "Ask him, Chloe."

She mock-whispered it. Brent glanced over . . . then quickly looked away. My face heated and I clutched my lunch bag to my chest.

Kari's long, dark hair brushed my shoulder. "He's a jerk," she whispered. "Ignore him."

"No, he's not a jerk. He just doesn't like me. Can't help that."

"Here," Miranda said. "I'll ask him for you."

"No!" I grabbed her arm. "P-please."

Her round face screwed up in disgust. "God, you can be such a baby. You're fifteen, Chloe. You have to take matters into your own hands."

"Like phoning a guy until his mother tells you to leave him alone?" Kari said.

Miranda only shrugged. "That's Rob's mother. *He* never said it."

"Yeah? You just keep telling yourself that."

That set them off for real. Normally, I'd have jumped in and made them quit, but I was still upset over Miranda's embarrassing me in front of Brent.

Kari, Beth, and I used to talk about guys, but we weren't totally into them. Miranda was—she'd had more boyfriends than she could name. So when she started hanging with us, it suddenly became really important to have a guy we liked. I worried enough about being immature, and it didn't help that she'd burst out laughing when I'd admitted I'd never been on a real date. So I invented a crush. Brent.

I figured I could just name a guy I liked and that would be enough. Not a chance. Miranda had outed me—telling him I liked him. I'd been horrified. Well, mostly. There'd also been a little part of me that hoped he'd go "Cool. I really like Chloe, too." Not a chance. Before, we used to talk in Spanish class sometimes. Now he sat two rows away, like I'd suddenly developed the world's worst case of BO.

We'd just reached the cafeteria when someone called my name. I turned to see Nate Bozian jogging toward me, his red hair like a beacon in the crowded hall. He bumped into a senior, grinned an apology, and kept coming.

"Hey," I said as he drew near.

"Hey yourself. Did you forget Petrie rescheduled film club for lunchtime this week? We're discussing avant-garde. I *know* you love art films."

I fake gagged.

"I'll send your regrets, then. And I'll tell Petrie you aren't interested in directing that short either."

"We're deciding that today?"

Nate started walking backward. "Maybe. Maybe not. So I'll tell Petrie—"

"Gotta run," I said to my friends and hurried to catch up with him.

The film club meeting started backstage as always, where we'd go through business stuff and eat lunch. Food wasn't allowed in the auditorium.

We discussed the short, and I *was* on the list for directors—the only freshman who'd made the cut. After, as everyone else watched scenes from avant-garde films, I mulled through my options for an audition tape. I snuck out before it ended and headed back to my locker.

My brain kept whirring until I was halfway there. Then my stomach started acting up again, reminding me that I'd been so excited about making the short list that I'd forgotten to eat.

I'd left my lunch bag backstage. I checked my watch. Ten minutes before class. I could make it.

Film club had ended. Whoever left the auditorium last had turned out the lights, and I didn't have a clue how to turn them on, especially when finding the switch would require being able to *see* it. Glow-in-the-dark light switches. That's how I'd finance my first film. Of course, I'd need someone to actually *make* them. Like most directors, I was more of an idea person.

I picked my way through the aisles, bashing my knees twice. Finally my eyes adjusted to the dim emergency lights, and I found the stairs leading backstage. Then it got tougher.

The backstage dissolved into smaller areas curtained off for storage and makeshift dressing rooms. There were lights, but someone else had always turned them on. After feeling around the nearest wall and not finding a switch, I gave up. The faint glow of more emergency lights let me see shapes. Good enough.

Still, it was pretty dark. I'm afraid of the dark. I had some bad experiences as a child, imaginary friends who lurked in dark places and scared me. I know that sounds weird. Other kids dream up playmates—I imagined bogeymen.

The smell of greasepaint told me I was in the dressing area, but the scent, mingled with the unmistakable odor of mothballs and old costumes, didn't calm me the way it usually did.

Three more steps and I did let out a shriek as fabric billowed around me. I'd stumbled into a curtain. Great. Exactly how loud had I screamed? I really hoped these walls were soundproof.

I swept my hand over the scratchy polyester until I

found the opening and parted the curtains. Ahead, I could make out the lunch table. Something yellow sat on the top. My bag?

The makeshift hall seemed to stretch before me, yawning into darkness. It was the perspective—the two curtained sides angled inward, so the hall narrowed. Interesting illusion, especially for a suspense film. I'd have to remember that.

Thinking about the corridor as a movie set calmed my nerves. I framed the shot, the bounce of my step adding a jerkiness that would make the scene more immediate, putting the viewer in the head of our protagonist, the foolish girl making her way toward the strange noise.

Something thumped. I started, and my shoes squeaked and *that* noise made me jump higher. I rubbed the goose bumps on my arms and tried to laugh. Okay, I did say *strange noise*, didn't I? Cue the sound effects, please.

Another noise. A rustling. So we had rats in our spooky corridor, did we? How clichéd. Time to turn off my galloping imagination and focus. *Direct* the scene.

Our protagonist sees something at the end of the corridor. A shadowy figure—

Oh, please. Talk about cheap thrills. Go for original . . . mysterious . . .

Take two.

What's that she sees? A child's lunch bag, bright yellow and new, out of place in this old, condemned house.

Keep the film rolling. Don't let my mind wander—

A sob echoed through the silent rooms, then broke off, dissolving into a wet snuffling.

Crying. Right. From my movie. The protagonist sees a child's lunch bag, then hears eerie sobs. Something moved at the end of the hall. A dark shape—

I flung myself forward, racing for my bag. I grabbed it and took off.

three

"CHLOE! HOLD UP!"

I'd just dumped my uneaten lunch in my locker and was walking away when Nate hailed me. I turned to see him edging sideways through a group of girls. The bell sounded and the hall erupted, kids jostling like salmon fighting their way upstream, carrying along anything in their path. Nate had to struggle to reach me.

"You took off from film club before I could grab you. I wanted to ask if you're going to the dance."

"Tomorrow? Um, yeah."

He flashed a dimpled grin. "Great. See you there."

A swarm of kids engulfed him. I stood there, staring after him. Had Nate just tracked me down to ask if I was going to the dance? It wasn't the same as asking me *to* the dance, but still . . . I was definitely going to need to rethink my outfit.

A senior whacked into me, knocking off my backpack and muttering something about "standing in the middle of the hall." As I bent to grab my bag, I felt a gush between my legs.

I snapped upright and stood frozen before taking a tentative step.

Oh God. Had I actually wet myself? I took a deep breath. Maybe I *was* sick. My stomach had been dancing all day.

See if you can clean up and if it's bad, take a cab home.

In the bathroom, I pulled down my pants and saw bright red.

For a couple of minutes, I just sat there, on the toilet, grinning like an idiot and hoping that the rumor about school bathroom cams wasn't true.

I balled up toilet paper in my panties, pulled up my jeans, and waddled out of the stall. And there it was, a sight that had mocked me since fall: the sanitary napkin dispenser.

I reached into my back pocket and pulled out a five-dollar bill, a ten, and two pennies. Back into the stall. Scavenge through my backpack. Find . . . one nickel.

I eyed the machine. Drew closer. Examined the scratched lock, the one Beth said could be opened with a long fingernail. Mine weren't long, but my house key worked just fine.

A banner week for me. Getting short-listed for the director spot. Nate asking me about the dance. My first period. And now my first criminal act.

After I fixed myself up, I dug into my backpack for my brush and emerged instead with the tube of hair color. I lifted it. My reflection in the mirror grinned back.

Why not add "first skipped class" and "first dye job" to the list? Coloring my hair at the school bathroom sink wouldn't be easy, but it would probably be simpler than at home, with Annette hovering.

Dying a dozen bright red streaks took twenty minutes. I'd had to take off my shirt to avoid getting dye on it, so I was standing over the sink in my bra and jeans. Luckily no one came in.

I finished squeezing the strands dry with paper towel, took a deep breath, looked . . . and smiled. Kari had been right. It did look good. Annette would freak. My dad might notice. Might even get mad. But I was pretty sure no one was going to hand me a twelve-and-under menu anymore.

The door creaked. I shoved the towels in the trash, grabbed my shirt, and dashed into a stall. I barely had time to latch the door before the other girl started crying. I glanced over and saw a pair of Reeboks in the next stall.

Should I ask whether she was okay? Or would that embarrass her?

The toilet flushed and the shadow at my feet shifted. The stall lock clicked open. When the taps started, though, her sobs got even louder.

The water shut off. The towel roll squeaked. Paper crumpled. The door opened. It shut. The crying continued.

A cold finger slid down my spine. I told myself she'd changed her mind, and was staying until she got things under control, but the crying was right beside me. In the next stall.

I squeezed my hands into fists. It was just my imagination.

I slowly bent. No shoes under the divider. I ducked farther. No shoes in any of the stalls. The crying stopped.

I yanked my shirt on and hurried from the bathroom before it could start again. As the door shut behind me, all went silent. An empty hall.

"You!"

I spun to see a custodian walking toward me, and I breathed a sigh of relief.

"Th-the bathroom," I said. "I was using the bathroom."

He kept coming. I didn't recognize him. He was maybe my dad's age, with a brush cut, wearing our school janitorial uniform. A temp, filling in for Mr. Teitlebaum.

"I—I'm heading to c-class now."

I started walking.

"You! Get back here. I want to talk to you."

The only other sound was my footsteps. *My* footsteps. Why couldn't I hear *his*?

I walked faster.

A blur passed me. The air shimmered about ten feet

ahead, a figure taking form in a custodian's shirt and slacks. I wheeled and broke into a run.

The man let out a snarl that echoed down the hall. A student rounded the corner, and we almost collided. I stammered an apology and glanced over my shoulder. The janitor was gone.

I exhaled and closed my eyes. When I opened them, the blue uniform shirt was inches from my face. I looked up . . . and let out a shriek.

He looked like a mannequin that had gotten too close to a fire. Face burned. Melted. One eye bulged, exposed. The other eye had slid down near his cheekbone, the whole cheek sagging, lips drooping, skin shiny and misshapen and—

The twisted lips parted. "Maybe now you'll pay attention to me."

I ran headlong down the hall. As I flew past one classroom door, it opened.

"Chloe?" A man's voice.

I kept running.

"Talk to me!" the horrible, garbled voice snarled, getting closer. "Do you know how long I've been trapped here?"

I flew through the doors into the stairwell and headed up.

Up? All the stupid heroines go up!

I veered across the landing and hit the next set of stairs.

The custodian limped up the flight below, fingers clutching the railing, melted fingers, bone peeking through—

I barreled through the doors and raced along the main hall.

"Listen to me, you selfish brat. All I want is five minutes—"

I swerved into the nearest empty classroom and slammed the door. As I backed into the center of the room, the custodian stepped through the door. Right *through* it. That awful melted face was gone, and he was normal again.

"Is that better? Now will you stop screaming and talk to—"

I darted to the window and started looking for a way to open it, then saw how far down it was. At least thirty feet . . . onto pavement.

"Chloe!"

The door flew open. It was the vice principal, Ms. Waugh, with my math teacher, Mr. Travis, and a music teacher whose name I couldn't remember. Seeing me at the window, Ms. Waugh threw out her arms, blocking the two men.

"Chloe?" she said, voice low. "Honey, you need to step away from that window."

"I was just—"

"Chloe . . ."

Confused, I glanced back toward the window.

Mr. Travis shot past Ms. Waugh and tackled me. As we

hit the floor, the air flew out of my lungs. Scrambling off, he accidentally kneed me in the stomach. I fell back, doubled over, wheezing.

I opened my eyes to see the custodian standing over me. I screamed and tried to get up, but Mr. Travis and the music teacher held me down while Ms. Waugh babbled into a cell phone.

The custodian leaned through Mr. Travis. "Now will you talk to me, girl? Can't get away."

I thrashed, kicking at the custodian, trying to pull away from the teachers. They only held me tighter. I vaguely heard Ms. Waugh calling that help was on the way. The custodian pushed his face into mine and it changed to that horrible melted mask, so close I was staring into his one bulging eye, almost out of its socket.

I chomped down on my tongue so I wouldn't scream. Blood filled my mouth. The more I fought, the harder the teachers restrained me, twisting my arms, pain stabbing through me.

"Can't you see him?" I shouted. "He's right there. Please. Please, please, please. Get him away from me. Get him away!"

They wouldn't listen. I continued to struggle, to argue, but they held me still as the burned man taunted me.

Finally, two men in uniforms hurried through the door. One helped the teachers restrain me while the other moved behind, out of my sight. Fingers tightened on my forearm.

Then a needle prick. Ice slid through my veins.

The room started to sway. The custodian faded, blinking in and out.

"No!" he yelled. "I need to speak to her. Don't you understand? She can hear me. I only want to . . ."

His voice faded as the paramedics lowered me onto a stretcher. It rose, swaying. Swaying . . . like an elephant. I'd rode one once, with my mom, at the zoo, and my mind slipped back there, Mom's arms around me, her laughter—

The custodian's howl of rage sliced through my memory. "Don't take her away. I need her!"

Swaying. The elephant swaying. Mom laughing . . .

FOUR

I SAT ON THE EDGE of my hospital bed and tried to persuade myself I was still asleep. That was the best explanation for what I was hearing. I could also chalk it up to *delusional*, but I preferred *dreaming*.

Aunt Lauren sat beside me, holding my hand. My eyes went to the nurses gliding past in the corridor. She followed my gaze, rose, and shut the door. Through a glaze of tears, I watched her and pictured Mom instead. Something inside me crumpled, and I was six years old, huddled on the bed, crying for my mother.

I rubbed my hands over the covers, stiff and scratchy, catching at my dry skin. The room was so hot every breath made my parched throat tighten. Aunt Lauren handed me my water, and I wrapped my hands around the cool glass. The water had a metallic taste, but I gulped it down.

"A group home," I said. The walls seemed to suck the words from my mouth, like a sound stage, absorbing them and leaving only dead air.

"Oh God, Chloe." She pulled a tissue from her pocket and wiped her nose. "Do you know how many times I've had to tell a patient he's dying? And somehow, this seems harder."

She shifted to face me. "I know how badly you want to go to UCLA for college. This is the only way we're going to get you there, hon."

"Is it Dad?"

She paused, and I knew she'd like to blame him. She'd wanted to raise me after my mom passed away, spare me a life of housekeepers and empty apartments. She'd never forgiven my father for refusing. Just like she'd never forgiven him for that night my mother died. It didn't matter that they'd been sideswiped in a hit-and-run—he'd been driving, so she held him responsible.

"No," she said finally. "It's the school. Unless you spend two weeks undergoing evaluation in a group home, it will go on your permanent record."

"What will go on my record?"

Her fist clenched around the tissue. "It's that da—" She caught herself. "It's the zero-tolerance policy." She spit the words with more venom than the curse.

"Zero tolerance? You mean violence? B-b-but I didn't—"

"I know you didn't. But to them, it's simple. You struggled

with a teacher. You need help."

In a home. For crazy kids.

I awoke several times that night. The second time, my father was in the doorway, watching me. The third, he was sitting beside my bed. Seeing my eyes open, he reached over and awkwardly patted my hand.

"It's going to be all right," he murmured. "Everything will be all right."

I fell back to sleep.

My father was still there the next morning. His eyes were bleary, the wrinkles around his mouth deeper than I remembered. He'd been up all night, flying back from Berlin.

I don't think Dad ever wanted kids. But he'd never tell me that, even in anger. Whatever Aunt Lauren thinks of him, he does his best. He just doesn't seem to know what to make of me. I'm like a puppy left to him by someone he loved very much, and he struggles to do right by it even if he isn't much of a dog person.

"You changed your hair," he said as I sat up.

I braced myself. When you run screaming through the school halls after dying your hair in the girls' bathroom, the first thing people say—well, after they get past the screaming-through-the-halls part—is "you were doing *what*?" Coloring your hair in a school bathroom isn't normal. Not for girls like me. And bright red streaks? While skipping class? It screams *mental breakdown.*

"Do you like it?" my father asked after a moment.

I nodded.

He paused, then let out a strained chuckle. "Well, it's not exactly what I would have chosen, but it looks all right. If you like it, that's what counts." He scratched his throat, peppered with beard shadow. "I guess your aunt Lauren told you about this group home business. She's found one she thinks will be okay. Small, private. Can't say I'm thrilled with the idea, but it's only for a couple of weeks. . . ."

No one would say what was wrong with me. They had me talk to a bunch of doctors and they ran some tests, and I could tell they had a good idea what was wrong and just wouldn't say it. That meant it was bad.

This wasn't the first time I'd seen people who weren't really there. That's what Aunt Lauren had wanted to talk to me about after school. When I'd mentioned the dream, she'd remembered how I used to talk about people in our old basement. My parents figured it was my creative version of make-believe friends, inventing a whole cast of characters. Then those friends started terrifying me, so much that we'd moved.

Even after that, I'd sometimes "seen" people, so my mom bought me my ruby necklace and said it would protect me. Dad said it was all about psychology. I'd believed it worked, so it had. But now, it was happening again. And this time, no one was chalking it up to an overactive imagination.

They were sending me to a home for crazy kids. They thought I was crazy. I wasn't. I was fifteen and had finally gotten my period and that had to count for something. It couldn't just be coincidence that I'd started seeing things the same day. All those stockpiled hormones had exploded and my brain misfired, plucking images from forgotten movies and tricking me into thinking they were real.

If I was crazy, I'd be doing more than seeing and hearing people who weren't there. I'd be acting crazy, and I wasn't.

Was I?

The more I thought about it, the more I wasn't sure. I felt normal. I couldn't remember doing anything weird. Except for dying my hair in the bathroom. And skipping class. And breaking into the napkin dispenser. And fighting with a teacher.

That last one didn't count. I'd been freaked out from seeing that burned guy and I'd been struggling to get away from him, not trying to hurt anyone. Before that, I'd been fine. My friends had thought I was fine. Mr. Petrie thought I was fine when he put me on the director short list. Nate Bozian obviously thought I was fine. You wouldn't be happy that a crazy girl was going to a dance.

He had been happy, hadn't he?

When I thought back, it all seemed fuzzy, like some distant memory that maybe I only dreamed.

What if none of that happened? I'd *wanted* the director spot. I'd *wanted* Nate to be interested in me. Maybe I'd imagined it all. Hallucinated it, like the boy on the street and the crying girl and the burned janitor.

If I was crazy, would I know it? That's what being crazy was, wasn't it? You thought you were fine. Everyone else knew better.

Maybe I was crazy.

My father and Aunt Lauren drove me to Lyle House on Sunday afternoon. They'd given me some medicine before I left the hospital and it made me sleepy. Our arrival was a montage of still shots and clips.

A huge white Victorian house perched on an oversized lot. Yellow trim. A swing on the wraparound porch.

Two women. The first, gray haired and wide hipped, coming forward to greet me. The younger one's dour eyes following me, her arms crossed, braced for trouble.

Walking up a long narrow flight of stairs. The older woman—a nurse, who introduced herself as Mrs. Talbot— chirping a guided tour that my fuzzy brain couldn't follow.

A bedroom, white and yellow, decorated with daisies, smelling of hair gel.

On the far side of the room, a twin bed with a quilt yanked over the bunched-up sheets. The walls over the bed decorated with pages ripped from teen magazines. The dresser covered with makeup tubes and bottles. Only the tiny desk bare.

My side of the room was a sterile mirror image—same bed, same dresser, same tiny desk, all wiped clean of personality.

Time for Dad and Aunt Lauren to go. Mrs. Talbot explained I wouldn't see them for a couple of days because I needed time to "acclimate" to my new "environment." Like a pet in a new home.

Hugging Aunt Lauren. Pretending I didn't see the tears in her eyes.

An awkward embrace from Dad. He mumbled that he'd stay in town, and he would come to visit as soon as they let him. Then he pressed a roll of twenties into my hand as he kissed the top of my head.

Mrs. Talbot telling me they'd put my things away, since I was probably tired. Just crawl into bed. The blind closing. Room going dark. Falling back to sleep.

My father's voice waking me. Room completely dark now, black outside. Night.

Dad silhouetted in the doorway. The younger nurse—Miss Van Dop—behind him, face set in disapproval. My father moving to my bedside and pressing something soft into my arms. "We forgot Ozzie. I wasn't sure you'd sleep without him." The koala bear had been on a shelf in my room for two years, banished from my bed when I'd outgrown him. But I took him and buried my nose in his ratty fake fur that smelled of home.

I awoke to the wheezy sleep breathing of the girl in the next bed. I looked over but saw only a form under the quilt.

As I turned onto my back, hot tears slid down my cheeks. Not homesickness. Shame. Embarrassment. Humiliation.

I'd scared Aunt Lauren and Dad. They'd had to scramble to figure out what to do with me. What was wrong with me. How to fix it.

And school . . .

My cheeks burned hotter than my tears. How many kids had heard me screaming? Peeked in that classroom while I'd been fighting the teachers and babbling about being chased by melted custodians. Seen me being taken away strapped to a stretcher.

Anyone who'd missed the drama would have heard about it. Everyone would know that Chloe Saunders had lost it. That she was nuts, crazy, locked up with the rest of the loonies.

Even if they let me return to school, I didn't think I'd ever have the guts to go back.

five

I WOKE TO THE *CLINK-CLINK* of metal hangers. A blond girl flipped through clothes that I was pretty sure were mine, hung up yesterday by Mrs. Talbot.

"Hello," I said.

She turned and smiled. "Nice stuff. Good labels."

"I'm Chloe."

"Liz. Like Lizzie McGuire." She waved at an old and faded magazine cutout on her wall. "Except, I don't go by Lizzie, 'cause I think it sounds kind of—" she lowered her voice, as if not to offend the picture Lizzie "—babyish."

She continued talking, but I didn't hear it because all I could think was, What's wrong with her? If she was at Lyle House, there was something wrong with her. Some "mental condition."

She didn't look crazy. Her long hair was brushed into a

gleaming ponytail. She wore Guess jeans and a Gap T-shirt. If I didn't know better, I'd think I'd woken up in a boarding school.

She kept talking. Maybe that was a sign.

She seemed harmless enough, though. She'd have to be, wouldn't she? They wouldn't put anyone dangerous in here. Or *really* crazy.

Oh no, Chloe. They don't put any really crazy people in here. Just the ones who hear voices and see burned-up janitors and fight with teachers.

My stomach started to ache.

"Come on," she said. "Breakfast's in five minutes, and they get real snippy if you're late." Liz put out a hand as I opened a dresser drawer. "You can wear your pajamas down to breakfast. The guys eat lunch and dinner with us, but they have breakfast later, so we get some privacy."

"Guys?"

"Simon, Derek, and Peter."

"The house is coed?"

"Uh-huh." She pursed her lips in the mirror and picked off a dry flake. "We all share the bottom floor, but the top one is divided."

She leaned out the door and showed me how short the hall was. "They get the other side. There's not even a joining door. Like we'd sneak over there at night if we could." She giggled. "Well, Tori would. And I might, if there was someone worth sneaking over for. Tori has dibs on Simon."

She scrutinized me in the mirror. "You might like Peter. He's cute but way too young for me. He's thirteen. Almost fourteen, I think."

"I'm fifteen."

She bit her lip. "Oh, geez. Um, anyway, Peter won't be around much longer. I heard he's going home soon." She paused. "Fifteen, huh? What grade?"

"Ninth."

"Same as Tori. I'm in tenth, like Simon, Derek, and Rae. I think Simon and Rae are still fifteen, though. And did I say I love your hair? I wanted to do that, with blue streaks, but my mom said . . ."

Liz kept up the commentary as we headed downstairs, moving on to the whole cast of characters. There was Dr. Gill, the psychologist, but she only came for her office hours, as did the tutor, Ms. Wang.

I'd met two of the three nurses. Mrs. Talbot—the older woman, whom Liz proclaimed "really nice," and the younger Miss Van Dop, who was, she whispered, "not so nice." The third nurse, Mrs. Abdo, worked weekends, giving the others each a day off. They lived in and looked after us. They sounded more like the housemothers I'd heard boarding school kids talk about, but Liz called them nurses.

At the bottom of the stairs, the overpowering stink of lemon cleaner hit me. It smelled like Gran's house. Even

Dad never seemed comfortable in his mother's immaculate house, under the glare that said you'd better not expect any birthday money if you spilled your soda on the white leather sofa. One look in this living room, though, and I breathed a sigh of relief. It was as clean as Gran's—the carpet spotless, the wood gleaming—but it had a worn, comfortable look that invited you to curl up on the sofa.

It was also painted the favored color for Lyle House—a pale yellow this time. Pillows covered the dark blue sofa and two rocking chairs. An old grandfather clock ticked in the corner. Every end table held a vase of daisies or daffodils. Bright and cheerful. Too bright and cheerful, really, like this bed-and-breakfast near Syracuse where Aunt Lauren and I stayed last fall—so desperate to be homey that it seemed more a stage set than someone's house.

No different from this, I guess—a business eager to convince you it *wasn't* a business, to make you feel at home. To make you forget you were in a place for crazy kids.

Liz stopped me outside the dining room so we could peek in.

On one side of the table sat a tall girl with short dark hair. "That's Tori. Victoria, but she likes Tori. With an *i*. She's my best friend. She gets moody, and I've heard that's why she's here, but I think she's fine." She jerked her chin toward the other person at the table—a pretty, copper-skinned girl with long dark curls. "That's Rachelle. Rae. She has this 'thing' for fire."

I stared at the girl. Thing for fire? Did that mean she *set* fires? I thought this place was supposed to be safe.

What about the boys? Were any of them violent?

I rubbed my stomach.

"Someone's hungry, I see," chirped a voice.

I glanced up to see Mrs. Talbot coming through what I guessed was the kitchen door, milk pitcher in hand. She smiled at me.

"Come in, Chloe. Let me introduce you."

Before breakfast, Miss Van Dop gave us all pills, then watched as we took them. It was creepy. No one said a word, just held out their hands, gulped their pill down with water, and returned to their conversations.

When I stared at mine, Miss Van Dop said the doctor would explain everything later, but for now, I should just take it. So I did.

After we'd eaten, we trooped upstairs to dress. Rae was in the lead, followed by Liz and Tori. Then me.

"Rachelle?" Tori called.

Rae's shoulders tightened and she didn't turn. "Yes, Victoria?"

Tori climbed two more steps, closing the gap between them. "You did get the laundry done, right? It's your turn, and I want to wear that new shirt my mom bought me."

Rae slowly turned. "Mrs. T. said I could do laundry today, since we had to take off while—" her gaze lit on me, and she offered a tiny, almost apologetic smile "—Chloe got settled."

"So you didn't do the laundry."

"That's what I said."

"But I want—"

"Your shirt. Got that part. So wear it. It's brand-new."

"Yeah, and other people probably tried it on. That's gross."

Rae threw up her hands and disappeared down the hall. Tori shot a scowl over her shoulder, as if this were my fault. As she turned, something flashed between us, and I stumbled back a step, grabbing the railing.

Her scowl twisted. "Geez, I'm not going to *hit* you."

Over her shoulder, a hand appeared, pale fingers wriggling like worms.

"Chloe?" Liz said.

"I—I—I—" I peeled my gaze from the disembodied hand. "I t-tripped."

"Listen—girl—" A man's voice whispered in my ear.

Liz came down the two steps between us and laid her fingers on my arm. "Are you okay? You're all white."

"I j-j-just thought I h-h-heard something."

"Why is she talking like that?" Tori asked Liz.

"It's called a stutter." Liz squeezed my arm. "It's okay. My brother stutters, too."

"Your brother is *five*, Liz. Lots of little kids do it. Not teenagers." Tori peered down at me. "Are you slow?"

"What?"

"You know, do you ride the looong bus—" she pulled her hands apart, then brought them together again "—or the short one."

Liz flushed. "Tori, that's not—"

"Well, she talks like a little kid, and she looks like one so . . ."

"I have a speech impediment," I said, enunciating carefully, as if she were the slow one. "I'm working to overcome it."

"You're doing great," Liz chirped. "You said that whole sentence without stuttering."

"Girls?" Mrs. Talbot peered around the hall doorway below. "You know you aren't supposed to fool around on the stairs. Someone could get hurt. Class is in ten minutes. Chloe, we're still waiting for notes from your teachers, so you won't be in class today. When you're dressed, we'll discuss your schedule."

Lyle House liked schedules the way a boot camp likes discipline.

We rose at 7:30. Ate, showered, dressed, and were in class by 9:00, where we did independent work assigned by our regular teachers, supervised by the tutor, Ms. Wang. Break at 10:30 for a snack—nutritious, of course. Back to class. Break for lunch at noon. Back to class from 1:00 until 4:30 with a twenty-minute break at 2:30. At some point during classes—the timing would vary—we'd have our individual hour-long therapy session with Dr. Gill; my first would be after lunch today. From 4:30 until 6:00, we had free time . . . kind of. In addition to classes and therapy, we had chores. A lot of chores from the looks of the list. These had to be done during our free time before and after dinner. Plus we had to squeeze in thirty minutes of physical activity every day. Then after a snack, it was off to bed at 9:00, lights-out at 10:00.

Nutritious snacks? Therapy sessions? Chore lists? Mandatory exercises? Nine o'clock bedtime?

Boot camp was starting to look good.

I didn't belong here. I really didn't.

After our talk, a phone call sent Mrs. Talbot scurrying off, calling back promises to return with my job list. Oh joy.

I sat in the living room trying to think, but the unrelenting cheerfulness was like a bright light shining in my eyes, making it hard to concentrate. A few days of yellow paint and daisies and I'd turn into a happy zombie, like Liz.

I felt a pang of shame. Liz had made me feel welcome and been quick to defend me against her friend. If being cheerful was a mental illness, it wasn't such a bad one to have—certainly better than seeing burned-up people.

I rubbed the back of my neck and closed my eyes.

Lyle House wasn't so bad, really. Better than padded

rooms and endless hallways filled with *real* zombies, shambling mental patients so doped up they couldn't be bothered to get dressed, much less bathe. Maybe it was the illusion of home that bothered me. Maybe, in some ways, I'd be happier with ugly couches and white walls and bars on the windows, so there'd be no false promises. Yet just because I couldn't see any bars didn't mean it was as open as it seemed. It couldn't be.

I walked to the front window. Closed, despite the sunny day. There was a hole where there'd probably been a latch for opening it. I looked out. Lots of trees, a quiet street, more older houses on big lots. No electric fences. No sign on the lawn proclaiming LYLE HOUSE FOR CRAZY KIDS. All very ordinary, but I suspected if I grabbed a chair and smashed the window, an alarm would sound.

So where was the alarm?

I stepped into the hall, glanced at the front door, and saw it, blinking away. No attempt to hide it. A reminder, I guess. This might look like your house, but don't try walking out the front door.

What about the back?

I went into the dining room and looked out the window into a large yard with as many trees as the front. There was a shed, lawn chairs, and gardens. The soccer ball on one wooden chair and the basketball hoop over a cement pad suggested we were allowed out—probably for that "thirty minutes of physical activity." Was it monitored? I couldn't see any cameras, but there were enough windows for the nurses to keep an eye on anyone in the yard. And the six-foot-high fence was a good deterrent.

"Looking for a way out?"

I spun to see Miss Van Dop. Her eyes glittered with what looked like amusement, but her face was solemn.

"N-no. I w-was just looking around. Oh, and while I was getting dressed, I noticed I don't have my necklace. I think I might have left it in the hospital, and I want to make sure I get it back. It's kind of special."

"I'll let your father know, but he'll have to hold it for you while you're here. We don't like our girls wearing jewelry. Now, as for looking around . . ."

In other words, nice try on the distraction, but it hadn't worked. She pulled out a dining room chair and motioned for me to sit. I did.

"I'm sure you saw the security system at the front door," she said.

"I—I wasn't—"

"Trying to escape. I know." The smile touched her lips. "Most of our residents aren't the sort of teenagers who run away from home, unless it's to make a statement. They're bright enough to know that whatever is out there is worse than what's in here. And what's in here isn't so bad. Not Disney World, but not prison either. The only escape attempts we've ever had are from kids trying to sneak out to meet friends. Hardly serious, but parents expect better security from us; and, while we pride ourselves on providing a homelike environment, I think it's important to point out the limits early."

She waited as if for a response. I nodded.

"The windows are armed with a siren, as are the exterior doors. You are allowed out the back only, and there is no gate. Because of the alarm, you must notify us before going out, so we can disable it and, yes, watch you. If you have any questions about what you can and cannot do, come to me. I won't sugarcoat it for you, Chloe. I believe honesty is the first step to establishing trust, and trust is critical in a place like this."

Again her gaze pierced mine, probing, making sure I understood the other side of that statement—that honesty went both ways and I was expected to keep up my end.

I nodded.

six

MRS. TALBOT SET ME up to peel carrots for lunch. I didn't dare tell her I'd never peeled one in my life. After hacking my thumb, I got the hang of it.

As I peeled, my mind started to wander . . . into places I'd rather not visit. So I called in my best defense: turn it all into a movie.

As traumatic experiences went, the last few days were my best film fodder ever. But what genre would it be? Straight horror? Or psychological suspense? Maybe a combination of elements, surprising the viewer with—

"Peeling duty already?" a voice whispered. "What'd you do to deserve that?"

This time, when I wheeled around, I didn't see a disembodied hand but a whole body. A guy, in fact, maybe a year older than me, a half foot taller and slender, with high cheekbones and dark blond hair worn in short, messy spikes. His almond-shaped brown eyes danced with amusement.

"You must be Chloe."

He reached out. I jumped back. The carrot leaped from my hands and bounced off his arm. A real arm. Attached to a real guy.

"I—I—"

He put a finger to his lips, then pointed at the dining room door. Beyond it, Mrs. Talbot was talking to Liz.

"I'm not supposed to be in here," he whispered. "I'm Simon, by the way."

I was suddenly aware that he was standing between me and the exit. His smile was friendly, and he was definitely cute, but cute didn't count with a guy who had you cornered in a group home.

He backed up to the walk-in pantry, lifted a finger telling me to wait, then disappeared inside. I could hear him rooting around in the shelves. When I peeked in, he was taking down a box of graham crackers.

A kitchen raid? I couldn't help smiling. Guess it didn't matter whether it was a group home or summer camp, guys and their stomachs didn't change. Simon pulled out an unopened sleeve of crackers.

"The other one's already open," I whispered, pointing.

"Thanks, but he'll want the whole thing. Right, bro?"

I followed his gaze over my shoulder, and let out a yelp. The guy standing behind me had to be six feet tall, with shoulders as wide as the door. Though he was as big as an adult, he'd never be mistaken for one. His face could be used as the "before" picture for acne cream. Dark hair hung in his eyes, lank and dull.

"I—I—I—" I swallowed. "I didn't see you there."

He reached past me and took the crackers from Simon. When he started to retreat, Simon grabbed the back of his shirt.

"We're still teaching him manners," he said to me. "Derek, Chloe. Chloe, my brother, Derek."

"Brother?" I said.

"Yeah." Derek's voice was a low rumble. "Identical twins."

"He's my foster brother," Simon said. "So I was just about to tell Chloe—"

"We done here?" Derek said.

Simon waved him away, then rolled his eyes. "Sorry. Anyway, I was just going to say welcome—"

"Simon?" Tori's voice echoed through the kitchen. "Aha. I thought I heard you." Her fingers closed around the pantry door. "You and Derek, always raiding the—"

She spotted me and her eyes narrowed.

"Tori?" Simon said.

Her expression flipped from simmering to simpering. "Yes?"

He jabbed a finger toward the dining room door. "Shhh!"

As she babbled apologies, I made my escape.

After I finished the carrots, Mrs. Talbot said I could have free time until lunch and directed me to the media room. If I was hoping for a big-screen TV with surround sound and a top-of-the-line computer, I was out of luck. There was a twenty-inch TV, a cheap DVD/VCR combo, an old Xbox, and an even older computer. One flip through the movie collection and I knew I wouldn't be spending much time here . . . unless I was suddenly nostalgic for the Olsen twins. The only movie rated above PG was *Jurassic Park*, and it was labeled "Please ask before viewing," like I had to show my school ID card to prove I was over thirteen.

I turned on the computer. It took five minutes to boot up. Windows 98. I spent another five minutes trying to remember how to use Windows. We had Macs at school and I'd used that as an excuse to finally persuade my dad to buy me an Apple laptop—complete with all the upgraded movie editing programs.

I searched for a browser. I hoped for Firefox, but wasn't getting anything better than plain old IE. I typed in a URL and held my breath, expecting to get a "cannot connect to the Internet message." Instead, the page popped up. Guess we weren't as cut off from the outside world as I'd feared.

I flipped through my favorite sites, killing time until I

worked up the nerve to check my in-box. A few minutes checking the weekend box office figures cleared my mind, then I typed in the URL to access my MSN account.

The browser chugged away for a minute, then brought up a "Page cannot be displayed" message. I tried Hotmail. Same thing.

"Chloe, there you are."

I turned as Mrs. Talbot walked in.

"I was just . . ." I waved at the screen. "I wanted to check my e-mail, but I keep getting this."

She walked over, glanced at the screen and sighed. "It's that Net Nanny software or whatever they use. It does more than block some Web sites, I'm afraid. You can send and receive e-mail through our account. You need to use the e-mail program that came with the computer, and get Miss Van Dop to type in the password so you can send it. A pain, I know, but we had a problem last year with a young man accessing sites he shouldn't have and when the board of directors found out . . ." She shook her head. "We're punishing everyone because of one bad apple, I'm sorry to say. Now, it's time for lunch."

I met the last housemate, Peter, over lunch. He said hello, asked how things were going, then turned his attention to his PSP as he ate. Like everything else at Lyle House, it was all very normal. Too normal. Every time someone moved, I tensed, waiting for her to start speaking in tongues or screaming about bugs crawling over his plate. No one did.

The food was decent enough. A homemade casserole, chock-full of vegetables and meat. Healthy, I was sure, like the milk and whole wheat rolls we had to go with it. For dessert we'd been promised Jell-O. Oh joy.

The sirens and screeching tires from Peter's game provided most of the meal's soundtrack. Rae was a no-show. Tori and Liz twittered together, too low for me to join in. Derek was too busy inhaling his food to talk.

So it was left to Simon to play host. He asked what part of the city I was from. When I admitted I hadn't been in any neighborhood very long, he said they'd moved around a lot, too—him and Derek. We started comparing worst-move-ever stories, and Tori jumped in with her own tale of moving horror—from her upstairs bedroom to her basement. Simon let her ramble for about two minutes before asking what grade I was in and at what school.

I knew he was just being polite—including the new girl in conversation—but if Tori had been a cartoon character, smoke would have billowed from her ears. I'd met girls like that. Territorial, whether it was about a hairbrush, a best friend, or a boy they had their eye on.

"Art school," she breathed. "Isn't that just *fascinating*. Tell me, Chloe. What do you study there? Ghost photography? Ghost writing?"

I choked on a chunk of meat.

"Oh." Tori turned doe eyes on Simon. "Didn't Chloe tell

you why she's here? She sees dead people."

Peter lifted his head from his game. "Really? Cool."

When I looked up, Derek's fork was stopped halfway to his mouth, green eyes piercing the curtain of hair as he stared at me, his lip curled, as if to say *What kind of freak thinks she sees ghosts?*

"It's not like that. I—I—I—"

"There she goes." Tori sighed. "Liz, slap her back. See if you can restart her."

Simon glared at her. "Stop being such a bitch, Tori."

She froze, mouth open, a still shot of humiliated horror. Derek returned to his lunch.

"I didn't mean it that way," Tori said, words tumbling out. "Like Peter said, it's kinda cool. If she does see ghosts, maybe she could help Liz with her, you know, poltergeist."

"Tori!" Liz shrieked, dropping her fork.

"Here we go," Derek grumbled.

Liz's eyes filled as she screeched back her chair. Tori retreated into stumbling apologies again. Simon grabbed Liz's glass before she knocked it flying. Peter hunched over his game. Derek took advantage of the chaos to scoop up the last of the casserole.

The kitchen door flew open and Mrs. Talbot appeared, but her words were beat back by the cacophony.

Rae appeared in the other doorway holding a basket of dirty laundry.

"Last call," she mouthed. "Any more?"

No one else noticed, much less heard her. I glanced around, and realized with all the commotion no one would notice if I left. So I did.

They knew. Everyone knew.

I was a freak. A crazy girl who saw ghosts. I belonged here.

Lunch churned in my stomach. I hurried up the stairs, thinking of my bed with its thin mattress that smelled of chemical vanilla, suddenly so inviting. Pull the blinds down, curl up under the covers with my iPod, and try to forget—

"Can I help you, Chloe?"

Two steps from the top, I stopped and turned to see Miss Van Dop below.

"I—I was just going to lie down for a minute. My head hurts and—"

"Then come and get some Tylenol."

"I—I'm kind of tired. I don't have classes, so I thought—"

"Come down, Chloe."

She waited until I was almost there then said, "At Lyle House, bedrooms are for sleeping."

"I—"

"I know you're probably tired and feeling overwhelmed, but you need activity and interaction, not isolation. Rae's getting a head start on the laundry before afternoon classes. If you've finished lunch, you can go help her."

I braced myself as I opened the basement door, expecting a descent down creaky wooden steps into a dark, damp basement, the kind of place I hated. Instead, I saw gleaming stairs, the passage brightly lit, the walls painted pale green with a flowery border. For the first time that day, I was glad of the too-bright cheeriness.

The laundry room had a tile floor, an old recliner, a washer and dryer, and a bunch of cupboards and shelves. Zero "old basement" creep factor.

The washing machine was running, but there was no sign of Rae.

I looked across the room, toward a closed door. As I walked to it, I picked up an acrid smell.

Smoke?

If Rae was smoking down here, I wasn't going to be the one to catch her. I turned to go back upstairs, and saw Rae squeezed between two towers of shelves.

Her lips formed a silent oath as she shook her hand, putting out a match. I looked for a cigarette. There wasn't one—just the smoldering match.

I heard Liz's voice again: *She has this "thing" for fire.*

My reaction must have shown because Rae jumped forward, getting between me and the door, hands flying up.

"No, no, it's not like that. I wasn't going to do anything. I don't—" She slowed, seeing she had my attention. "I don't start fires. They wouldn't let me stay here if I did. Ask anyone. I just like fire."

"Oh."

She noticed me staring at the matchbook and pocketed it.

"I, uh, noticed you didn't get lunch," I said. "Can I bring you something?"

Her face brightened. "Thanks. But I'll grab an apple before class. I use any excuse to avoid eating with Queen Victoria. You saw what she's like. With me, it's food. If I take a big helping or seconds or dessert, she gets her jabs in."

I must have looked confused, because she waved a hand down her body.

"Yes, I could stand to lose a few pounds, but I don't need her as my personal dietitian." She moved to a pile of unsorted laundry. "My advice? Steer clear of her. She's like these monsters I saw in an old sci-fi film, vampires from space, only they didn't drink blood, they sucked out all your energy."

"*Lifeforce*. Tobe Hooper. Psychic vampires."

She grinned, showing a crooked canine. "Psychic vampires. I'll have to remember that one."

Earlier I'd thought I didn't belong here because I didn't feel crazy. I bet none of them did either. Maybe mental illness was like stuttering. I'd spent my life trying to convince people that just because I stammered didn't mean there was anything else wrong with me. I just had a problem that I was working hard to overcome.

Like seeing people who weren't there.

Like being attracted to fire.

It didn't mean you were schizo or anything.

The sooner I got over myself, the better off I'd be at Lyle House. The sooner I'd *get* better . . . and get out.

I looked at the piles of laundry. "Can I help?"

She showed me how—another thing I'd never done. Even at camp, someone did it for us.

After a few minutes of working together, she said, "Does it make sense to you?"

"What?"

"Putting a girl in a place like this because she likes fire."

"Well, if that's all . . ."

"There's more, but it's small stuff, related to the fire thing. Nothing dangerous. I don't hurt myself or anyone else."

She returned to her sorting.

"Do you like manga?" she asked after a minute. "Anime?"

"Anime's cool. I'm not really into it, but I like Japanese movies, animated or not."

"Well, I'm into it. I watch the shows, read the books, chat on the boards, and all that. But this girl I know, she's completely into it. She spends most of her allowance on the books and DVDs. She can recite dialogue from them." She caught my gaze. "So would you say *she* belongs here?"

"No. Most kids are that way about something, right?

With me, it's movies. Like knowing who directed a sci-fi movie made before I was born."

"But no one would say that makes you crazy. Just crazy about movies. Fascinated by them. Just like—" she took the matchbook from her pocket and waggled it "—me and fire."

The door at the top of the stairs clicked.

"Girls?" Mrs. Talbot called. "Are you still down there?"

Her footsteps tapped down before we could answer. As her shadow rounded the corner, I snatched the matchbook from Rae's outstretched hand and hid it under the shirt I'd been folding.

"Rae?" Mrs. Talbot said. "Your classes are starting. Chloe—"

"I'll finish here, then come up."

Mrs. Talbot left. I passed Rae back her matchbook and she mouthed her thanks, then followed the nurse up the stairs. And I was left alone in the basement.

seven

I TOSSED A PAIR OF pink underwear marked *Liz* into her pile, then stopped. Did we wash the guys' underwear, too? I really hoped not. I sifted through the pile, finding only ones for Rae, Liz, and Tori, and exhaled in relief.

"Girl . . ."

A man's voice over my head. I stiffened but forced myself to keep sorting. No one was here. Or, if someone was, he wasn't real. This was how I needed to handle it. Not jump like a scorched cat. Tough it out. Hear the voices, see the visions, and ignore them.

". . . come here . . ."

The voice had moved across the room. I lifted a red lace thong marked *Tori* and thought of my little girl cotton undies.

". . . over here . . ."

I tried to focus on how I could get better underwear before anyone else washed mine, but my hands started to tremble from the effort of ignoring the voice. *Just one look. Just one—*

I glanced across the room. No one there. I sighed and returned to sorting.

". . . door . . . closed . . ."

I looked at the closed door. The one I'd noticed earlier, which was proof that the voice was really just my overactive imagination.

Why do you need proof? What else would it be?

Great. Two voices to ignore.

"Open the door . . . something . . . show you . . ."

Ha! Now there was a classic movie scene: *Just come look behind the closed door, little girl.* I laughed, but the sound quavered, squeaking at the end.

Get a grip. Toughen up or they'll never let you out.

My gaze snuck to the door. It looked like an ordinary closet. If I really believed the voice was in my head, then what was stopping me from opening it?

I strode to the door, forcing myself to put one foot in front of the other, knowing if I stopped, I'd lose my nerve.

"Good . . . come . . ."

I grasped the doorknob, the metal cold under my fingers.

". . . open . . ."

I turned the handle slowly. It went a quarter turn,

then stopped. I jiggled it.

"Locked." My voice echoed through the laundry room.

I jangled it again, then twisted sharply. The door didn't budge.

"Key . . . find . . . unlock . . ."

I pressed my fingers to my temples. "The door is locked and I'm going upstairs," I answered.

As I turned, I smacked into a wall of solid flesh and for the second time that day gave a girlie yelp. I looked up to see the same face that had made me shriek the last time.

I stumbled back and would have fallen if the door wasn't right behind me. Derek made no move to catch me, just stood there, hands in his pockets as I recovered.

"Who were you talking to?" he asked.

"Myself."

"Huh."

"Now, if you'll excuse me . . ."

When he didn't budge, I sidestepped to get around him. He moved into my path.

"You saw a ghost, didn't you?" he said.

To my relief, I managed to laugh. "Hate to break it to you, but there's no such thing as ghosts."

"Huh."

His gaze traveled around the laundry room, like a cop searching for an escaped convict. When he turned that piercing look on me, its intensity sucked the backbone out of me.

"What do you see, Chloe?"

"I—I—I don't s-s-s—"

"Slow down." He snapped the words, impatient. "What do they look like? Do they talk to you?"

"You really want to know?"

"Yeah."

I chewed my lip, then lifted onto my tiptoes. He bent to listen.

"They wear white sheets with big eye holes. And they say 'Boo!' " I glowered up at him. "Now get out of my way."

I expected him to sneer. Cross his arms and say, *Make me, little girl.*

His lips twitched and I steeled myself, then I realized he was smiling. Laughing at me.

He stepped aside. I swept past him to the stairs.

Dr. Gill was a small woman with a long rodent nose and bulging ratlike eyes that studied me as if *I* were the rat—one whose every twitch had to be scribbled into her notebook. I'd had therapists before. Two of them, both after my mom died. I'd hated the first one, an old man with bad breath who'd closed his eyes when I talked, like he was taking a nap. When I complained, I got the second one, Dr. Anna, a woman with bright red hair who'd joked with me and reminded me of my mom and helped me get on with my life. After ten minutes with Dr. Gill, I knew she fell somewhere in the middle. She seemed nice enough, and listened carefully, but she wasn't going to start cracking jokes any-time soon.

We talked about how I'd slept; how I was eating; what I thought of the others; and, mostly, how I felt about being here. I lied about the last. I wasn't stupid. If I wanted to get out, I couldn't moan that I didn't belong or complain that someone made a horrible mistake.

So I said that I knew my dad and aunt had done the right thing by putting me in Lyle House, and that I was deter-mined to get better, whatever it took.

Dr. Gill's rat face relaxed. "That's a very mature atti-tude. I'm glad to hear it."

I nodded, and tried to look sincere.

"Now, Chloe, have you ever heard of schizophrenia?"

My heart stopped. "Sch-schizophrenia?"

"Yes. Do you know anything about it?"

My mouth opened and closed, brain refusing to fill it with words.

"Chloe?"

"Y-you think I'm schizo?"

Her mouth tightened. "We don't use that word, Chloe. In fact, we prefer not to use labels at all. But a diagnosis is a necessary part of the process. A patient must know her con-dition, understand and accept it before we can begin treat-ment."

"B-but I just got here. How c-can you know already—"

"Do you remember at the hospital? The doctors you

spoke to? The tests they ran?"

"They found schizophrenia?"

She shook her head. "While scientists are working on a way to definitively diagnose schizophrenia, we don't have anything conclusive yet. Those tests, though, ruled out other possibilities, such as tumors or drug use. Taking those results and combining them with your symptoms, the most likely diagnosis is schizophrenia."

I stared at the floor. "You think I have schizophrenia."

"Do you know what it is?" She spoke slowly, like she was starting to question my intelligence.

"I've seen *A Beautiful Mind*."

More lip pursing. "That's Hollywood's version, Chloe."

"But it's based on a true story, right?"

"*Based*." Her voice softened. "I know from your file that you enjoy movies, and that's wonderful. But they aren't a good place to learn about mental illness. There are many forms and degrees of schizophrenia and yours isn't the same as that one."

Wasn't it? I saw people who weren't there, just like the guy in the movie.

Dr. Gill continued. "What you are experiencing is what we'd call undifferentiated schizophrenia, meaning you're displaying a limited number of the primary symptoms—in your case, seeing visions and hearing voices. Visual and auditory hallucinations."

"What about paranoia?"

"We see no evidence of that. You show no signs of disorganized behavior or disorganized speech patterns—"

"What about stuttering?"

She shook her head. "That's unrelated. You display none of the other symptoms, Chloe."

"Will I? Eventually?"

"Not necessarily. We'll have to be vigilant, of course, but we've caught this early. Usually a diagnosis isn't made until a patient is in her late teens or twenties. It's like catching a disease in its early stages, when we have the best chance to minimize its progression."

"And get rid of it."

A moment of silence as she fingered a long corded necklace. "Schizophrenia . . . is not like the flu, Chloe. It is permanent."

Blood thundered in my ears, drowning out her next words. She leaned forward, touching my knee.

"Chloe, are you listening to me?"

I nodded.

She moved back. "Schizophrenia is not a life sentence. But it is a lifelong condition. Like having asthma. With lifestyle changes and medication, it can be controlled and you can lead an otherwise normal life, to the point where no one will realize you have it unless you choose to tell them." She leaned back, meeting my gaze. "Earlier you said you were determined to do whatever it took to get through this. I know you were hoping for a quick fix, but this is going to require that same level of maturity and determination. Are you still prepared to do that, Chloe?"

I had more questions. Did it usually happen this fast, with no warning? One day you're walking around, totally normal, and the next you're hallucinating and running screaming through the halls? Then, bang, you get told you have schizophrenia, case closed?

It all seemed too sudden. But when I looked at Dr. Gill, watching me expectantly, waiting to get on to the next phase, I was afraid if I said anything, it would sound like I was still in denial; and if I did that, I'd never get out of Lyle House.

So I nodded. "I just want to get better."

"Good. Then we'll begin."

Dr. Gill explained about the medication. It was supposed to stop my hallucinations. Once they had the dose adjusted, there shouldn't be any significant side effects, but at first I might experience partial hallucinations, depression, and paranoia. Great. Sounded like the cure was as bad as the disease.

Dr. Gill assured me that by the time I left the group home, taking the pills would be no different than taking daily asthma medicine. "That's how you need to think of schizophrenia, Chloe. As a medical condition. You did nothing to cause it."

And could do nothing to cure it.

"You'll go through a period of depression, anger, and even denial. That's natural, and we'll deal with that in our sessions. You'll meet with me for an hour a day."

"Are there group sessions, too?" I asked.

"No. Someday you may decide you want to explore the dynamics of group therapy and we can discuss that later, but at Lyle House, we believe that privacy is critical. You need to fully accept your condition before you'll be comfortable sharing it with others."

She laid her notebook on the desk and crossed her hands on her knee. "And that leads to our final topic for today. Privacy. As I'm sure you've guessed, all the residents here are coping with mental issues. But that is all anyone needs to know. We will not share details of your condition, your symptoms, or your treatment with anyone here. If anyone pressures you for details, you are to come to us right away."

"They already know," I murmured.

"What?"

The outrage blazing from her eyes told me I should have kept my mouth shut. I knew from past therapy that it was important to share anything that was bothering me, but I didn't need to start my stay at Lyle House by tattling.

"N-not about the schizophrenia. Just . . . someone knew about me seeing things. Ghosts. Which I *never* said. To anyone."

"Who was it?"

"I—I'd rather not say. It was no big deal."

She unfolded her hands. "Yes, it is a big deal, Chloe. But I also appreciate that you don't want to get anyone into trouble. I have a good idea who it was. She must have been eavesdropping when we were discussing your hallucinations and jumped to her own conclusions about . . ." A dismissive wave of her hands. "Ghosts. I'm sorry this happened, but I promise it will be handled discreetly."

"But—"

"She won't know you told us anything, but it must be dealt with." She eased back into her seat. "I'm sorry this happened on your first day. Young people are, by nature, curious, and as hard as we strive to provide privacy, it isn't always possible in such tight living quarters."

"It's okay. No one made a big deal of it."

She nodded. "We have a very good group of young people here. In general, they are very respectful and accepting. That's important at Lyle House. You have a difficult road ahead and we're all here to make that journey as smooth as possible."

Schizo.

It didn't matter how many times Dr. Gill compared it to a disease or physical disability, it wasn't the same thing. It just wasn't. I had schizophrenia.

If I saw two guys on the sidewalk, one in a wheelchair and one talking to himself, which one would I rush to open a door for? And which would I cross the road to avoid?

Dr. Gill said it was just a matter of taking my meds and learning to cope. If it was that easy, why *were* there people wandering the streets talking to themselves? Crazy-eyed homeless people shouting at thin air?

Seeing people who weren't there. Hearing voices that didn't exist.

Schizo.

Just like me.

After my session, I ducked into the media room to think. I was curled up on the love seat, hugging a pillow to my chest, when Simon sailed in.

Not seeing me, he crossed the room and grabbed a baseball cap from the computer desk. Humming under his breath, he tossed the hat in the air and caught it.

He looked happy.

How could he be happy here? Comfortable, maybe. But happy?

He flipped the cap over in his hand and tugged it on. He stopped, gaze fixed on the window. I couldn't see his expression, but he went very still. Then a sharp shake of his head. He turned and saw me. A flash of surprise, then a broad grin.

"Hey."

"Hi."

He stepped closer, smile fading. "You okay?"

I'm fine sprang to my lips, but I couldn't force it out. I wasn't fine. I wanted to say I wasn't. I wanted it to be okay to say I wasn't. But the concern in his voice went no deeper than his grin, neither touching his eyes. They stayed distant, like he was making an effort to be nice because he was a nice guy and it was the right thing to do.

"I'm fine," I said.

He twisted the bill of his cap, watching me. Then he shrugged. "Okay. But a word of advice? Don't let them catch you holing up in here. It's like going to your room during the day. You'll get a lecture on moping around."

"I'm not—"

He lifted his hands. "Their words, not mine. I'm just warning you. You can get away with turning on the TV and pretending you're watching it, but they'll be happier if you're up and about, hanging with us. We're not such a bad bunch. Not too crazy."

He gave a blazing grin that made my stomach flip. I sat up, struggling for something to say, something to keep him here. I did want to talk. Not about Dr. Gill. Not about schizophrenia. About anything *but* that. Simon seemed normal and I desperately needed normal.

But his gaze had already shunted to the door. Sure, he thought I should hang out . . . with someone else. He was just giving advice to the new girl.

The doorway darkened and Simon's smile flashed fresh.

"Hey, bro. Don't worry. I didn't forget you. Just talking to Chloe."

He waved my way. Derek looked in, so expressionless you'd think Simon was gesturing at the furniture.

The scene in the basement flashed back—Derek accusing me of talking to ghosts. Had he told Simon? Probably. I bet they had a good laugh at the crazy girl.

"We're heading out back," Simon said. "Kick around the ball for our break. You're welcome to join us."

The invitation came lightly, automatically, and he didn't even wait for a response before he brushed past Derek with, "I'll get Talbot to disarm the door."

Derek stayed where he was. Still watching me.

Staring at me.

Like I was a freak.

Like I was schizo.

"Take a picture," I snapped. "It'll last longer."

He didn't so much as blink. Didn't leave either. Just kept studying me, as if I hadn't said a word. He'd leave when he was ready. And he did, walking out without a word.

When I left the media room, only Mrs. Talbot was around. The other kids had returned to class after their break. She sent me into the kitchen to peel—potatoes this time.

Before I started, she gave me another pill. I wanted to ask when I could expect them to start working, but if I did, then I'd have to admit I was still hearing voices. I wasn't seeing anything, though. Just that hand this morning, right after I took the pills. So maybe they *were* working. Maybe it didn't get any better than this. What would I do then?

Fake it. Block the voices and pretend I wasn't hearing them. Learn to—

A scream echoed through the house.

I jumped, the peeler clattering into the sink. As my heart thumped, I listened for a reaction. No reaction would mean the voice had been in my head. See, I was learning already.

"Elizabeth Delaney! Get back here!"

A door slammed. Footsteps raced down the hall, punctuated by sobs. The hairs on my neck rose as I thought of the crying girl at school. But I forced myself to the door and cracked it open just in time to see Liz lurch up the stairs.

"Enjoying the show?"

I jumped and caught Tori's glower before she hurried after her friend. Miss Van Dop strode from the living room into the hall.

"I have had it!" the other voice boomed from the classroom. "I expect some behavioral problems tutoring in a place like this, but that girl needs professional help."

"Ms. Wang, please," Miss Van Dop said. "Not in front of—"

"She threw a pencil at me. Whipped it. Like a weapon. Another half inch and she'd have taken my eye out. She broke the skin. Blood. From a pencil! All because I dared to suggest that a tenth grade student should be able to understand basic algebra."

Miss Van Dop tugged her into the hall, but the woman broke away and stormed into another room.

"Where's the director's number? I'm quitting. That girl is a menace. . . ."

A shadow glided past me and I turned to see Derek at my shoulder. As the dining room door swung shut behind him, I caught a glimpse of books and a calculator spread across the table. He must have been there the whole time, doing independent work.

As he looked down at me, I expected some sarcastic comment about eavesdropping, but he only muttered, "Welcome to the madhouse," then brushed past me into the kitchen to swipe an extra snack.

eight

A FTER THAT, CALM DESCENDED. Like the calm before the storm, only in reverse. The nurses put dinner in the oven, then sequestered themselves in Dr. Gill's office, on a conference call, not to be disturbed.

No one had disagreed with Ms. Wang's explanation of events. No one tried to say it had been an accident. No one even seemed surprised that Liz had almost put someone's eye out.

When dinner time came, Mrs. Talbot served the food, then retreated into the office again. Liz joined us, wan and quiet. Simon snuck her a juice box, though we were supposed to be having milk. Tori hovered over her, coaxing her to eat. Even Rae and Peter made efforts at conversation, as if to distract her. Only Derek and I didn't participate.

After dinner Tori reminded Liz it was movie night, when

they could get a DVD delivered. She gave Liz the honor of choosing, but Liz seemed overwhelmed by the responsibility and looked to us for help. Simon made suggestions, but said he wouldn't be watching it—he and Derek had a project due the next day. Liz finally settled on a romantic comedy. While she and Tori went to tell the nurses, Rae announced she had to fold the now-clean laundry. I offered to help.

We each carried a basket to the room Rae shared with Tori. I could tell neither was pleased with the arrangement. I swore I saw pencil marks on the windowsill to divide the room in half.

Tori's side was so clean it looked like mine when I'd first walked in. Nothing on the walls. Nothing on the bed or the floor. Every surface was bare, except two picture frames on the dresser. One held a shot of Tori and her parents and the other of a huge Siamese cat.

Rae's half had enough clutter for both of them. Hooded sweatshirts on the bedposts, textbooks balancing precariously on the desk, makeup left open on the dresser, drawers leaking clothing. The room of someone who didn't see why she had to put things away when she'd only be using them again the next day. Her walls were covered with taped photos.

Rae set her basket on Tori's bed, then closed the door. "Okay, I could beat around the bush, but I hate that, so I'm going to come right out and ask. Did I hear right? That you're here because you see ghosts?"

The words *I don't want to talk about it* rose to my lips. But I *did* want to talk about it. I longed to pick up the phone and call Kari or Beth, but I wasn't sure how much they'd heard about what happened and whether they'd understand. The person who seemed least likely to make fun of me or gossip about my problem was right here, asking for my story. So I gave it to her.

When I finished, Rae knelt there, holding up a shirt for at least thirty seconds before realizing what she was doing and folding it.

"Wow," she said.

"No wonder I'm in here, huh?"

"And it started right before you got your first period? Maybe that's it. Because you were kinda late, all that stuff built up, and then . . . bam."

"Super PMS?"

She laughed. "So have you looked it up?"

"Looked what up?"

"The custodian."

When I frowned, she went on. "You got chased by a guy in a custodian's uniform, right? And he was burned, like he died in some fire or explosion. If it really happened, it would have made the papers. You could look it up online."

I won't say the thought hadn't occurred to me, but I'd only given it permission to flit through my brain, like a streaker at a football game, moving too fast for me to get a good look.

What if I was *really* seeing ghosts?

My brain flashed *don't go there* neon warnings, but some deeper part was fascinated, *wanted* to go there.

I rubbed my temples.

Ghosts aren't real. Ghosts are for crazy people. What I saw were hallucinations, and the sooner I accepted that, the sooner I'd get out of here.

"It'd be cool if it was," I said carefully. "But Dr. Gill said seeing visions is a clear sign of a mental illness."

"Ah, the label. God, they love their labels here. Can't even let a girl get through her first day without slapping one on. Mine's pyromania." She caught my look. "Yeah, I know. We aren't supposed to share. Protecting our privacy. I think that's crap. They just don't want us comparing notes."

She lined up socks and started matching them. "You don't agree."

"Maybe with something like pyromania. It sounds almost . . . cool. But there are other things, labels, that we might not want to share."

"Like what?"

I concentrated on mating the socks for a minute. I wanted to tell her. Like the stuff about the ghosts. As scared as I was of sounding like a freak, I wanted to tell someone, to see what she said, get a second opinion.

"They say I have schizophrenia."

I studied her reaction. Just a small frown of confusion.

"Isn't that multiple personality?" she asked.

"No. Schizophrenia is, like, you know, schizo."

Her expression didn't change. "So it's seeing things and stuff?"

I lifted a white sail of a T-shirt, with faintly dingy armpits. No need to check the name. I folded it and added it to Derek's pile. "There's a whole lot of other symptoms, but I don't have them."

"None of them?"

"Guess not."

She eased back, uncrossing her legs. "See, that's my problem with it. You have one weird episode and they slap on a label, even if you just have the one problem. It's like coughing and they decide you've got pneumonia. I bet there are a lot more symptoms to pyromania, too. Ones I don't have."

Her gaze fixed on a red and a blue sock, and she stared intently at them, as if she could will them to turn purple and match. "So what else comes with schizophrenia?"

"Dr. Gill didn't say exactly."

"Huh."

"I guess I could look it up on the Internet. I should."

"*We* should. Schizophrenia and pyromania. I'd like to know more. To be sure, you know? Especially with the way things are going with Liz . . ." She rubbed her mouth with the back of her hand, still staring at the mismatched socks.

"I think you're going to have the room to yourself soon. Maybe real soon."

"They're transferring her?"

"Probably. They've been talking about it for a while. This place is for kids who have problems, but they're not too bad and they're getting better. A couple weeks after I got here, they transferred a guy named Brady. He wasn't getting worse or anything. Not like Liz. He just didn't want to get better. He didn't think there was anything wrong with himself. So off he went . . . Taught me a lesson. I might not like their labels and their meds, but I'll keep my mouth shut, play the game, and get out of here the *right* way."

"And go home."

A moment of silence, neither of us moving. Then she yanked a blue sock from my hand and waved it in front of my face.

"Whoops." I hadn't even realized I'd been holding it.

She folded the blue pair together, then shoved the lone red sock under Tori's bed. "Done. It should be movie time soon." She piled folded laundry into one basket. "Notice how quick Simon was to get out of watching the movie? Couple of real scholars, those two. Anything to avoid hanging out with the crazy kids."

"I got that impression. Simon seems nice but . . ."

She handed me one basket and took the other. "He's as much of a diva as Tori. They'd be a great pair. Derek might be a jerk, but at least he's honest about it. Simon makes nice during the day when he has to hang with us, then bolts the minute he can escape with his brother. Acts like he doesn't belong here. Like he doesn't have any problems and it's all a huge mistake."

"What *is* he in here for?"

"Believe me, I'd love to know. Him and Derek, both. Simon never goes to therapy, but Derek gets more than anyone. No one ever comes to visit them, but sometimes you'll hear them going on about their dad. Simon's dad, I think. If he's so great, why'd he dump them here and take off? And how do two guys from the same family, but not blood brothers, both have mental problems? I'd love to see their files."

I'd be lying if I said I wasn't curious about Simon. And maybe Derek, if only because I had the feeling I might need some ammunition against him. But I wouldn't want anyone reading *my* file and I wasn't going to help Rae read theirs.

"We couldn't risk taking a peek tonight anyway," she said. "With what's going on with Liz, they'll be on high alert. I don't want to get kicked out for corrupting the new kid."

"Maybe I'd get tossed out for corrupting you."

She caught my grin and laughed. "Oh, yeah, you're trouble, girl. I can tell."

She scooted me from the room and shut the door behind us.

nine

I'M NOT KEEN ON ROMANTIC comedies. This may be like a guy admitting he doesn't like car chases, but Rae nodded off a few times, too, so I guessed this wouldn't have been her choice either.

I stayed awake by deconstructing the screenplay, which was so predictable I'd bet my college fund the writer was a student of screenwriting guru Robert McKee.

But as I watched the silly movie and munched popcorn, I finally relaxed. Talking to Rae had helped. She'd didn't think I was crazy. She didn't even think I was schizophrenic.

For the first time since my breakdown, things didn't look so bad. Maybe life as I knew it hadn't really ended in that classroom. Maybe I was overreacting and going all drama queen.

Did the kids at school know what had happened to me? A few saw me run down a hall. More saw me carried out on a stretcher, unconscious. Big deal. I could return in a few weeks and most probably wouldn't even notice I'd been gone.

Tomorrow, I'd e-mail Kari, tell her I was sick, and see what she said. That's probably exactly what she heard, that I had something like mono.

I'd get through this. Whatever I thought of their diagnosis, now wasn't the time to argue. I'd take my meds, lie if I had to, get released from Lyle House, and get on with my life.

"Chloe? Chloe?"

Liz's voice echoed through the deep caves of dreamland, and it took me a few minutes to find the way out. When I opened my eyes, she was leaning over me, bathing me in toothpaste breath, her long hair tickling my cheek. The hand clutching my arm kept trembling even after she stopped shaking me.

I pushed up on my elbows. "What's wrong?"

"I've been lying here for hours, trying to think of some way to ask you, some way that won't sound weird. But I can't. I just can't."

She backed away, her pale face glowing in the darkness, hands tugging at her nightshirt neckline, like it was choking her.

I scrambled up. "Liz?"

"They're going to send me away. Everyone knows they are, and that's why they're being so nice to me. I don't want to go, Chloe. They'll lock me up and—" She hiccuped deep breaths, hands cupped over her mouth. When she looked at me, her eyes were so wide the whites showed around her dark irises. "I know you haven't been here long, but I really need your help."

"Okay."

"Really?"

I stifled a yawn as I sat up. "If there's anything I can do—"

"There is. Thank you. Thank you." She dropped to her knees and pulled a bag from under her bed. "I don't know what all you need, but I did one at a sleepover last year, so I gathered up everything we used. There's a glass, some spices, a candle—" Her hand flew to her mouth. "Matches! Oh, no. We don't have any matches. They keep them locked up because of Rae. Can we do it without lighting the candle?"

"Do what?" I rubbed my hands over my face. I hadn't taken a sleeping pill but still felt that weird fogginess, like I was swimming through a sea of cotton balls. "What exactly are we doing, Liz?"

"A séance, of course."

The sleep fog evaporated, and I wondered if this was a prank. But I could tell by her expression that it wasn't. I remembered Tori's words at lunch.

"The . . . poltergeist?" I said carefully.

Liz flew at me so fast I smacked backward into the wall, hands flying up to ward her off. But she only pounced down beside me, eyes wild.

"Yes!" she said. "I have a poltergeist. It's so obvious, but they won't see it. They keep saying it's me doing all this stuff. But how would I throw a pencil that hard? Did anyone see me throw it? No. I get mad at Ms. Wang and the pencil flies and hits her and everyone says 'Oh, Liz threw it,' but I didn't. I never do."

"It's the . . . poltergeist."

"Right! I think it's trying to protect me because every time I get mad, things start flying. I've tried to talk to it, to make it stop. But it can't hear me because I can't talk to ghosts. That's why I need you."

I struggled to keep my expression neutral. I'd seen a documentary on poltergeist activity once. It usually *did* happen around girls like Liz—troubled teens desperate for attention. Some people thought the girls were playing pranks. Others believed the energy the girls gave off—hormones and rage—actually made things move.

"You don't believe me," she said.

"No, I didn't say—"

"You don't *believe* me!" She rose to her knees, eyes blazing. "Nobody believes me!"

"Liz, I—"

Behind her, the hair gel bottles rocked. Empty hangers in the closet chattered. I dug my fingers into the mattress.

"O-o-okay, Liz. I s-s-see—"

"No, you *don't!*"

She slammed her hands down. The bottles jetted into the air, smashing against the ceiling with such force the plastic exploded. Hair gel rained down.

"Do you see?"

"Y-y-yes."

Her hands flew up again, like a conductor hitting the crescendo. A picture leaped from the wall. It smashed onto the hardwood floor, glass spraying. Another fell. Then a third. A sliver of glass shot into my knee. A button of blood welled up and streamed down my leg.

Out of the corner of my eye, I saw the picture above my bed quaver. It sprang from its moorings.

"No!" Liz cried.

I dove. Liz hit my side, shoving me out of the picture's path. It struck her shoulder. She twisted. We both rolled from the bed, hitting the floor hard.

I lay on my side, catching my breath.

"I'm so sorry," she gasped. "I didn't mean— Do you see what happens? I can't control it. I get mad and everything . . ."

"You think it's a poltergeist."

She nodded, her lip quivering.

I had no idea what was going on. Not a poltergeist

though—that was nuts—but if she thought it was, then maybe if she thought I'd told it to stop, it really *would* stop.

"Okay," I said. "Get the candle and we'll—"

The door shot open. Mrs. Talbot's bathrobed form stood silhouetted in the doorway. She flipped on the light. I drew back, blinking.

"Oh my God," she breathed, barely above a whisper. "Elizabeth. What have you done?"

I jumped to my feet. "It wasn't her. I—I—I—"

For once, I wasn't stammering. I just couldn't think of more words. Her gaze swept across the room, taking in the glass littering the floor, the hair gel dripping from the ceiling, the exploded makeup painting the wall, and I knew there was no reasonable explanation.

Her gaze fell to my leg and she let out a squeak.

"It's okay," I said, drawing my leg up and swiping the blood. "It's nothing. I cut myself. Shaving. Earlier."

She picked her way past me, eyes fixed on the glass-carpeted floor.

"No," Liz whispered. "Please no. I didn't mean it."

"It's okay, hon. We're going to get you help."

Miss Van Dop strode in, carrying a needle. She sedated Liz as Mrs. Talbot tried to calm her, telling her they were only transferring her to a better hospital, one more suitable, one that could help her get well faster.

When Liz was unconscious, they shooed me from the room. As I backed into the hall, a hand walloped me in the back, slamming me into the wall. I turned to see Tori looming over me.

"What did you do to her?" she snarled.

"Nothing." To my shock, the word came out clear, defiant even. I pulled myself up straight. "*I'm* not the one who told her I could help."

"Help?"

"By contacting her poltergeist."

Her eyes went wide, with that same horrified expression as when Simon told her to stop acting like a bitch. She turned away and stumbled into her room.

ten

THE PARAMEDICS CAME FOR LIZ. I watched her go, asleep on the stretcher, just like I'd been taken from school. Deluxe transportation for crazy kids.

Miss Van Dop insisted I take half a sleeping pill. I gave in, but when she tried to follow it with an extra dose of my antihallucination medicine, I hid that pill under my tongue.

I hadn't seen or heard anything since lunchtime. While that might have been the meds kicking in, I couldn't help hoping Rac's wild theory was right—that my "break with reality" was only a temporary mental vacation, brought on by stress and hormones. With any luck, I was already making the return trip to sanity.

I had to test that theory. So I'd save the pill and, if I saw anything, I'd take it.

I offered to help clean the room, but Mrs. Talbot took me

downstairs for a glass of milk, then settled me on the sofa. I drifted off, waking when she came to trundle me back to bed, and was asleep again before I could pull up the covers.

I awoke to the fruity smell of Liz's hair gel. I floated there, dreaming I was trapped in a vat of cotton candy, the sweet smell making my stomach churn as I fought through the sticky strands. Finally I broke free, eyes flying open, gulping air.

"Chloe?"

I blinked. It sounded like Liz's voice, timid and wavering.

"Are you awake, Chloe?"

I rolled onto my side. Liz sat on the edge of her bed, wearing her Minnie Mouse nightshirt and gray socks covered with purple and orange giraffes.

She wiggled her toes. "Funky, huh? My little brother got them for me last Christmas."

I pushed up, blinking harder. The cotton candy from the sleeping pill still encircled my brain, sticky and thick, and I couldn't seem to focus. Sunlight streamed through the venetian blind, making the giraffes on Liz's socks dance as she waggled her toes.

"I had the weirdest dream last night," she said, gaze fixed on her feet.

You and me both, I thought.

"I dreamed they took me away and I woke up in this hospital. Only I wasn't in a bed but on a table. A cold, metal table. And there was this woman there, like a nurse, wearing one of those masks. She was bending over me. When I opened my eyes, she jumped."

Her gaze shot my way, and she managed a tiny smile. "Kinda like you do sometimes. Like I startled her. She calls this guy over, and I ask where I am, but they just keep talking. They're mad because I wasn't supposed to wake up and now they don't know what to do. I try to sit, but I'm tied down."

Liz bunched her nightshirt in her hands, kneading it. "All of a sudden I couldn't breathe. I couldn't move, couldn't yell, and then . . ." She shuddered, arms wrapping around herself. "I woke up here."

I sat up. "I'm going to help you, Liz. Okay?"

She scuttled back on the bed, pulling her knees up. She opened her mouth, but she was shaking too badly to form words. I stood, the wood floor icy beneath my feet, and crossed over to sit beside her.

"Do you want me to try talking to your poltergeist?"

She nodded, chin drumming against her chest. "Tell it to stop. Tell it I don't need its help. I can look after myself."

I reached out to lay my hand on her arm. I saw my fingers make contact, but they kept moving. Kept going. Through her arm.

As I stared in horror, Liz looked down. She saw my hand pass through her. And she started to scream.

eleven

I TUMBLED OFF HER BED, hitting the floor so hard pain jolted through my spine. When I scrambled up, Liz's bed was empty, the comforter wrinkled only where I'd been sitting.

I took a slow look around the bedroom. Liz was gone.

Gone? She'd never been here. They'd taken her away last night. I hadn't dreamed that part—hair gel still freckled the ceiling.

I pressed my palms to my eyes and backed up until I hit my bed, sitting down on it and inhaling deeply. After a moment, I opened my eyes. Sticky strands of sleep were still woven around my brain.

I'd been dreaming.

No, not dreaming. Not imagining things. Hallucinating.

Dr. Gill was right. I had schizophrenia.

But what if it wasn't? What if Rae was right, and I was seeing ghosts?

I shook my head sharply. No, that was crazy talk. That would mean Liz was dead. That was nuts. I was hallucinating, and I had to accept it.

I reached under my mattress, pulled out the pill I'd stuffed there the night before, and swallowed it dry, gagging in protest.

I had to take my meds. Take them and get better or I'd be shipped off to a real mental hospital, like Liz.

Only Rae joined me for breakfast. Tori was still in her room, and the nurses seemed content to leave her there.

I picked at my cereal, scooping one Cheerio at a time so it looked like I was eating. I kept thinking of how scared Liz had been. Terrified of being sent away. Then talking about her dream of being tied down, unable to breathe . . .

A hallucination. In real life, things like that don't happen.

And in real life, teenage girls can't make bottles explode and pictures fly off the walls. . . .

"Miss Van Dop?" I said when she came in to lay the breakfast table for the boys. "About Liz . . ."

"She's fine, Chloe. She's gone to a better place."

Those words sent a shiver through me, my spoon clattering against the bowl.

"I'd like to talk to her if I could," I said. "I didn't get a chance to say good-bye. Or thank her for helping me my first day."

Miss Van Dop's severe face softened. "She needs to settle in, but we'll call her in a few days and you can speak to her then."

See? Liz was fine. I was being paranoid.

Paranoia. Another symptom of schizophrenia. I pushed back the stab of dismay.

The nurse turned to go.

"Miss Van Dop? Sorry. I, um, I was talking to Mrs. Talbot yesterday, about e-mailing a friend. She said I needed to speak to you."

"Just use the e-mail program to write your letter and click send. It'll sit in the out-box until I enter the password."

Some instructions from my school had arrived, so after breakfast, I showered and dressed as the guys ate, then headed off to class with Rae.

Tori stayed in her room and the nurses let her. That surprised me, but I guessed it was because she was upset over Liz. I remembered Liz saying Tori was here because she was moody. There'd been a girl at drama camp a couple years ago whom I'd overheard counselors calling "moody." She'd always seemed to be either really happy or really sad, with no in-between.

With Tori absent, I was the only ninth grader. Peter was

in eighth; Simon, Rae, and Derek in tenth. It didn't seem to matter much. Kind of like running a one-room schoolhouse, I guess. We shared a room with eight desks and we all worked on our separate assignments as Ms. Wang went around, helping and quietly giving short lessons.

Maybe knowing Ms. Wang had been partly responsible for Liz's leaving influenced my opinion of her, but she seemed to be one of those teachers who trudges through her job, watching the clock, waiting for the day to end . . . or a better job to come along.

I didn't get much work done that morning. I couldn't concentrate, couldn't stop thinking about Liz, what she'd done, what had happened to her.

The nurses hadn't seemed at all surprised by the damage in our room. That's just what Liz did, like with the pencil. She got mad and threw things.

But she hadn't thrown that stuff. I'd seen pictures fly from the wall when she'd been nowhere near them.

Or had I?

If I *was* schizophrenic, how was I supposed to know what I'd really seen or heard? And if paranoia was another symptom, how could I even trust my own gut feeling that said something bad had happened to Liz?

Rae was in session with Dr. Gill for the first part of the morning. When she returned, I spent the rest of the class eagerly awaiting break time, so I could talk to her. Not about

Liz and my fears. Just talk to her. About class, last night's movie, the weather . . . anything that would clear Liz from my head.

But she was having problems with a work sheet, and Ms. Wang made her stay through the break. So I promised to grab her a snack, then trudged out, heading for the kitchen, sentenced to another hour or two trapped in my own head, thinking about Liz.

"Hey." Simon jogged up beside me in the hall. "You okay? You seem quiet this morning."

I managed a wan smile. "I'm always quiet."

"Yeah, but after last night, you have an excuse. Probably didn't get much sleep, huh?"

I shrugged.

Simon reached for the kitchen door. A hand appeared over my head and grabbed it for him. I didn't jump this time, just glanced back, and murmured a good morning to Derek. He didn't answer.

Simon headed into the pantry. Derek stayed in the kitchen, watching me. Studying me, again, with that spookily intense look of his.

"What?" I didn't mean to snap, but the word came out harsh.

Derek reached for me. I stumbled back . . . and realized he was reaching for the fruit bowl, which I was blocking. My cheeks burned as I darted out of the way, mumbling an apology. He ignored that, too.

"So what happened last night?" he asked as he grabbed two apples in one big hand.

"Hap-p-p-?"

"Slow down."

My face heated more—with anger now. I didn't like it when adults told me to slow down. From another kid, it was worse. Rude with a grating edge of condescension.

Simon stepped from the pantry, a box of granola bars in hand.

"You should have an apple," Derek said. "That's not—"

"I'm good, bro."

He flipped one granola bar to Derek, then held out the box for me. I took two, with thanks, and turned to leave.

"Might help if you talk about it," Simon called after me.

I turned back. Simon was unwrapping his granola bar, gaze averted, trying to look casual. Derek didn't bother. He leaned back against the counter, chomping into his apple, staring at me, expectant.

"Well?" Derek said when I stayed silent. He gestured for me to hurry up, spill all the gory details.

I'd never been one for gossip. Maybe that's not what they wanted—maybe they were just curious, concerned even. But it felt like gossip, and Liz deserved better.

"Rae's waiting for me," I said.

Simon stepped forward, raising a hand as if to stop me. Then he glanced at Derek. I didn't catch the look that passed between them, but it made Simon pull back, nod a good-bye to me, and busy himself unwrapping the rest of his bar.

The door was still swinging shut behind me when Simon whispered, "Something happened."

"Yeah."

I let the door close, and stood there. Derek said something else, but his low rumble swallowed the words.

"I don't know," Simon said. "We shouldn't—"

"Chloe?"

I wheeled as Mrs. Talbot stepped into the hall from the living room.

"Is Peter around?" she asked. Her broad face beamed.

"Uh, in class I think."

"Could you tell him I need to see him in the living room? I have a surprise for him."

I glanced at the kitchen door, but the guys had gone silent. I nodded to Mrs. Talbot and hurried off.

Peter's parents had come to take him home.

He'd known it would be coming soon, but they'd wanted to surprise him, so we had a little party, complete with cake. Low-fat, organic, frosting-free carrot cake. Then his parents went upstairs to help him pack, while Simon, Derek, and Rae returned to class and I had my session with Dr. Gill.

Twenty minutes later, from her office window, I watched

his parents' minivan back out the drive and disappear down the street.

Another week and I'd be doing the same. I just had to stop thinking about Liz and ghosts and concentrate on getting out.

twelve

AFTER LUNCH, IT WAS time for math. That was one class where the tutor needed to know exactly where I was in the program and my math teacher hadn't sent over my work yet, so I was allowed to skip it for now. Math was also the class Derek had been sitting out the day before, and he did so again, taking his course work into the dining room as Ms. Wang gave a short lesson. I guessed he was doing remedial work and needed the quiet. He went his way and I went mine, into the media room to write that e-mail to Kari.

Getting the words right took time. The third version finally seemed vague but not like I was obviously avoiding anything. I was about to hit Send when I stopped.

I was using a communal account. What would come up in the sender field? Lyle Group Home for Mentally

Disturbed Teens? I was sure it wouldn't be *that*, but even just "Lyle House" would throw Kari off, maybe enough for her to look it up.

I switched to the browser and searched for "Lyle House." Over a million hits. I added "Buffalo" and that cut my hits in half, but a scan of the first page showed they were all just random hits—a mention of a house on Lyle in Buffalo, a list of Lyle Lovett songs including the words "house" and "buffalo," a House representative named Lyle talking about Buffalo Lake.

I moved my mouse over the Send button again, and stopped again.

Just because Lyle House didn't have a cheerful Web site with a daisy border didn't mean Kari couldn't find it in the phone book.

I saved the e-mail as a text document with an obscure name. Then I deleted the message. At least with a phone call, I could probably block call display. There were no telephones in the common area, so I'd have to ask to use the nurses' phone. I'd do that later, when Kari would be home from school.

I shut down Outlook and was about to turn off the browser when a search result caught my eye—one about a Buffalo man named Lyle who'd died in a house fire.

I remembered what Rae had said last night about looking up my burned custodian. Here was my chance to settle the battle between the side that said *you're hallucinating—*

take your meds and shut up and the side that wasn't so sure.

I moused to the search field, deleted the words, then sat there, fingers poised over the keys, every muscle tensed, as if bracing for an electric shock.

What was I afraid of?

Finding out I really did have schizophrenia?

Or finding out I didn't?

I lowered my fingers to the keys and typed. *A. R. Gurney school arts Buffalo death custodian.*

Thousands of hits, most of them random matches to A. R. Gurney, the Buffalo playwright. Then I saw the words *tragic accident* and I knew.

I forced my mouse up the screen, clicked, and read the article.

In 1991, forty-one-year-old Rod Stinson, head custodian at Buffalo's A. R. Gurney School of the Arts, had died in a chemical explosion. A freak accident, caused by a part-time janitor refilling a container with the wrong solution.

He'd died before I'd been born. So there was no way I could have ever heard about the accident.

But just because I couldn't remember hearing about it didn't mean I hadn't caught a snatch of it, maybe someone talking in class, and stored it deep in my subconscious, for schizophrenia to pull out and reshape as a hallucination.

I scanned the article. No picture. I backed out to the search page and went to the next. Same basic information, but this one did have a picture. And there was no question it was the man I'd seen.

Had I seen the photo somewhere?

You have an answer for everything, don't you? A "logical explanation." Well, what would you think if you were seeing this in one of your movies?

I'd run to the screen and smack this silly girl who was staring the truth in the face, too dumb to see it. No, not too dumb. Too stubborn.

You want a logical explanation? String the facts together. The scenes.

Scene one: girl hears disembodied voices and sees a boy who disappears before her eyes.

Scene two: she sees a dead guy with some kind of burns.

Scene three: she discovers that the burned custodian is real and died in her school, just the way she saw it.

Yet this girl, our supposedly intelligent heroine, doesn't believe she's seeing ghosts? Give yourself a shake.

Still I resisted. As much as I loved the world of cinema, I knew the difference between reality and story. In movies, there are ghosts and aliens and vampires. Even someone who doesn't believe in extraterrestrials can sit in a movie theater, see the protagonists struggling with clues that suggest alien invasion, and want to scream "Well, duh!"

But in real life, if you tell people you're being chased by melted school custodians, they don't say "Wow, you must be seeing ghosts." They put you someplace like this.

I stared at the picture. There could be no question—

"Is that who you saw?"

I spun in my chair. Derek was there at my shoulder. For someone his size, he could move so quietly I'd almost think *he* was a ghost. Just as silent . . . and just as unwelcome.

He pointed to the headline over the janitor's article. "A. R. Gurney. That's your school. You saw that guy, didn't you?"

"I don't know what you're talking about."

He fixed me with a look.

I clicked off the browser. "I was doing schoolwork. For when I go back. A project."

"On what? 'People who died at my school'? You know, I always heard art schools were weird. . . ."

I bristled. "Weird?"

"You want something to research?" As he leaned over to take the mouse, I caught a whiff of BO. Nothing flower wilting, just that first hint that his deodorant was about to expire. I tried to move away discreetly, but he noticed and glowered, as if insulted, then shifted to one side, pulling in his elbows.

He opened a fresh browser session, typed a single word, and clicked *Search*. Then he straightened.

"Try that. Maybe you'll learn something."

I'd been staring at the search term for at least five minutes. One word. *Necromancer.*

Was that even English? I moved the cursor in front of

the word and typed "define." When I hit Enter, the screen filled.

Necromancer: one who practices divination by conjuring up the dead.

Divination? As in foretelling the future? By talking to dead people . . . from the past? That made no sense at all.

I skipped to the next definition, from Wikipedia.

Necromancy is divination by raising the spirits of the dead. The word derives from the Greek nekrós *"dead" and* manteía *"divination." It has a subsidiary meaning reflected in an alternative and archaic form of the word,* nigromancy *(a folk etymology using Latin* niger, *"black"), in which the magical force of "dark powers" is gained from or by acting upon corpses. A practitioner of necromancy is a necromancer.*

I reread the paragraph three times and slowly deciphered the geek talk, only to realize it didn't tell me anything more than the first definition. On to the next one, also from Wikipedia.

In the fictional universe of Diablo 2, the Priests of Rathma . . .

Definitely not what I was looking for, but I ran a quick search and I discovered a role-playing game class called necromancers, who could raise and control the dead. Was that where Derek got it? No. He might be creepy, but if he'd misplaced the boundary between real life and video games, he'd be in a real mental hospital.

I returned to Wikipedia, skimmed the rest of the definitions, and found only variations on the first. A necromancer foretells the future by talking to the dead.

Curious now, I deleted *define* and searched on *necromancer*. The first couple of sites were religious ones. According to them, necromancy was the art of communicating with the spirit world. They called it evil, a practice of black magic and Satan worship.

Did Derek think I was involved in black magic? Was he trying to save my soul? Or warn me that he was watching? I shivered.

Aunt Lauren's women's health clinic had once mistakenly been the target of a militant prolife group. I knew firsthand how scary people could get when they thought you did something that crossed their beliefs.

I flipped back to the list of search results and picked one that seemed more academic. It said that necromancy was another—older—name for mediums, spiritualists, and other people who could talk to ghosts. The meaning came from an ancient belief that if you could talk to the dead, they could predict the future because they could see everything—they'd know what your enemy was doing or where you could find buried treasure.

I switched to the next site on the list, and a horrible painting filled my screen—a mob of dead people, rotting and hacked up, being led by a guy with glowing eyes and an evil grin. The title: *The Army of the Dead*.

I scrolled down the page. It was filled with stuff like that, men surrounded by zombies.

I quickly switched to another page. It described the "art of necromancy" as the raising of the dead. I shuddered and flipped to another. A religious site now, quoting some old book ranting about "foul necromancers" who committed crimes against nature, communicating with spirits and re-animating the dead.

More sites. More old engravings and paintings. Grotesque pictures of grotesque men. Raising corpses. Raising spirits. Raising demons.

Fingers trembling, I turned off the browser.

thirteen

I STEPPED CAUTIOUSLY FROM the media room, expecting to find Derek lurking around the corner, waiting to pounce.

The rumble of his voice made me jump, but it came from the dining room, where he was asking Mrs. Talbot when Dr. Gill would be ready to see him. I hurried into class. They weren't done with math yet, and Ms. Wang waved for me to take the seat next to the door.

When the lesson finally ended, Derek lumbered in. I struggled to ignore him. Rae waved me to the desk beside hers. I bolted for it. Derek never even looked my way, just took his regular seat beside Simon, their heads and voices lowering as they talked.

Simon laughed. I strained to hear what Derek was saying. Was he telling Simon about his "joke"? Or was I getting paranoid?

* * *

After English, school was done for the day. Derek disappeared with Simon, and I followed Rae to the dining room, where we did our homework.

I could barely finish a page on sentence diagramming. It was like deciphering a foreign language.

I was seeing ghosts. Real ghosts.

Maybe it would be different for someone who already believed in ghosts. I didn't.

My religious training was limited to sporadic church and Bible school visits with friends, and one brief stint at a private Christian school when my dad hadn't been able to get me into a public school. But I believed in God and in an afterlife the same way I believed in solar systems I'd never seen—that matter-of-fact acceptance that they existed even if I'd never thought much about the specifics.

If ghosts existed, did that mean there was no heaven? Were we all doomed to walk the earth forever as shades, hoping to find someone who could see or hear us and . . . ?

And what? What did the ghosts want from me?

I thought of the voice in the basement. I knew what that one wanted—a door opened. So this spirit had been wandering for years, finally finds someone who can hear him and his earth-shattering request is "Hey, could you open that door for me?"

What about Liz? I must have dreamed that. Anything

else . . . I couldn't wrap my head around it.

But one thing was certain. I needed to know more, and if the pills were stopping me from seeing and hearing the ghosts clearly, then I had to stop taking them.

"It's not going to happen to you."

I turned from the living room window as Rae walked in.

"What happened to Liz, getting transferred, that won't happen with you." She sat on the couch. "That's what you're worried about, right? Why you haven't said ten words all day?"

"Sorry. I'm just . . ."

"Freaked out."

I nodded. This was true, even if it wasn't about what she thought. I sat in one of the rocking chairs.

"Like I said last night, Chloe, there's a trick to getting out of here." She lowered her voice. "Whatever you think? About their labels? Just nod and smile. Say 'Yes, Dr. Gill. Whatever you say, Dr. Gill. I just want to get better, Dr. Gill.' Do that, and you'll be following Peter out that front door any day now. We both will. Then I'll send you a bill for my advice."

I struggled to smile. From what I'd seen so far, Rae was a model patient. So why was she still here?

"How long is the average stay?" I asked.

She reclined on the sofa. "A couple months, I think."

"M-months?"

"Peter was here about that long. Tori a bit more. Derek and Simon, about three months."

"Three months?"

"I think so. But I could be wrong. Before you, Liz and I were the newbies. Three weeks for each of us, me a few days more than her."

"I—I was told I'd only be in for two weeks."

She shrugged. "I guess it's different for you then, lucky girl."

"Or did they mean two weeks was the *minimum*?"

She stretched her foot to nudge my knee. "Don't look so glum. The company's good, isn't it?"

I managed a smile. "Some of it."

"No kidding, huh? With Peter and Liz gone, we're stuck with Frankenstein and the divas. Speaking of which, Queen Victoria is up and about . . . relatively speaking."

"Hmm?"

She lowered her voice another notch. "She's stuffed full of meds and totally out of it." I must have looked alarmed because she hurried on. "Oh, that's not normal. They don't do that to anyone but Tori, and she wants it. She's the pill princess. If she doesn't get hers on time, she *asks* for them. Once, on the weekend, they ran out and had to page Dr. Gill for a refill and whoa boy—" She shook her head. "Tori ran to our room, locked the door, and wouldn't come out until someone brought her the medication.

Then she tattled to her mom and there was this huge uproar. Her mom's connected to the people who run Lyle House. Anyway, she's totally doped up today, so she shouldn't give us any trouble."

When Mrs. Talbot rounded us up for dinner, I realized I hadn't told Rae about taking her advice and looking up the dead janitor.

Tori joined us for dinner—in body, at least. She spent the meal practicing for a role in the next zombie movie, expressionless, methodically moving fork to mouth, sometimes even with food on it. I was torn between feeling sorry for her and just being creeped out.

I wasn't the only one left uncertain. Rae tensed with every mouthful, as if waiting for "old Tori" to leap out and jab her about her eating. Simon gamely tried to carry on a conversation with me and tentatively slanted questions Tori's way, as if afraid she was just playing possum, looking for sympathy.

After that endless meal, we all fled, gratefully, to our chores—Rae and I on dinner cleanup, the guys on garbage and recycling detail. Later Rae had a project to work on, and Ms. Wang had warned the nurses that she wanted Rae to do it without help.

So after telling Miss Van Dop that I'd be right back, I headed up to my room for my iPod. When I opened the door, I found a folded note on the floor.

Chloe,

We need to talk. Meet me in the laundry room at 7:15.

Simon

I folded the note into quarters. Had Derek put Simon up to this when I didn't freak out over him calling me a necromancer? Did he hope I might give a more gratifying response to his brother?

Or did Simon want to resume our discussion from the kitchen, when they'd asked about Liz? Maybe I wasn't the only one worried about her.

I went downstairs just past seven, and used the extra time to ghost hunt, prowling the laundry room, listening and looking. The one time I wanted to see or hear a ghost, I didn't.

Could I contact it? Or was it a one-way street, and did I have to wait until one chose to speak to *me*? I wanted to test that by calling out, but Derek had already caught me talking to myself. I wasn't taking that risk with Simon.

So I just wandered, my mind automatically sliding behind a camera lens.

". . . here . . ." a voice whispered, so soft and dry it sounded like the wind through long grass. ". . . talk to . . ."

A shadow loomed over my shoulder. I braced myself to see a vision of horror as I looked up into . . . Derek's face.

"You always this jumpy?" he said.

"Wh-where did you come from?"

"Upstairs."

"I'm waiting for some—" I stopped and studied his expression. "It's you, isn't it? You had Simon send—"

"Simon didn't send anything. I knew you wouldn't come for me. But Simon?" He glanced at his watch. "For Simon, you're early. So did you look it up?"

So that's what this was about. "You mean that word? *Nec*—" I pursed my lips, testing it. "*Necromancer*? Is that how you say it?"

He waved the pronunciation off. Unimportant. He leaned against the wall, trying for casual, uninterested maybe. His flexing fingers betrayed his eagerness to hear my answer. To see my reaction.

"Did you look it up?" he asked again.

"I did. And, well, I don't quite know what to say."

He rubbed his hands against his jeans, as if drying them. "Okay. So, you searched for it and . . ."

"It wasn't what I expected."

He brushed his jeans again, then closed his hands. Crossed his arms. Uncrossed them. I looked around, drawing it out, making him rock forward, almost bouncing with impatience.

"So . . ." he said.

"Well, I have to admit . . ." I took a deep breath. "I'm not really into computer games."

His eyes closed to slits, face screwed up. "Computer games?"

"Video games? RPGs? I've played some, but not the kind you're talking about."

He looked at me, wary, as if suspecting I really did belong in a home for crazy kids.

"But if you guys are into them?" I flashed a bright smile. "Then I'm certainly willing to give them a shot."

"Them?"

"The games. Role playing, right? But I don't think the necromancer is for me, though I do appreciate the suggestion."

"Suggestion . . ." he said slowly.

"That I play a necromancer? That's why you had me look it up, right?"

His lips parted, eyes rounding as he understood. "No, I didn't mean—"

"I suppose it could be cool, playing a character who can raise the dead, but it's just, you know, not really *me*. A little too dark. Too emo, you know? I'd rather play a magician."

"I wasn't—"

"So I don't have to be a necromancer? Thanks. I really do appreciate you taking the time to make me feel welcome. It's *so* sweet."

As I fixed him with a sugary smile, he finally realized I was having him on. His face darkened. "I wasn't inviting you to a game, Chloe."

"No?" I widened my eyes. "Then why would you send me to those sites about necromancers? Show me pictures of madmen raising armies of rotting zombies? Is that how you get your kicks, Derek? Scaring the new kids? Well, you've had your fun, and if you corner me again or lure me into the basement—"

"Lure you? I was trying to talk to you."

"No." I lifted my gaze to his. "You were trying to scare me. Do it again and I'll tell the nurses."

When I scripted the lines in my head, they'd been strong and defiant—the new girl standing up to the bully. But when I said them, I sounded like a spoiled brat threatening to tattle.

Derek's eyes hardened into shards of green glass and his face twisted into something not quite human, filling with a rage that made me stumble back out of its path and bolt for the stairs.

He grabbed for me, fingers clamping around my forearm. He yanked so hard I yelped, shoulder wrenching as I sailed off my feet. He let go and I crashed to the floor.

For a moment, I just lay there, crumpled in a heap, cradling my arm and blinking hard, unable to believe what had just happened. Then his shadow fell across me, and I scrambled to my feet.

He reached for me. "Chloe, I—"

I staggered back before he could touch me. He said something. I didn't hear it. Didn't look at him. Just ran for the stairs.

I didn't stop until I was in my room. Then I sat cross-legged on my bed, gulping oxygen. My shoulder burned. When I rolled up my sleeve, I saw a red mark for each of his fingers.

I stared at them. No one had ever hurt me before. My parents had never struck me. Never spanked me or even threatened to. I wasn't the kind of girl who got into fistfights or catfights. Sure, I'd been pushed, jostled, elbowed . . . but grabbed and thrown across a room?

I yanked down my sleeve. Was I surprised? Derek had made me nervous from that first encounter in the pantry. When I realized he'd sent the note, I should have gone upstairs. If he'd tried to stop me, I should have screamed. But no, I had to be cool. Be clever. Bait him.

Yet I had no proof except marks on my arm that were already fading. Even if I still had them when I showed the nurses, Derek could say I'd lured him into the basement and flipped out, and he'd had to grab my arm to restrain me. After all, I was a diagnosed schizophrenic. Hallucinations and paranoia went with the territory.

I had to handle this myself.

I *should* handle this myself.

I'd led the proverbial sheltered life. I'd always known that meant I lacked the life experience I'd need to be a screenwriter. Here was my chance to start getting it.

I'd handle this. But to handle it, I needed to know exactly what I was up against.

* * *

I took Rae aside.

"Do you still want to see Simon and Derek's files?" I asked.

She nodded.

"Then I'll help you get them. Tonight."

fourteen

W
E FOUND MRS. TALBOT setting out the evening
snack. Carrot sticks and dip. Yum. Whatever
complaints I had about Annette, at least I could
always count on brownies at home.

"Hungry, girls? I'm not surprised. No one ate very much
at dinner."

She held out the plate. We each took a stick and
dipped it.

"Chloe and I were thinking, Mrs. T," Rae said. "About
Tori."

She set the plate on the table, eyes downcast as she
nodded. "I know, dear. She's taking Liz's leaving very
hard. They were close. I'm sure she'll feel better once
they can talk, but until then she may feel a little down
while we get her . . . medication adjusted. We'll need you

girls to be extra nice to her."

"Sure." Rae licked dip off her finger. "We were wondering, though, whether it might be easier for her if she had the room to herself. I could sleep in Chloe's."

Mrs. Talbot handed Rae a napkin. "I don't want to isolate her too much but, yes, she'd probably be happier alone for now."

"Just for now?"

The nurse smiled. "No, you can move in with Chloe permanently, if that's what you'd both like."

While Tori was downstairs watching television, Rae started to move, as if afraid Miss Van Dop or Dr. Gill would veto the change.

She handed me a stack of T-shirts. "It's Simon, isn't it?"

"Hmm?"

"You want to know what Simon is in for."

"I don't—"

She draped her jeans over her arms and waved me out. "You two have been chatting every meal. At first, I thought maybe he was using you to throw Tori off his trail, but she wasn't paying any attention today, and he kept talking."

"I'm not—"

"Hey, you like him. That's fine." She opened Liz's bottom drawer. It was empty—every trace of her cleaned out while we'd been in class. "I don't care for the guy, but that's just my opinion. Maybe he's just stuck up with me because

I'm not in his league."

"League?"

She held up a pair of jeans and pointed to the label. "You see anyone else in this place wearing jeans from Wal-Mart? It's a private home. You gotta pay for it, and I bet it costs more than Motel 6. I'm the designated charity case."

"I—"

"It's cool. You treat me fine. So did Peter and—" a somber look around her new room "—Liz. Derek's a jerk to everyone, so I don't take it personally. If I'm only getting the cold shoulder from Simon and Tori, I can live with it. That's why I think those two are perfect for each other, but if you like him and he likes you? None of my business. But you're smart to run a background check."

She headed back to her old room, me at her heels. "My friend's mom did that with a guy she was supposed to marry. Found out he had three kids he'd never mentioned." She grinned over her shoulder. "I'm pretty sure Simon doesn't have kids, but you never know."

As we finished clearing out her drawers, I considered letting it go at that. But I didn't want her thinking I was the kind of girl who gets into a new place and immediately starts scoping out the guys. If I wasn't ready to tell the nurses about Derek, I should tell someone. That way, I'd have backup for my story if I needed it later.

"It's not Simon," I said as we returned to her room, clothing finished. "It's Derek."

She'd been in the middle of plucking a photo from the wall and fumbled it, cursing as I rescued the fallen photograph.

"Derek? You like—"

"God, no. I meant Derek's the one I'm checking out— and not *that* way."

She exhaled and leaned against the wall. "Thank God. I know some girls go for the jerks, but that's just nasty." She flushed as she took the picture from me and reached for another. "I shouldn't say that. It's not his fault, the whole . . ." She faltered for a word.

"Puberty smackdown."

A grin. "Exactly. I should feel sorry for the guy, but it's hard when his attitude is as ugly as his face." She stopped, photo in hand, and glanced over her shoulder at me. "Is that it? Did he . . . do something?"

"Why? Does he have a history of that?"

"Depends on what *that* is. Being rude, yes. A jerk, yes. He ignores us except when he doesn't have a choice and, believe me, no one complains. So what did he do?"

I considered my words. I didn't want her to insist I talk to the nurses, so I left out the throwing-me-across-the-room part and just said he'd been following me, popping up when I was alone.

"Ah, he likes you." She handed me a photo to hold.

"No, it isn't like that."

"Uh-huh. Well, you'd probably rather it *wasn't* like that,

but it sure sounds like it. Maybe you're his type. At my school, there's this guy I like, on the basketball team. He's even taller than Derek, but he always goes for tiny girls like you."

I took another photo from her. "That's not it. I'm absolutely certain of it."

She opened her mouth and I felt a flash of annoyance. Why is it that every time a girl says a guy is bothering her, it's fluffed off with *oh, he just likes you*, as if that makes it okay?

Seeing my expression, Rae snapped her mouth closed and took down another picture.

I said, "He freaks me out and I want to see what his file says. Whether there's any reason to be spooked. Whether he has, you know, a problem."

"That's smart. And I'm sorry. If he scares you, that's serious. I don't mean to make jokes. We'll get the facts tonight."

fifteen

BEDTIME AT LYLE HOUSE was nine, with the lights out and the no-talking rule coming into effect an hour later when the nurses retired.

Each side of the upper level had a bedroom for its assigned nurse. Liz had said there was no door linking the boys' and girls' areas, but according to Rae, there was one between the nurses' rooms, which gave them quick access to the whole upper floor in an emergency.

So while Rae swore Mrs. Talbot was a quick and sound sleeper, we had to take Miss Van Dop into account, too. An early break-in was too risky. Rae set the alarm on her sports watch for 2:30 and we went to sleep.

At 2:30, the house was still and silent. Too still and too silent. Every creaking floorboard sounded like a gunshot.

And in an old house, *most* boards creak.

Rae followed me into the kitchen, where we took two juice boxes from the fridge and set them on the counter. Then I opened the pantry door, turned on the light, and returned to the hall, leaving both doors half open.

Dr. Gill's office was at the west end, near the boys' stairs. Rae had checked out the lock a week ago. It was only a regular interior key lock, not much tougher than the kind you can pick with a coin. Or so she said. I'd never had any reason to open a household lock—probably because I didn't have siblings. So I watched and took mental notes. All part of gaining life experience.

Rae had watched Dr. Gill get her file out once, during her session, so she knew where they were kept. The office had an all-in-one printer, which made things easy. I stood guard. The only hitch came when she copied the pages, the *swoosh-shoosh* of the scanner head loud enough to make me nervous. But the files must have been short because by the time I looked in, she was returning them to the folder, copies made.

She passed me two sheets, folded in half, then she returned the file to the drawer. We backed out of the room. As she reengaged the lock, the unmistakable sound of a creaking floorboard made us both freeze. A long moment of silence passed. Then a fresh creak. Someone was coming down the boys' stairs.

We took off, padding barefooted down the hall. At the

half-open kitchen door, we darted inside, then into the open pantry.

"Come on," I stage-whispered. "Just pick something already."

"I can't find the Rice Krispie bars. I know there were some last week."

"The guys probably—" I stopped, then hissed. "Someone's coming. Get the light!"

She flipped the switch as I closed the door all but a crack. As I peered through the gap, Derek stopped inside the kitchen door. He left the light off as he looked around, moonbeams from the window casting a glow on his face. His gaze swept the kitchen and came to rest on the pantry door.

I pushed it open and stepped out.

"Cracker?" I said, holding up a box.

He looked at me and, in a flash, I was back in the basement, sailing through the air. My smile fell away and I shoved the box into his hands.

"We were getting a snack," Rae said.

He kept watching me, eyes narrowing.

"I'll get the juice," Rae said, squeezing past.

Derek looked over at the boxes we'd left on the counter. Proof that we'd only been raiding the kitchen. It had been my plan, and I thought it was so clever, but as his gaze swung back my way, the hairs on my neck rose and I knew he didn't buy it.

I stepped forward. For a second, he didn't move and all

I could hear was his breathing, feel the sheer size of him, looming there.

He stepped aside.

As I passed, he took a cracker sleeve from the box and held it out. "Forgot these."

"Right. Thanks."

I took one and fled into the hall, Rae behind me. Derek followed us out but headed the other way, toward the boys' side. When I turned to go up the stairs, I glanced down the hall. He'd stopped outside Dr. Gill's office and stood looking at the door.

We lay in bed with the lights out for fifteen minutes, long enough for Derek to either tell the nurses on us or just go back to bed. My fingers kept brushing the pages I'd stuffed in my pajama waistband. Finally, Rae scooted over to my bed, flashlight in hand.

"That was a close call," she said.

"Do you think he'll tell the nurses?"

"Nah. He was getting a snack himself. He wouldn't dare tattle."

So Derek had just happened to get up for a snack while we were breaking into Dr. Gill's office? I hated coincidence, but surely the printer hadn't made enough noise for him to hear it upstairs.

I pulled the sheets out and smoothed them on the mattress.

"That's Derek's," Rae whispered as she turned on the flashlight.

I tugged the second page free and held it out. "You want Simon's?"

She shook her head. "That's Derek's second page. There wasn't one for Simon."

"You couldn't find it?"

"No, there *wasn't* one. The dividers in the drawer are marked with our names, then the file folders are marked again. There wasn't a divider or a file for Simon."

"That's—"

"Weird, I know. Maybe they keep it someplace else. Anyway, you wanted Derek's, so I figured I shouldn't waste time searching for Simon's. Now, let's see what Frankenstein is in for." She moved the beam to the top of the page. "Derek Souza. Birth date, blah, blah, blah."

She shifted the light to the next section. "Huh. He was brought to Lyle House by a children's services agency. No mention of that father they're always talking about. If child services is involved, then you can bet he's no dad of the year. Oh, here it is. Diagnosis . . . antisocial personality disorder." She snorted a laugh. "Yeah? Tell me something I didn't know. Is that really an illness? Being rude? What kind of meds do they give you for that?"

"Whatever it is, they aren't working."

She grinned. "Got that right. No wonder he's been stuck here so long—"

The hall light clicked on. Rae dove for her bed, leaving the flashlight behind. I turned it off as the bathroom door closed. When I made a motion to toss it to her, she shook her head, then leaned out and whispered, "You finish up. Find anything interesting? Tell me in the morning."

Whoever was in the bathroom—Tori or Mrs. Talbot—seemed to take forever. By the time the toilet flushed, Rae was asleep. I waited a few minutes, then turned on the flashlight and read.

With each sentence, the ball of dread in my stomach grew. Antisocial personality disorder had nothing to do with being rude. It meant someone who showed a complete disregard for others, who lacked the ability to empathize—to put himself in another person's shoes. The disorder was characterized by a violent temper and fits of rage, which only made it worse. If you didn't understand that you were hurting someone, what would make you stop?

I flipped to the second page, labeled "background."

Performing a standard background check on DS has proved difficult. No birth certificate or other identifying records could be found. They likely exist, but the lack of concrete information on his early life makes a proper search impossible. According to DS and his foster brother, SB, Derek came to live with them at approximately five years of age. DS does not recall—or refused to share—the details of his life before this, though his responses suggest he may have been raised in an institutional setting.

Simon's father, Christopher Bae, appears to have taken de facto custody of DS, with no record of a formal adoption or fostering arrangement. The boys were enrolled in school as "Simon Kim" and "Derek Brown." The reason for the false names is not known.

School records suggest DS's behavioral problems began in seventh grade. Never an outgoing or cheerful child, he became increasingly sullen, his withdrawal punctuated by bouts of misplaced anger, often culminating in violent outbursts.

Violent outbursts . . .
The bruises on my arms throbbed and I absently rubbed them, wincing.

No incidents have been properly documented, making a complete forensic study of the disorder's progression impossible. DS seems to have avoided expulsion or other serious disciplinary action until an altercation described by witnesses as "a normal school yard fight." DS violently attacked three youths in what officers suspected was a chemically fueled rage. An adrenaline surge may also explain the display of extraordinary strength reported by witnesses. By the time authorities interceded, one youth had suffered spinal fractures. Medical experts fear he may never walk again.

The single-spaced page of background detail continued, but the words vanished, and all I could see was the floor whipping past as Derek flung me across the laundry room.

Extraordinary strength . . .

Violent outbursts . . .

May never walk again . . .

They'd taken Liz away for throwing pencils and hair gel bottles, and they kept Derek? A huge guy with a history of violent rages? With a disorder that meant he didn't care who he hurt or how badly?

Why hadn't someone warned me?

Why wasn't he locked up?

I shoved the pages under my mattress. I didn't need to read the rest. I knew what it would say. That he was being medicated. That he was being rehabilitated. That he was cooperating and had shown no signs of violence while at Lyle House. That his condition was under control.

I shone the flashlight on my arm. The finger marks were turning purple.

sixteen

EVERY TIME I DRIFTED off, I'd get stuck in that weird place between sleep and waking, where my mind sifted through the memories of the day, confusing them and twisting them. I'd be back in the basement, Derek grabbing my arm and throwing me across the room. Then I'd wake up in a hospital, with Mrs. Talbot at my side, telling me I'd never walk again.

When the wake-up rap came at the door, I buried my head under my pillow.

"Chloe?" Mrs. Talbot opened the door. "You need to get dressed before you come down today."

My stomach seized. With Liz and Peter gone, had they decided we should all eat breakfast together? I couldn't face Derek. I just couldn't.

"Your aunt is coming by at eight to take you out to breakfast. You need to be ready for her."

I released my death grip on the pillow and got up.

"You're mad at me, aren't you, Chloe?"

I stopped moving my scrambled eggs around my plate and looked up. Worry clouded Aunt Lauren's face. Dark half-moons under each eye said she hadn't been getting enough sleep. I'd missed those smudges earlier, hidden under her makeup until we got under the fluorescent lights of Denny's.

"Mad about what?" I asked.

A short laugh. "Well, I don't know. Maybe because I dumped you in a group home with strangers and disappeared."

I set down my fork. "You didn't 'dump' me. The school insisted I go there and the home insisted you and Dad stay away while I adjusted. I'm not a little kid. I understand what's going on."

She exhaled, the sound loud enough to be heard over the roar of the busy restaurant.

"I have a problem," I continued. "I have to learn to deal with it, and it isn't your fault or Dad's."

She leaned forward. "It isn't yours either. You understand that, too, right? It's a medical condition. You didn't do anything to cause it."

"I know." I nibbled my toast.

"You're being very mature about this, Chloe. I'm proud of you."

I nodded and kept nibbling. Seeds from the raspberry jam crackled between my teeth.

"Oh, and I have something for you." She reached into her purse and pulled out a sandwich bag. Inside was my ruby necklace. "The nurses called from the home and told me you were missing it. Your dad forgot to take it from the hospital when you left."

I took it, fingering the familiar pendant through the plastic, then passed it back. "You'll have to keep it for me. I'm not allowed to have jewelry at the home."

"Don't worry, I've already spoken to the nurses. I told them it was important to you, and they've agreed to let you have it."

"Thanks."

"Make sure you wear it, though. We don't want it going missing again."

I took the necklace out of the bag and put it on. I knew it was a silly superstition, but it did make me feel better. Reassured, I guess. A reminder of Mom and something I'd been wearing so many years that I'd felt a little odd without it.

"I can't believe your father left it at the hospital," she said, shaking her head. "God only knows when he would have remembered, now that he's jetted off again."

Yes, my dad was gone. He'd called me on Aunt Lauren's cell phone to explain that he'd had to leave for Shanghai last night on an emergency business trip. She was furious with him, but I couldn't see how it mattered when I was living at the group home. He'd already arranged to take a month off when I got out, and I'd rather he was around then.

My aunt talked about her plan for a "girls' New York trip" when I was released. I didn't have the heart to tell her I'd rather just go home, see Dad, hang with my friends. Getting back to my normal life would be the best post—Lyle House celebration I could imagine.

My normal life . . .

I thought of the ghosts. Would my life ever be normal again? Would *I* ever be normal again?

My gaze tripped over the landscape of faces. Was anyone here a ghost? How would I know?

What about that guy in the back wearing a heavy metal shirt, looking like he'd just stepped off the set of VH1's *I Love the 80's*? Or the old woman with long gray hair and a tie-dyed shirt? Or even the guy in a suit, waiting by the door? Unless someone smacked into them, how did I know they weren't ghosts, just waiting for me to notice them?

I lowered my gaze to my orange juice.

Oh, there's a plan, Chloe. Spend the rest of your life avoiding eye contact.

"So how are you adjusting? Getting along with the other kids?"

Her words were a slap, reminding me I had bigger problems than ghosts.

She was smiling, the question meant as a joke. *Obviously*, I would be getting along with the kids. I might not be the most outgoing girl, but I could be counted on not to make waves or cause trouble. As I looked up, her smile faded.

"Chloe?"

"Hmm?"

"Is there a problem with the other kids?"

"N-no. Everything's f-f-f—" My teeth clicked as I snapped my jaw shut. To anyone who knew me well, my stutter was a stress-o-meter. There was no sense saying everything was fine if I couldn't even get the lie out.

"What happened?" Her hand gripped her fork and knife, as if ready to wield them against whoever was responsible.

"It's noth—"

"Don't tell me it's nothing. When I asked about the other kids, you looked like you were going to be sick."

"It's the eggs. I put too much hot sauce on them. The other kids are fine." Her eyes bored into mine, and I knew I wasn't getting away with that. "There's just this one, but it's no big deal. You can't get along with everyone, right?"

"Who is it?" She waved off the server tentatively approaching with her coffeepot. "Don't roll your eyes at me, Chloe. You're at that home to rest, and if someone's bothering you—"

"I can handle it."

She released her death-grip on the cutlery, set them down, and smoothed her place mat. "That's not the point, hon. You have enough to worry about right now. Tell me who this boy is and I'll make sure he doesn't bother you any-more."

"He won't—"

"So it is a boy. Which one? There are three—no, only two now. It's the big boy, isn't it? I saw him this morning. I tried to introduce myself, but he walked away. Darren, Damian . . ."

I stopped myself before correcting her. She'd already tricked me into admitting my tormentor was a boy. I really wished that, for once, she'd just listen to my problems, maybe offer some advice, not leap in trying to fix every-thing.

"Derek," she said. "That's his name. When he ignored me this morning, Mrs. Talbot said he was like that. Rude. Am I right?"

"He's just . . . not very friendly. But that's fine. Like I said, you can't get along with everyone, and the other kids seem okay. One girl's kind of stuck up, like my roommate at camp last year. Remember her? The one who—"

"What did this Derek do to you, Chloe?" she said, refus-ing to be distracted. "Did he touch you?"

"N-no, of c-course n-not."

"Chloe." Her voice sharpened, my stuttering giving me

away. "This is not something you hide. If he did anything inappropriate, I swear—"

"It wasn't like that. We were talking. I tried to walk away and he grabbed my arm—"

"He *grabbed* you?"

"For, like, a second. It just freaked me out. I overreacted."

She leaned forward. "You did not overreact. Anytime someone lays an unwanted hand on you it is your right to object and to complain and . . ."

And so it went, through the rest of breakfast. A lecture on "inappropriate touching," like I was five years old. I didn't know why she was so upset. It's not like I'd even shown her the bruises. The more I argued, though, the madder she got, and I started thinking maybe this wasn't really about a boy bothering me or grabbing my arm. She was angry at my dad for taking off and at my school for making me go to this group home, and because she couldn't go after them, she'd found someone she *could* go after, a problem she *could* fix for me.

"Please don't," I said as we sat in the car, idling in the driveway. "He didn't *do* anything. Please. It's hard enough—"

"Which is why I'm not going to make this any harder for you, Chloe. I'm not stirring up trouble; I'm settling it down." She smiled. "Preventative medicine."

She squeezed my knee. When I looked out the window, she sighed and turned off the engine. "I promise I will be discreet. I've learned how to handle problems like this delicately, because the last thing a victim needs is to be blamed for tattling."

"I'm not a vic—"

"This Derek boy will never know who complained. Even the nurses won't know you said a word to me. I'm going to carefully raise concerns based on my own professional observations."

"Just give me a couple of days—"

"No, Chloe," she said firmly. "I'm talking to the nurses and, if necessary, to the administrators. It would be irresponsible of me not to."

I turned to face her, mouth opening to argue, but she was already out of the car.

When I returned, Tori was back. Back in class and back in attitude.

If I'd been scripting this scene, I'd have been tempted to go for a character reversal. The young woman sees her only friend taken away, partly because of a snide remark she made. When her housemates rally around, trying to lift her depression with support and concern, she realizes she hasn't lost her only friend and vows to be a kinder, gentler person.

In real life, though, people don't change overnight.

Tori started the first class by informing me that I was sitting in Liz's seat, and I'd better not act like she wasn't coming back. Afterward, she followed Rae and me into the hall.

"Did you have a good breakfast with your auntie? Parents too busy for you, I guess?"

"I'm sure Mom would have made it. But it's kind of hard for her, being dead and all."

A great slap-down comeback. Tori didn't even blink.

"So what did you do to deserve a pass already, Chloe? Was that your reward for helping them get rid of Liz?"

"She didn't—" Rae began.

"Like you're any better, *Rachelle*. You couldn't even wait until Liz's bed was cold before you bunked down with your new buddy. So, Chloe, what's with the special treatment?"

"It's not special," Rae said. "Your mom takes you out all the time. In Chloe's case, it's probably a reward for good behavior. With you, it's just because your mom's on the board of directors."

At our age, being "well behaved" isn't exactly a goal to strive for. But Tori's nostrils flared, her face twisting, as if Rae had lobbed the worst possible insult.

"Yeah?" she said. "Well, we don't see your parents coming around, do we, Rachelle? How many times have they visited or called since you've been here? Let's see . . . oh, right, zero." She made an O with her thumb and forefinger. "And it has nothing to do with bad behavior. They just don't care."

Rae shoved her into the wall. Tori let out an ear-shattering shriek.

"She burned me!" she said, clutching her shoulder.

"I *pushed* you."

Ms. Wang hurried from the classroom, followed by Simon and Derek, who'd stayed behind to discuss an assignment.

"Rae burned me. She has matches or something. Look, look . . ." Tori pulled down the collar of her T-shirt.

"Leave your clothes on, Tori," Simon said, raising his hands to his eyes. "Please."

Derek let out a low rumble that sounded suspiciously like a laugh.

Rae held up her hands. "No matches. No lighters. Nothing up my sleeve . . ."

"I see a very faint red mark, Tori, from being pushed," Ms. Wang said.

"She burned me! I felt it! She's hiding matches again. Search her. *Do* something."

"How about you do something, Tori?" Simon said as he brushed past us. "Like get a life."

She wheeled—not on him but on Rae—lunging at her before being grabbed by Ms. Wang. The nurses came running.

Yep, Tori was back.

seventeen

I'D SPENT THAT FIRST class braced for Miss Van Dop or Dr. Gill to stride in and yank Derek out for a "conference." I should have trusted my aunt. When we'd come back from breakfast, she'd quietly taken Mrs. Talbot aside, saying only that she wanted to discuss my progress. No one thought anything of it. And no one had burst into the class and dragged Derek out.

Tori's episode was the only bump in an otherwise quiet morning. Derek attended classes and ignored me. He went to his session with Dr. Gill before lunch. When he came out, I was in the hall, waiting to use the bathroom. Simon was inside, as he always was before a meal. I'd never known a guy to be so conscientious about washing up before eating.

I was considering running upstairs to the girls' bathroom when Dr. Gill's door opened, and Derek's dark form filled it. I braced myself. He stepped out and looked at me. My heart pounded so hard I was sure he could hear it, just as sure as I was that he'd just gotten bawled out. Our eyes met. He nodded, grunted something that sounded like "hi," and was about to brush past me when the bathroom door opened.

Simon walked out, head down. He saw me and shoved something into his back pocket. "Whoops. Guess I'm hogging the bathroom again, causing lines."

"Just Chloe." Derek pushed open the door for me. He didn't seem angry at all. Nicer than normal, even. My aunt must have handled it fine. I should have known she would.

As I went inside, Simon said to Derek, "Hey, lunch is this way."

"Start without me. I gotta get something from our room."

A pause. Then "Hold up," and Simon's footsteps followed Derek's up the stairs.

After lunch, it was my turn to take out the trash. Life experience, I kept telling myself as I wheeled the wagon to the shed, swatting away flies buzzing in for a closer look. All life experience. You never know when I'd need a critical scene with the protagonist hauling trash.

My laugh fluttered across the yard. The sun was shining, heat beating down on my face, tree and daffodils blossoming, the faint smell of newly cut grass almost masking the stink of rotting garbage.

A pretty good start to my afternoon. Better than I'd expected—

I stopped. There, in the yard behind ours, was a ghost. A little girl, no more than four.

She had to be a ghost. She was alone in the yard, playing outside in a frilly dress—a wedding cake confection of bows and ribbons, with more ribbons wound in her corkscrew curls and more bows on her shiny patent leather shoes. She looked like Shirley Temple off an old movie poster.

I tossed the bags into the shed, where they'd be safe from marauding raccoons and skunks. The bags thumped as they hit the wooden floor, but the girl, only twenty feet away, didn't look up. I closed the shed, walked behind it to the fence, and crouched, getting closer to her level.

"Hello," I said.

She frowned, as if wondering who I was talking to.

I smiled. "Yes, I can see you. That's a pretty dress. I had one like that when I was about your age."

One last hesitant glance over her shoulder, then she sidled closer. "Mommy bought it for me."

"My mom bought mine, too. Do you like it?"

She nodded, her smile lighting up her dark eyes.

"I bet you do. I loved mine. Do—?"

"Amanda!"

The girl jumped back, landing on her rear and letting out a wail. A woman in slacks and a leather coat broke into a run, keys jangling in her hand, the back door whooshing shut behind her.

"Oh, Amanda, you got your pretty dress all dirty. I'm going to have to reschedule your special photos." The woman shot me a glare, scooping up the little girl and carrying her toward the house. "I told you not to go near that fence, Amanda. Never talk to the kids over there. *Never*, do you hear me?"

Don't talk to the crazy kids. I longed to shout back that we weren't crazy. I'd mistaken her kid for a ghost, that's all.

I wondered whether they had books about this sort of thing. *Fifty Ways to Tell the Living from the Dead Before You Wind Up in a Padded Room*. Yep, I'm sure the library carried that one.

I couldn't be the only person in the world who saw ghosts. Was it something I'd inherited, like blue eyes? Or was it something I'd contracted, like a virus?

There had to be others. How would I find them? Could I? Should I?

The thump of footsteps told me someone was coming. A living person. That was one lesson I'd already learned: ghosts can yell, cry, and talk, but they don't make any noise when they move.

I was still behind the shed, hidden from view. Like being in the basement, only here, no one would hear me scream for help.

I dashed forward just as a shadow rounded the shed. Simon.

He strode toward me, his face dark with anger. I stiffened, but stood my ground.

"What did you say?" His words came slow, deliberate, as if struggling to keep his voice steady.

"Say?"

"To the nurses. About my brother. You accused him of something."

"I didn't tell the nurses any—"

"Your aunt did, then." His fingers drummed against the shed. "You know what I'm talking about. You told her, she told the nurses, then Dr. Gill took Derek into a special conference before lunch and warned him not to bother you. If he does, they're sending him away."

"Wh-what?"

"A word from you, and he's gone. Transferred." A vein in his neck throbbed. "He's been *perfect* since he got here. Now, all of a sudden, after one problem with you, he's put on notice. If he so much as *looks* at you funny, he's gone."

"I—I—I—"

"Something happened with you two last night, didn't it? Derek came upstairs completely freaked out. Said he was talking to you and screwed up. That's all he'd tell me."

I considered the truth—that I hadn't meant to tattle on Derek. I'd been quiet at breakfast and my aunt had figured out I was upset. But that might sound as if I'd been sulking, wanting her to drag it out of me.

And Simon's attitude pissed me off. He'd all but

accused me of making up stories, unfairly targeting his poor, misunderstood brother.

"It was hot at the restaurant," I said. "So I rolled up my sleeves."

"What?"

I pushed my left one up, showing four bruises, dark as ink spots. Simon paled.

"My aunt wanted to know what happened. When I wouldn't tell her, she tricked me into admitting it was a boy. She met Derek this morning and he was rude, so she decided it had to be him. I never confirmed it. If he's in trouble, it is *not* my fault. I had every right to tell someone and I didn't."

"Okay, okay." He rubbed his mouth, still staring at my arm. "So he grabbed your arm. That's what it looks like. Right? He just grabbed harder than he thought."

"He threw me across the room."

Simon's eyes widened, then he lowered his lids to hide his surprise. "But he didn't *mean* to. If you saw how freaked out he was last night, you'd know that."

"So that makes it okay? If I lose my temper and smack you, it's all right, because I didn't mean to, didn't *plan* to."

"You don't understand. He just—"

"She's right." Derek's voice preceded him around the corner.

I shrank back. I couldn't help it. As I did, a look passed through Derek's eyes. Remorse? Guilt? He blinked it away.

He stopped behind Simon's shoulder, at least five feet from me.

"I wanted to talk to you last night. When you tried to leave, I pulled you back and . . ." He trailed off, gaze shunting to the side.

"You *threw* me across the room."

"I didn't— Yeah, you're right. Like I said. No excuse. Simon? Let's go."

Simon shook his head. "She doesn't understand. See, Chloe, it's not Derek's fault. He's superstrong and—"

"And you weren't wearing your kryptonite necklace," Derek said. His mouth twisted in a bitter smile. "Yeah, I'm big. I got big fast. Maybe I don't know my own strength yet."

"That's not—" Simon began.

"No excuse, like you said. You want me to stay away from you? Wish granted."

"Derek, tell her—"

"Drop it, okay? She's not interested. She's made that very, very clear. Now let's go before someone catches me with her and I get stomped again."

"Chloe!" Mrs. Talbot's voice rang through yard.

"Perfect timing," Derek muttered. "Must have ESP."

"Just a second," I called back, moving sideways so she could see me.

"Go on," Derek said when the back door banged shut. "You don't want to be late for your meds."

I glowered, then turned away, circling wide around them

as I started for the door. Simon murmured something under his breath, as if to Derek.

Smoke rose in my path. I stumbled back. It hovered over the ground, like a low patch of fog.

"Simon!" Derek hissed.

I turned, pointing at the fog. "What is that?"

"What's what?" Derek followed my finger. "Huh. Must be a ghost. No, wait, you don't see ghosts. You hallucinate. Guess it's a hallucination then."

"That's not—"

"It's nothing, Chloe." He pushed his hands in his pockets, rocking back on his heels. "Just your imagination, like everything else. Now run along and take your meds and be a good girl. Don't worry, I'll stay out of your way from now on. Seems I made a mistake. A *big* mistake."

He meant he misjudged me. That I wasn't worthy of his interest. My fists clenched.

"Watch it, Chloe. You wouldn't want to hit me. Then *I'd* have to tattle on *you*."

Simon stepped forward. "Cut it out, Derek. She didn't tattle—"

"He knows that," I cut in, holding Derek's gaze. "He's baiting me. He's a jerk and a bully and whatever 'secrets' he's taunting me with, he can keep them. He's right. I'm not interested."

I wheeled, strode to the wagon, and grabbed the handle.

"Here," Simon called. "I'll take that—"

"She's got it."

I turned to see Derek's hand on Simon's shoulder.

Simon shrugged his brother off. "Chloe—"

I wheeled the wagon back to the house.

eighteen

W HEN I CAME IN THE back door, I almost mowed
down Tori.

"Have fun putting out the trash?" she asked.

I glanced back through the frilly curtains to see Simon
near the shed. I could have said he'd been helping or, better
yet, point out that Derek was there, too, if she looked closer.

But I didn't much see the point.

Derek blamed me for getting him into trouble. Simon
blamed me for getting Derek into trouble.

If Tori was going to blame me for poaching her non-
boyfriend, so be it. I couldn't work up the energy to care.

Rae was quiet all afternoon. Tori's comments about her parents not visiting seemed to have brought her down. At
break, we got permission to go upstairs before classes and

move the rest of her photos to our room.

"Thanks for helping with this," she said. "I know, I don't have to clear out right now, but if I leave one of these, Tori's liable to toss it out and say she thought I didn't want it anymore."

I looked at the top photo, one of a blond girl about three years old and a slightly older boy, who looked Native American. "Cute. Friends? Kids you babysit?"

"No, my little brother and sister."

I'm sure my face turned bright red as I stammered an apology.

Rae laughed. "No need to be sorry. I'm adopted. My mother was from Jamaica. Or so I'm told. She was just a kid when she had me, so she had to give me up. That—" she pointed to a photo of a Caucasian couple on the beach "—is my mom and dad. And that—" she pointed to a Hispanic girl mugging for the camera with Donald Duck "—is my sister, Jess. She's twelve. That—" She waved to a solemn-faced boy with red hair "—is my brother, Mike. He's eight. A very multicultural family, as you can tell."

"Five kids? Wow."

"Jess and I were adopted. The others are fosters. Mom likes kids." She paused. "Well, in theory anyway."

We walked to my room. She took the stack of photos from me and put them on her new dresser.

As she moved her Nintendo DS aside, her fingers tapped the scratched plastic. "You know how some kids are when they get a new gizmo? For weeks or even months, it's the coolest, best, most interesting whatsit they've ever owned and they can't stop talking about it. They carry it everywhere. Then, one day, they're all hyped up over some new gadget. There's nothing wrong with the old one. It just isn't cool and new anymore. Well, that's how my mom is." She turned and walked to the bed. "Only with her, it isn't gadgets. It's kids."

"Oh."

"When they're little, they're great. When they get older . . . not so much." Rae sat on the bed and shook her head. "Yeah, I'm probably being too hard on her. You know how it is. When you're little, your mom is so cool and she can't do anything wrong and then you get older—" She stopped and blushed. "No, I guess you wouldn't know what that's like, would you? Sorry."

"It's okay." I sat on my bed.

"Your dad never got married again?"

I shook my head.

"So who looks after you?"

As we headed down to class, I told her about Aunt Lauren, and the endless succession of housekeepers, making her laugh with my impressions, and forgot everything else . . . at least for a little while.

That afternoon, during my session with Dr. Gill, I put on an Oscar-worthy performance. I admitted that, as she'd suspected, I *had* thought I might be seeing ghosts. Now, after hearing her diagnosis and letting my medication take effect, I understood that I'd been hallucinating. I was a schizophrenic. I needed help.

She totally bought it.

All I had to do now was keep up the act for a week or so, and I'd be free.

When classes ended, Rae and I did our homework together in the media room. Simon passed the door a couple of times and I thought maybe he wanted to talk to me, but when I stuck my head out the door, he'd disappeared upstairs.

As I worked, I thought about that patch of fog in the yard. If Derek hadn't seen it, too, I might have mistaken it for a ghost.

Why had he shushed Simon? Was Simon somehow causing my "hallucinations"? Some kind of special effects?

Sure, that would explain the ghosts I'd seen at school—holographic projections created by a guy I'd never met. Right.

But something was going on.

Or, at least, that's what Derek wanted me to believe.

By refusing to explain and making a big deal of refusing, Derek wanted me to do exactly what I was doing right now—driving myself nuts wondering what he wasn't telling me. He wanted me to go to him, begging for answers, so he could taunt and torment me some more.

There was no way Simon or Derek could have created the ghosts at school, but that fog would be a simple effect to pull off. Maybe Derek had done it. That's why Simon had protested, and Derek had shut him up.

Was Simon afraid of his brother? He pretended to defend him and act like best buds, but what choice did he have? He was stuck with Derek until his father returned.

Where was his father?

Why had he enrolled Simon and Derek in school under false names?

Why was Simon even here, if he didn't have a file?

Too many questions. I needed to start finding answers.

We were clearing the table after dinner when Mrs. Talbot came into the dining room with a man she introduced as Dr. Davidoff, the head of the board that ran Lyle House. With only a thin circle of hair and a huge, sharp nose, he was so tall that he seemed to be permanently leaning down to hear better. With the hair and the nose, he bore an unfortunate resemblance to a vulture, head tucked down, eyes beady behind his glasses.

"This must be little Chloe Saunders." He beamed with the false heartiness of a middle-aged guy who doesn't have kids and never stops to think that a fifteen-year-old girl might not like being called "little" Chloe Saunders.

He awkwardly clapped me on the back. "I like your

hair, Chloe. Red stripes. Very cool."

He said "cool" like I say a Spanish word when I'm not sure of the pronunciation. Rae rolled her eyes behind his back, then came around front.

"Hey, Dr. D."

"Rachelle. Oh, sorry, *Rae*, right? Are you keeping out of trouble?"

Rae flashed a perky smile, one custom-made for adults she had to suck up to. "Always, Dr. D."

"That's my girl. Now, Chloe, Dr. Gill tells me you had quite a breakthrough today. She's very pleased with your progress and how quickly you've fit into the therapeutic routine and accepted your diagnosis."

I tried not to squirm. He meant well, but being a good patient wasn't something I wanted to be publicly congratulated on. Especially when Derek had stopped eating to watch.

Now run along, take your meds and be a good girl.

Dr. Davidoff continued. "Normally, I don't meet with our young people until they've been here at least a week, but since you're speeding right along, Chloe, I don't want to hold you back. I'm sure you're eager to get back to your friends and school as soon as possible."

"Yes, sir." I copied Rae's perky smile, ignoring Derek's heavy gaze.

"Come along then and we'll chat in Dr. Gill's office."

He put his hand on one shoulder to propel me out.

Tori stepped in front of us. "Hello, Dr. Davidoff. That new medicine you have me on is working great. I'm really doing well."

"That's good, Victoria."

He absently patted her arm, then led me out.

The session was similar to the first one I'd had with Dr. Gill, filling in background. Who was Chloe Saunders? What had happened to her? How did she feel about it?

I'm sure he could get all this from Dr. Gill's notes, and she'd stayed late today to sit in, but it was like in a cop movie, where the detective interviews the suspect, asking all the same questions as the last guy. It's not the information that's important, but how I tell it. What's my emotional reaction? What extra details did I add this time? What did I leave out?

For all his false heartiness, Dr. Davidoff was Dr. Gill's supervisor, meaning he was here to check her work.

Dr. Gill had sat stiff and tense, leaning forward, squinting at me as she raced to capture every word, every gesture, like a student afraid to miss a key point for the exam. Dr. Davidoff took his time, getting a coffee for himself and a juice box for me, relaxing in Dr. Gill's chair, chatting me up before we started.

When he asked whether I'd had any hallucinations since I'd been here, I said yes, I'd seen a disembodied hand the second morning and heard a voice later that day.

I didn't mention yesterday but said honestly that all had been fine today.

I sailed through the session without a hitch. At the end, he told me I was doing "fine, just fine," patted me on the back, and led me from the office.

As I passed the open media room door, I glanced inside. Derek was at the computer, his back to me as he played what looked like a war strategy game. Simon was also playing a game, on his Nintendo DS, as he sprawled sideways in the recliner, legs draped over the arm.

He noticed me and straightened, lips parting as if ready to call after me.

"If you're going for a snack, grab me a Coke," Derek said, attention fixed on the screen. "You know where they're hidden."

Simon paused, gaze shunting between us. His brother was giving him the perfect excuse to sneak out and talk to me, but he still hesitated, as if sensing a setup or a test. There was no way Derek knew I was here, behind his back. Yet Simon slouched in his chair.

"You want a Coke, get it yourself."

"I didn't *ask* you to get me one. I said *if* you were going."

"I'm not."

"Then say so already. What's with you tonight?"

I continued down the hall.

* * *

I found Rae in the dining room, homework spread across the table.

"You've got a DS, don't you?" I asked.

"Yep. Only Mario Karts on it, though. You want to borrow it?"

"Please."

"It's on my dresser."

I walked past the media room doorway again. The guys were still there, looking like they hadn't budged since I last passed. Again Simon glanced up. I waved Rae's DS and gestured. He grinned and shot me a discreet thumbs-up.

Now to find a place within range . . . I had a DS at home and knew I should be able to connect with another one within fifty feet. The media room was sandwiched between the front hall and the classroom, both off-limits for hanging out. But it was also right under the bathroom. So I went up, started PictoChat and prayed I could connect to Simon.

I could.

I used the stylus to write my message: *u want to talk?*

He drew a check mark, then wrote *D* followed by a picture that, after a moment I realized was an eye. Yes, he wanted to talk, but Derek was keeping an eye on him.

Before I could reply, he sent another. *D 8?* a box with "soap" drawn in it, surrounded by bubbles. It took a moment, but I finally interpreted that as "Derek has a shower around eight."

He erased it and drew an *8* followed by *yard*. Meet him outside at eight.

I sent back a check mark.

nineteen

A T 7:50, I WAS HELPING Rae empty the dishwasher. From the hall, I heard Simon ask if he could go out back and shoot hoops while Derek showered. Mrs. Talbot warned that it was getting dark, and he couldn't stay out for long, but she turned off the alarm and let him go. Once the dishwasher was empty, I told Rae I'd catch up with her later, then slipped out after him.

As Mrs. Talbot warned, dusk was already falling. Huge shade trees bordered the deep yard, casting even more shadow. The basketball net was on a patch of concrete beyond the reach of the porch light, and I could see only the white flash of Simon's shirt and hear the *thump-thump-thump* of the dribbled ball. I circled the perimeter.

He didn't see me, just kept dribbling, gaze fixed on the ball, face solemn.

Keeping to the shadows, I moved closer and waited for him to see me. When he did, he jumped, as if startled, then waved me to an even darker spot on the other side of the net.

"Everything okay?" I asked. "You looked . . . busy."

"Just thinking." His gaze swept the fence line. "Can't wait to get out of here. Just like everyone else I guess, but . . ."

"Rae said you've been here awhile."

"You could say that."

A shadow passed behind his eyes, like he was scanning his future, seeing no sign of release. At least I had someplace to go. They'd been in child services. Where would they go from here?

He bounced the ball hard and managed a smile. "Wasting our time, aren't I? I've got about ten minutes before Derek tracks me down. First off, I wanted to say I'm sorry."

"Why? You didn't do anything."

"For Derek."

"He's your brother, not your responsibility. You can't help what he does." I nodded toward the house. "Why didn't you want him seeing us talking? Will he get mad?"

"He won't be happy, but—" He caught my expression and let out a sharp laugh. "You mean, Am I afraid he'll beat the crap out of me? No way. Derek isn't like that at all. If he gets mad, he just treats me the same way he treats everyone else—ignores me. Hardly fatal but, no, I don't *want* to piss him off if I can help it. It's just . . ." He bounced the ball, gaze fixed on it. After a moment, he stopped and flipped it into his hands. "He's already mad that I defended him—he hates that—and now if I'm talking to you, trying to explain things, when he doesn't want them explained . . ."

He twirled the ball on his fingertip. "See, Derek's not really a people person."

I tried not to look shocked.

"When he decided you might really be seeing ghosts, I should have said, *Sure, bro, let me talk to her*. I'd have handled it . . . well, different. Derek doesn't know when to back off. To him, it's as simple as adding two plus two. If you can't figure it out yourself and you don't listen when he tells you the answer, he'll keep slamming you until you wake up."

"Running away screaming doesn't help."

He laughed. "Hey, if Derek kept coming at me, I'd be screaming, too. And you didn't run anywhere today. You stood up to him, which, believe me, he's not used to." A grin. "Good on ya. That's all you have to do. Don't take his crap."

He took another shot. This one dropped gracefully through the hoop.

"So Derek thinks I'm a . . . necromancer?"

"You're seeing ghosts, right? A dead guy who talked to you, chased you, asked for your help?"

"How did you—?" I stopped myself. My heart thumped, breath coming hard and fast. I'd just convinced Dr. Gill that

I'd accepted my diagnosis. As much as I longed to trust Simon, I didn't dare.

"How did I know? Because that's what ghosts do to necromancers. You're the only person who can hear them, and they all have something to say. That's why they're hanging out here, in limbo or whatever." He shrugged as he tossed the ball. "I'm not real clear on the specifics. Never actually met a necromancer. I just know what I've been told."

I inhaled and exhaled before saying, as casually as I could, "I guess that makes sense. That's what you'd expect ghosts would do to people who think they can talk to the dead. Mediums, spiritualists, psychics, whatever."

He shook his head. "Yes, mediums, spiritualists, and psychics *are* people who *think* they can talk to the dead. But necromancers *can*. It's hereditary." He smiled. "Like blond hair. You can cover it up with red streaks, but underneath, it's still blond. And you can ignore the ghosts, but they'll still come. They know you can see them."

"I don't understand."

He flipped the ball and caught it on his open palm. Then he murmured something. I was about to say I couldn't hear him when the ball rose. Levitating.

I stared.

"Yeah, I know, it's about as useless as that patch of fog," he said, gaze fixed on the levitating ball, as if concentrating. "Now, if I could lift it more than a couple of inches, maybe to the top of that hoop, and slam-dunk it every time, that'd be a trick. But I'm not Harry Potter and real magic doesn't work that way."

"That's . . . magic?" I said.

The ball dropped into his hand. "You don't believe me, do you?"

"No, I—"

He cut me off with a laugh. "You think it's some kind of trick or a special effect. Well, movie girl, get your butt over here and test me."

"I—"

"Get over here." He pointed at the spot beside him. "See if you can find the strings."

I slid closer. He said some words, louder now, so I could hear them. It wasn't English.

When the ball didn't move, he cursed. "Did I mention I'm not Harry Potter? Let's try that again."

He repeated the words, slower, his gaze glued to the ball. It rose two inches.

"Now check for strings or wires or whatever you think is holding it up."

I hesitated, but he prodded and teased me until I moved closer and poked a finger between the ball and his hand. When I didn't hit anything, I slid all my fingers through, then waggled them. Simon's fist closed, grabbing my hand and I yelped as the ball bounced off across the concrete pad.

"Sorry," he said, grinning, his fingers still holding mine. "I couldn't resist."

"Yes—I'm skittish, as your brother has probably pointed out. So how did you . . ." I looked at the ball, coming to rest on the grass. "Wow."

His grin grew. "You believe me now?"

As I stared at the ball, I struggled for other explanations. None came.

"Can you teach me how to do that?" I said finally.

"Nah. No more than you can teach me how to see ghosts. Either you have it or you—"

"Playing basketball in the dark, Simon?" asked a voice across the yard. "You should have called me. You know I'm always up for a little—"

Tori stopped short, seeing me now. Her gaze moved to my hand, still in his.

"—one-on-one," she finished.

I yanked my fingers away. She kept staring.

"Hey, Tori," Simon said as he retrieved the ball. "What's up?"

"I saw you playing and thought maybe you could use a partner." Her gaze swung my way, expression unreadable. "I guess not."

"I should get inside," I said. "Thanks for the pointers, Simon."

"No, hold up." He took a step after me, then glanced at Tori. "Uh, right. You're welcome. And it is getting dark, isn't it? It must be snack time by now . . ."

He hurried into the house.

I lay in bed, unable to sleep again. This time, though, it wasn't bad dreams that kept me awake but thoughts pinging through my head, so shrill and insistent that by midnight, I was seriously considering a real kitchen raid—to grab the travel tube of Tylenol I'd seen there.

I was a necromancer.

Having a label should have come as a relief, but I wasn't sure this one was any better than *schizophrenic*. At least schizophrenia was a known and accepted condition. I could talk to people about it, get help coping with it, take my meds, and make the symptoms go away.

Those same meds might cover the symptoms of necromancy, but as Simon said, it would be like coloring my hair—I'd still be the same underneath, my true nature waiting to pop up as soon as the medication wore off.

Necromancy.

Where had it come from? My mother? If so, why didn't Aunt Lauren know about it? From my father? Maybe he hadn't worked up the nerve to warn me and that's why he'd seemed so guilty in the hospital, so eager to make me happy and comfortable. Or maybe neither of my parents or my aunt knew anything about it. It could be a recessive gene, one that skipped generations.

Simon was lucky. His dad must have told him about the

magic, showed him how to use it. My envy evaporated. Lucky? He was stuck in a group home. His magic didn't seem to be doing him any good here.

Magic. The word came so casually, as if I'd already accepted it. Had I? *Should* I?

I'd spent days denying that I saw ghosts, and now, suddenly, I had no problem believing in magic? I should be demanding more demonstrations. Coming up with alternate explanations. But I'd done that with myself, and now, having realized that I really did see the dead, there was almost a comfort in accepting that I wasn't the only one out there with weird powers.

And what about Derek? Simon said Derek was unnaturally strong. Was that magical? I'd felt that strength. I'd read his file, and I knew even the authorities had been stumped for a cause.

As bizarre as it sounded, the explanation that made the most sense was the most far-fetched one. There were people out there with powers found only in legends and movies. And we were part of that.

I almost laughed. It was like something out of a comic book. Kids with supernatural powers, like superheroes. Superheroes? Right. Somehow, I didn't think seeing ghosts and levitating basketballs was going to help us save the world from evil anytime soon.

If both Derek and Simon had powers, is that how they'd ended up together, as foster brothers? What had their dad told them? Did his disappearance have something to do with being magical? Was that why the guys had enrolled in school under fake names and kept moving around? Is that what our kind had to do? Hide?

The questions crowded my brain, none of them willing to leave without answers . . . answers I couldn't get at two in the morning. They bounced around like Simon's basketball. After a while, I swore I could see them—orange balls bouncing through my head, back and forth, back and forth, until I fell asleep.

A voice sliced through the heavy blanket of sleep, and I bolted up, fighting my way to consciousness.

I gulped air as I surveyed the room, ears and eyes straining. All was still and silent. I glanced over at Rae. She was sound asleep.

A dream. I started lying back down.

"Wake up."

The whisper floated through the half-open door. I lay down, resisting the urge to pull the covers higher.

I thought you weren't going to cower anymore? That's the plan, right? Not to ignore the voices but get answers, take control.

A deep breath. Then I slipped out of bed and walked to the door.

The hall was empty. I could hear only the *tick-tick-tick* of the grandfather clock downstairs. As I turned, a pale shape flickered near a closed door down the hall. A closet, I'd presumed earlier. What was it with ghosts and closets in this house?

I crept down the hall and eased the door open. Dark stairs led up.

The attic.

Uh-uh, this was as bad as a basement, maybe even worse. I wasn't following some ghost up there.

Good excuse.

It's not an—

You don't want to talk to them. Not really. You don't want to know the truth.

Great. Not only did I have to deal with Derek's taunts and jibes but now even my inner voice was starting to sound like him.

I took a deep breath and stepped inside.

twenty

SLID MY HAND ALONG the wall, searching for a light switch, then stopped. Was that a good idea? With my luck, Tori would head to the bathroom, see the attic light on, and investigate . . . only to find me up there talking to myself.

I left the light off.

One hand on the railing, the other gliding along the opposite wall, I climbed the stairs, ascending into blackness.

My hand slipped off the end of the railing, and I pitched forward. I'd reached the top. A trickle of moonlight came from the tiny attic window, but even after I paused to let my eyes adjust, I could only make out vague shapes.

I walked with my hands out, feeling my way. I smacked into something, and it sent up a cloud of dust. My hands flew over my nose to stifle a sneeze.

"Girl . . ."

I stiffened. It was the ghost from the basement, the one who kept insisting I open the locked door. I took a deep breath. Whoever he was, he couldn't hurt me. Even that janitor, as hard as he tried, couldn't do anything more than scare me.

I had the power here. I was the necromancer.

"Who are you?" I asked.

". . . contact . . . get through . . ."

"I can't understand you."

". . . blocked . . ."

Something was blocking him from making contact? Leftover meds in my system?

". . . basement . . . try . . ."

"Try that door again? Forget it. No more basements. No more attics. If you want to talk to me, do it on the main level. Got it?"

". . . can't . . . block . . ."

"Yes, you're blocked. I think it's something I was taking, but it should be better tomorrow. Talk to me in my room. When I'm alone. Okay?"

Silence. I repeated it, but he didn't answer. I stood there, shivering, for at least five minutes before trying one last time. When he didn't respond, I turned toward the stairs.

"Chloe?"

I wheeled so fast I knocked into something at knee

level, my bare legs scraping against wood, hands hitting the top with a thud, enveloping me in a cloud of dust. I sneezed.

"Bless you." A giggle. "Do you know why we say that?"

Blood pounded in my ears as I recognized the voice. I could make out Liz, a few feet away, dressed in her Minnie Mouse nightshirt.

"It's because when we sneeze, our soul flies out our nose and if no one says 'bless you,' the devil can snatch it." Another giggle. "Or so my nana always said. Funny, huh?"

I opened my mouth but couldn't force words out.

She looked around, nose wrinkling. "Is this the attic? What are we doing up here?"

"I—I—I—I—"

"Take a deep breath. That always helps my brother." Another look around. "How did we get up here? Oh, right. The séance. We were going to do a séance."

"Séance?" I hesitated. "Don't you remember?"

"Remember what?" She frowned. "Are you okay, Chloe?"

No, I was pretty sure I wasn't. "You . . . never mind. I—I was just talking to a man. Can you see him? Is he here?"

"Um, no. It's just us." Her eyes went round. "Are you seeing ghosts?"

"Gh-ghosts?"

"Chloe?"

This voice was sharp and I spun to see Mrs. Talbot feeling her way over to me. I turned back to Liz. No one was there.

"Chloe, what are you doing up here?"

"I—I—I—I thought I heard . . . a mouse. Or a rat. Something was moving around up here."

"And you were talking to it?" Tori stepped through the attic doorway.

"N-no, I—I—"

"Oh, I'm pretty sure I heard you say *ghost*. And you were definitely talking to someone. It seems you aren't quite as cured as you said you were."

Mrs. Talbot brought me a sleeping pill and waited while I took it. The whole time, she didn't say a word to me, but as I heard her feet tapping double time down the stairs, I knew there would be a lot of words for Dr. Gill and Dr. Davidoff.

I'd blown it.

Tears burned my eyes. I swiped them back.

"You really can see ghosts, can't you?" Rae whispered.

I said nothing.

"I heard what happened. You aren't even going to admit it to me now, are you?"

"I want to get out of here."

"News flash. We *all* do." An edge crept into her voice. "It's fine to lie to *them*. But I thought you were seeing ghosts even before you did. Who gave you the idea of looking up that guy you saw at your school? You looked him up, didn't you? You just didn't bother to tell me."

"That's not—"

She rolled over, her back to me. I knew I should say something, but I wasn't sure what.

When I closed my eyes, I saw Liz again and my stomach clenched.

Had I really seen her? Talked to her? I struggled for some other explanation. She couldn't be a ghost because I'd seen and heard her clearly—not like the ghost who'd called me up there. And she couldn't be dead. The nurses had promised we could talk to her.

When could we talk to her?

I struggled to get up, suddenly needing to know now. But I was so tired that I couldn't think straight and hovered there, propped up on my elbows, as the sleeping pill kicked in.

Something about Liz. I wanted to check. . . .

My head fell back to the pillow.

twenty-one

THE NEXT MORNING WHEN I was called into a meeting with the doctors, I did my best damage control. I claimed I really had gotten past the I-see-dead-people stage and accepted my condition, but had woken up hearing a voice in the night, calling me to the attic. I'd been confused, sleep drunk, *dreaming* of seeing ghosts, not really seeing them.

Dr. Gill and Dr. Davidoff didn't fully appreciate the distinction.

Then Aunt Lauren arrived. It was like when I'd been eleven, caught peeking at test scores, egged on by the new classmates I'd been eager to impress. Being hauled to the principal's office had been bad enough. But the disappointment on Aunt Lauren's face had hurt worse than any punishment.

That day, I saw the same disappointment, and it didn't hurt any less.

In the end, I managed to persuade them all that I'd had a minor setback, but it was like the little boy crying wolf. The next time I said I was improving, they'd be a lot slower to believe me. No quick track to release now.

"We're going to need you to provide urine samples for the next week," Dr. Gill said.

"Oh, that's ridiculous," Aunt Lauren said. "How do we know she wasn't sleepwalking and dreaming? She can't control her dreams."

"Dreams are the windows to the soul," Dr. Gill said.

"That's the eyes," my aunt snapped.

"Anyone versed in psychiatry will tell you it's the same for dreams." Dr. Gill's voice was level, but her look said she was sick of parents and guardians questioning her diagnoses and defending their children. "Even if Chloe is only dreaming she sees ghosts, it suggests that, subconsciously, she hasn't accepted her condition. We need to monitor her with urine tests."

"I—I don't understand," I said. "Why do I need urine tests?"

"To ensure you're receiving the proper dosage for your size, activity level, food intake, and other factors. It's a delicate balance."

"You don't believe—" Aunt Lauren began.

Dr. Davidoff cleared his throat. Aunt Lauren pressed

her lips into a thin line and started picking lint from her wool skirt. She rarely backed down from an argument, but these doctors held the key to my future.

I already knew what she'd been going to say. The urine tests weren't to check my dosage. They were to make sure I was taking my pills.

Since I'd missed morning classes, I was assigned lunch duty. I was setting the table, lost in my thoughts, when a voice said, "I'm behind you."

I spun to see Derek.

"I can't win," he said. "You're as skittish as a kitten."

"So if you sneak up and announce yourself, that's going to startle me less than if you tap me on the shoulder?"

"I didn't sneak—"

He shook his head, grabbed two rolls from the bread basket, then rearranged the others to hide the theft. "I just wanted to say that if you and Simon want to talk, you don't need to do it behind my back. Unless you want to."

"We were just—"

"I know what you were doing. Simon already told me. You want answers. I've been trying to give them to you all along. You just have to ask."

"But you said—"

"Tonight. Eight. Our room. Tell Mrs. Talbot you'll be with me for math tutoring."

"Your side is off-limits. Is she going to let me go up

there, alone, with a boy?"

"Just tell her it's for math. She won't question it."

Because he had problems with math, I supposed.

"Will that be . . . okay? You and I aren't supposed to—"

"Tell her Simon will be there. And talk to Talbot, not Van Dop."

twenty-two

RAE AND I DIDN'T SPEAK much all day. She wasn't
nasty; Rae wasn't like that. She sat beside me in
class and asked questions, but there was no chatter,
no giggling or goofing off. Today we were classmates, not
friends.

Before dinner, when we'd normally hang out or do
homework together, she took her books, retreated to the dining room, and closed the door.

After dinner, I followed her into the kitchen with my
dirty plates.

"It's my turn to do laundry," I said. "Would you have a
minute to show me how to use the machine?" I lowered my
voice. "And I'd like to talk to you."

She shrugged. "Sure."

* * *

"I'm sorry I didn't tell you," I said as she demonstrated the dials on the washer. "I'm . . . I'm having a hard time with it."

"Why? You can talk to the dead. How cool is that?"

It wasn't cool at all—it was terrifying. But I didn't want to sound like I was whining. Or maybe I just didn't want to sound like a wimp.

I dumped in the first load and added soap.

"Whoa, whoa! You'll give this place a bubble carpet." She took the soap box from me and scooped some of the detergent back out of the machine. "If you can prove you're seeing ghosts, why not just tell them?"

A perfectly logical question, but at the thought, some deep-rooted instinct screamed *Don't tell! Never tell!*

"I—I don't want to tell anyone the truth. Not yet. Not here."

She nodded and set the box aside. "Gill is a pencil pusher with all the imagination of a thumbtack. She'd keep you locked up in here until you stopped this 'ghost nonsense.' Better to save the spooky stuff for when you get out."

We sorted a basket of laundry in silence, then I said, "The reason I asked to talk to you down here is, well, there's a ghost."

She took a slow look around, wrapping a T-shirt around her hand like a boxer taping up for a fight.

"Not right now. I mean, there *was* a ghost in here. The same one I heard upstairs last night." Before Liz showed up. All day I'd been struggling not to think of Liz. If I was seeing her, didn't that mean . . .

Why hadn't I asked Mrs. Talbot when I could talk to Liz? Was I afraid of the answer?

"—he say?"

I shook it off and turned to Rae. "Hmm?"

"What did the ghost say?"

"It's hard to tell. He keeps cutting out. I think it's the meds. But he said he wanted me to open that door."

I pointed. Her head whipped around so fast she winced and rubbed her neck.

"That door?" Her eyes glittered. "The *locked* basement door?"

"Yes, cliché, I know. Whoooo, don't go into the locked room, little girl."

Rae was already striding to the door.

I said, "I thought maybe, we could, you know, check it out. Like open it."

"Duh, *of course*. I'd have done that days ago." She jiggled the handle. "How can you live with the suspense?"

"For starters, I'm pretty sure there's nothing in there."

"Then why's it locked?"

"Because it's for storing stuff they don't want us messing with. Lawn furniture. Winter bedding. Christmas decorations."

"The bodies of Lyle House kids who never went home . . ."

She grinned, but I froze, thinking of Liz.

"Geez, I'm *kidding*. You are such a girl."

"No, I've just seen too many movies."

"That, too." She walked back to the laundry shelves and rooted through a box. "Another crappy lock, so easy a six-year-old with a credit card can pick it."

"Not many six-year-olds have credit cards."

"I bet Tori did. That's who this house is made for." She lifted a sponge, shook her head, and dropped it back into the box. "Rich kids whose only use for a credit card is buying a new pair of Timbs. They stick cheap locks on the doors, knowing you guys will turn the handle and say 'huh, locked' and walk away."

"That's—"

She stopped me with a look. "Unfair? Uh, that's exactly what you did, girl." She brandished a stiff piece of cardboard, a tag ripped off a new shirt.

"It's not perfect," she murmured as she slid it between the door and the frame. "But it'll—" She jiggled the cardboard and swore. "Or maybe it—" she swiped it down sharply, a ripping sound as it tore in half "—won't."

More curses, some of them quite creative.

"There's a piece caught . . . Here, let me."

I grabbed the edge between my fingernails, which would have been much easier if I had any. When I'd woken in the hospital, my nails had been filed to the pink, like they'd been worried I'd commit suicide by scratching. I managed to get hold of the cardboard, pulled . . . and ripped out another chunk, leaving the rest wedged in where no nails, however long, could reach it.

"Get the feeling someone doesn't want us going in there?" Rae said.

I tried to laugh, but ever since she'd mentioned "bodies," there'd been a sour taste in my mouth.

"We're going to need the key," she pronounced, straightening. "It might be on the ring with the one for the shed in the kitchen."

"I'll get it."

When I slipped into the kitchen, Derek was pawing through the fruit basket. The door hadn't made any noise opening and he had his back to me. The perfect chance for payback. I took three slow, silent steps toward him, barely daring to breathe—

"The key you want isn't on that ring," he said, not looking my way.

I froze. He dug out an apple, took a bite, then walked to the fridge, reached behind it, and pulled off a magnetized set of keys.

"Try these." He dropped them in my hand and walked past me to the kitchen door. "I have no idea what you guys are doing down there, but next time you want to secretly open a locked door, don't whale on it hard enough to bring down the house."

When I brought the keys downstairs, I didn't tell Rae that Derek knew what we were up to. She might have decided to abort the plan. Anyway tattling wasn't Derek's style. Or so I hoped.

As Rae tried the keys, I rubbed the back of my neck, grimacing against the dull throb of a threatening headache. Was I really that anxious about what lay behind the door? I rolled my shoulders, trying to shake it off.

"Found it," she whispered.

She swung open the door to reveal . . .

An empty closet. Rae stepped inside. I followed. We were in a space so small we could both barely fit.

"Okay," Rae said. "This is weird. Who builds a closet, doesn't put anything in it, then locks it? There's gotta be a catch." She rapped on the wall. "Yow! It's concrete. Painted concrete. Scraped my knuckles good." She touched the adjoining walls. "I don't get it. Where's the rest of the basement?"

I rubbed my temple, now throbbing. "It's a half basement. My aunt lived in an old Victorian place before she got sick of the renovations and moved into a condo. She said when her house was built, it didn't have a basement at all, just a crawl space under the house. Then someone dug out a room for the laundry. She used to have real bad problems with flooding and stuff. Maybe that's why this is empty and locked. So no one uses it."

"Okay, so what does your spook want you to see? Overlooked storage space?"

"I told you it was probably nothing."

The words came out more sharply than I intended. I rolled my shoulders and rubbed my neck again.

"What's wrong?" Rae laid her hand on my arm. "God, girl, you're covered in goose bumps."

"Just a chill."

"Maybe it's a cold spot."

I nodded, but I didn't feel cold. Just . . . anxious. Like a cat sensing a threat, its fur rising.

"There's a ghost here, isn't there?" she said, looking around. "Try contacting it."

"How?"

She shot me a look. "Start with 'hello.'"

I did.

"More," Rae said. "Keep talking."

"Hello? Is anyone there?"

She rolled her eyes. I ignored her. I felt foolish enough without having my dialogue critiqued.

"If someone's here, I'd like to talk to you."

"Close your eyes," Rae said. "Focus."

Something told me it had to be a lot more complicated than "close your eyes, focus, and talk to them." But I didn't have a better idea. So I gave it a shot.

"Nothing," I said after a moment.

When I opened my eyes, a figure flashed past so fast it was only a blur. I wheeled, trying to follow, but it was gone.

"What?" Rae said. "What'd you see?"

I closed my eyes and struggled to pull a replay tape from

memory. After a moment, it came. I saw a man dressed in a gray suit, clean shaven, wearing a fedora and horn-rimmed glasses, like someone out of the fifties.

I told her what I'd seen. "But it was just a flash. It's the meds. I had to take them today and they seem to . . . block transmission. I only get flashes."

I turned slowly, eyes narrowing as I concentrated as hard as I could, looking for even the faintest shimmer. As I circled, my elbow hit the door, knocking it against the wall with an oddly metallic clank.

Motioning Rae aside, I pulled the door forward to peek behind it. She squeezed in to take a look.

"Seems we missed something, huh?" she said, grinning.

The closet was so small that when the door opened, it had blocked the left wall. Now, looking behind it, I saw there was a metal ladder fastened to that wall. It led up a few steps to a small wooden door halfway up the wall, the gray paint blending with the concrete. I stepped onto the ladder. The door was secured only with a latch. One hard push and it swung open into darkness.

A musty stink billowed out.

The smell of the moldering dead.

Right. Like I knew what the dead smelled like. The only body I'd ever seen had been my mother's. She hadn't smelled dead. She'd smelled like Mom. I shook the memory off.

"I think it's a crawl space," I said. "Like at my aunt's

old place. Let me take a look."

"Hey." She plucked at the back of my shirt. "Not so fast. It looks awfully dark in there . . . too dark for someone who sleeps with the blinds open."

I ran my hand over the floor. Damp, packed dirt. I felt along the wall.

"A dirt crawl space," I said. "With no light switch. We're going to need a flashlight. I saw one—"

"I know. My turn to get it."

twenty-three

WHEN RAE GOT BACK, she spread her empty hands wide and said, "Okay, guess where I hid it."

She even turned around for me, but I could see no bulge big enough to hide a flashlight. With a grin, she reached down the front of her shirt into the middle of her bra, and pulled out a flashlight with flourish.

I laughed.

"Cleavage is great," she said. "Like an extra pocket."

She smacked the flashlight into my hand. I shone it into the crawl space. The dirt floor extended through the darkness as far as the beam pierced. I waved the flashlight. The beam bounced off something to my left. A metal box.

"There's a box," I said. "But I can't reach it from here."

I climbed the remaining two steps and crawled in. The

space stunk of dirt and stale air, as if no one had been there in years.

The ceiling was really low, so I had to waddle hunched over. I maneuvered to the box. It was dull gray metal with the kind of lid that lifted off, like a gift box.

"Is it locked?" Rae whispered. She had climbed the ladder and was peering in.

I passed the light around the perimeter of the lid. No sign of a lock.

"Well, open it," she said.

Kneeling, I gripped the flashlight between my knees. My fingertips slid under the lid's rim.

"Come on, come on," Rae said.

I ignored her. This room was what the ghost had wanted me to see. I was sure of it. And this box was the only thing I could see in this barren, dark space.

I'd seen boxes like this in movies, and what lay inside was never good. Body parts were usually involved.

But I had to know. The lid started coming off, then stopped. I jiggled it. One side came up, but the other caught. I slid my fingertips around the edge, trying to find what it was catching on. It was a piece of paper.

I tugged, and the paper ripped, leaving me with a corner. There was handwriting on it, but only fragments of words. I found the part of the paper still stuck in the box and pulled, prying the lid with my other hand. One sharp tug, and the paper came free . . . and so did the lid, flying off and landing in my lap. Before I could think about whether I wanted to look, I *was* looking, staring straight down into the box.

"Papers?" Rae said.

"It looks like . . . files."

I reached into a folder marked *2002* and pulled out a sheaf of papers. I read the first.

"Property taxes." I flipped through the other pages. "It's just records of stuff they needed to keep. They put them into a fireproof box and stored it here. The door's probably only locked so we don't snoop."

"Or this isn't what the ghost was telling you about. That means there must be something else down here."

We spent ten minutes crawling around, and finding nothing more than a dead mole that stunk so bad I nearly puked.

"Let's go," I said, crouched on my heels with my arms crossed. "There's nothing here, and it's freezing."

Rae shone the flashlight in my face. I swatted it out of the way.

"No need to get snippy," Rae said. "I was just going to say it's not cold."

I took her hand and wrapped it around my arm. "I'm *cold*. Those are goose bumps, all right? Feel them?"

"I didn't say you weren't—"

"I'm going. Stay if you want."

I started crawling away. When Rae grabbed my foot, I

yanked hard, almost toppling her over.

"What's with you?" she said.

I rubbed my arms. Tension strummed my nerves. My jaw ached, and I realized I was clenching my teeth.

"I just—I was okay before but now . . . I just want to get out."

Rae crawled up beside me. "You're sweating, too. Sweat and goose bumps. And your eyes are all glittery, like you have a fever."

"Maybe I do. Can we just—?"

"There's something here, isn't there?"

"No, I—" I stopped and looked around. "Maybe. I don't know. It's just— I need to go."

"Okay." She handed me the flashlight. "Lead the way."

The moment my fingers closed around the flashlight, the light started to dim. Within seconds, it was giving off only a faint yellowish glow.

"Tell me that's the batteries going," Rae whispered.

I quickly handed it back to her. The light surged, but only for a second. Then it went out, plunging us into darkness. Rae let out an oath. A swish. Light flared. Rae's face glowed behind the match flame.

"Knew these things would come in handy someday," she said. "Now . . ."

She stopped, her gaze going to the flame. She stared at it like a child mesmerized by a campfire.

"Rae!" I said.

"Oh, uh, sorry." A sharp shake of her head. We were almost at the door when I heard the distant sound of the basement door opening.

"The match!" I whispered.

"Right."

She extinguished it. Not by waving it or blowing it, but by cupping the flame in her hand. Then she tossed the dead match and the matchbook over her shoulder.

"Girls?" Mrs. Talbot called from the top of the stairs. "Is your homework done?"

Homework. Simon and Derek. I checked my watch. 7:58.

I scrambled out of the crawl space.

twenty-four

I KNEW RAE WAS DISAPPOINTED by what we'd found—or hadn't. I felt a weird kind of guilt, like a performer who failed to entertain. But she never doubted I'd seen a ghost or that he'd told me to open that door, and I was grateful for that.

I returned the key, washed, then found Mrs. Talbot and told her I was going upstairs for math tutoring with Derek and that Simon would be there. She hesitated but only for a moment, then sent me off.

I retrieved my newly arrived math text from my room and went around to the boys' side. The door was open. Simon sprawled on the bed, reading a comic. Derek was hunched over the too-small desk, doing homework.

The room was a reverse image of ours, set at the back of the house instead of the front. Simon's walls were covered in what looked like pages ripped from a comic book, but when I squinted, I realized they were hand drawn. Some were black-and-white, but most were in full color, everything from character sketches to splash panels to full pages, done in a style that wasn't quite manga, wasn't quite comic book. More than once Simon had gotten in trouble for doodling in class. Now I could see what he'd been working on.

Derek's walls were bare. Books were stacked on his dresser and magazines lay open on the bed. Shoved to the back corner of his desk was some kind of contraption full of wires and pulleys. A school project, I supposed, but if I had to build anything that complicated next year, I was doomed.

I rapped on the doorframe.

"Hey." Simon slapped down the comic as he sat up. "I was just going to tell Derek we should go downstairs, make sure the nurses weren't giving you a hassle. They didn't, did they?"

I shook my head.

Derek set his math text on the bedside table, as a prop, then put his binder over it. "I'll be in the shower. Start without me."

"Won't the nurses hear the water running?"

He shrugged, and shoved back his hair, lank and stringy now, the dull sheen of oil glistening under the lights. "Tell them I was already in there. I'll only be a few minutes."

He headed for the door, circling as wide around me as

he could manage, which made me wonder how badly he *needed* that shower. I wasn't about to sniff and find out.

If he was showering at night, that might be part of his problem. Kari said she always used to have a bath in the evening, but she'd had to switch to morning showers or her hair would be gross by dinner. I wouldn't dare suggest this to Derek, but as he passed, I couldn't resist an innocent, "Why don't you just shower in the morning?"

"I do," he muttered as he left.

Simon put away his comic. "Come on in. I don't bite."

He lay back in the middle of his bed, springs squeaking, then patted a spot at the edge.

"I'd say this is the first time I've had a girl in my bed . . . if I didn't mind sounding like a total loser."

I reached over to put my books on the beside table, hiding my blush. As I opened my text, to look like we were working on it, I knocked the binder off Derek's. I glimpsed the cover and did a double take.

College Algebra with Trigonometry.

I flipped through the pages.

"If you can understand any of that, you're way ahead of me," Simon said.

"I thought Derek was in tenth grade."

"Yeah, but not in algebra. Or geometry. Or chemistry, physics, or biology, though he's only in twelfth grade in the sciences."

Only twelfth . . . ?

When he said that no one would question us working on math together, he hadn't meant that *he* needed help. Great. It was bad enough Derek thought I was a flighty blond, jumping at every noise. Apparently he figured I wasn't too bright, either.

I put the binder back on top of Derek's text.

"Tori . . . she didn't give you a hard time or anything, did she?" he asked. "About yesterday."

I shook my head.

He exhaled and crossed his arms behind his head. "Good. I don't know what her problem is. I've made it clear that I'm not interested. At first, I tried being nice about it, brushing her off. When she didn't take a hint, I told her I wasn't interested. Now, I'm downright rude to her and she still won't back off."

I twisted around to see him better. "I guess that would be hard having someone really like you and you aren't interested back."

He laughed. "The only person Tori really likes is Tori. I'm just a stand-in until she can get back to her football captains. Girls like Tori need to have a guy—any guy—and here I'm her only option. Peter was way too young and Derek's—Derek's not her type. Trust me, if another guy walks in here, she'll forget I exist."

"I don't know about that. I think she might really—"

"Puh-lease. Do I look like diva bait to you?" He turned onto his side, head propped on his arm. "Oh, sure, when

Derek and I start at a new school, I'll get some attention from the clique girls. Like"—he raised his voice to a falsetto—"'Hey, Simon, I was, like, wondering if you could maybe, you know, help me with my homework after school? 'Cause it's, like, math and, like, you're Chinese, right? I bet you're sooo good at it.'"

He rolled his eyes. "First, my Dad's Korean and my mom was Swedish. Second, I totally suck at math. I don't like cuckoo clocks or skiing or fancy chocolate either."

I sputtered a laugh. "I think that's Swiss."

"Huh. So what's Swedish?"

"Um, I don't know. Meatballs?"

"Well, I kind of like those. But probably not Swedish ones."

"So what do you like?"

"In school? History. Don't laugh. And I'm not bad in English. I write mean haiku, which, by the way, is Japanese."

"I knew that." I glanced up at the drawings on his walls. "You must ace art, though. Those are amazing."

His eyes lit up, amber glinting in the deep brown.

"Not sure about *amazing*, but thanks. Actually, I don't ace art. Last year, I barely passed. I pissed off the teacher because I kept handing in my comics. I was doing the assignments, just taking the techniques and using them for my stuff. She thought I was being a smart-ass."

"That's not fair."

"Well, when I kept handing in my stuff even after the first couple of warnings, I probably *was* being a smart-ass. Or just stubborn. Anyway, I'm not that great in school overall—a solid B minus student. Derek's the genius. My best class is gym. I'm into cross-country, hurdles, B-ball, soccer . . ."

"Oh, I played soccer." I stopped. "Well, a while ago. A long while ago. Like back when we'd all chase the ball like a swarm of bumblebees."

"I remember those days. I'll have to give you some brushup lessons, so we can start a team. The Lyle House soccer club."

"A very small club."

"No, a very *exclusive* club."

I leaned back on my elbows, reclining on the bed. The last time I'd talked one-on-one like this with a guy was . . . well, probably back before I stopped thinking of them as "other kids" and started thinking of them as "boys."

"Speaking of exclusive clubs," I said, "I hope you asked me up here planning to answer some questions."

"My company isn't enough?" His brows shot up in mock outrage, ruined by the gleam in his eyes. "Okay, you've been patient long enough. What do you want to know?"

"Everything."

We grinned at each other.

"Okay, you're a necromancer and I'm a sorcerer. You speak to the dead and I cast spells."

"Is that why you're here? You did something?"

"Nah." He paused, a shadow crossing his face. "Well, kind of, but not magic. Something happened. With Der—" He cut himself short. From Derek's file, I knew why *he* was here, though I wasn't about to admit it. "Anyway, something happened, and then my dad disappeared and it's a very long story, but the short version is that we're stuck here until someone figures out what to do with us."

And until Derek was "cured," I supposed. That's why Simon didn't have a file or go to therapy. He wasn't here for any problem. When their dad left, the authorities must have brought Derek here, and decided to leave Simon with him.

"So what else is there? What other kind of . . ." I struggled for a word.

"Supernaturals. The different types are called races. There aren't very many. The biggies would be necros, sorcerers, witches—which are the girl spellcasters. Similar, but a different race, and not as strong as sorcerers, or so everyone says. What else? Half-demons, but don't ask me about them because I know next to nothing. Derek knows more. Oh, and shamans. They're good healers and they can astral project."

"Astral . . .?"

"Leave their bodies. Move around like a ghost. Cool for cheating on tests or sneaking into the girls' locker room . . . for guys who'd do that kind of thing . . ."

"Uh-huh. You said Derek knows more about half-demons. Is that what he is?"

He glanced toward the hall, head turning as if making sure he could still hear the water running.

"You dragged it out of me, okay?"

"Huh?"

He turned onto his side, moving close enough to brush my leg. His voice dropped. "About Derek. What he is. If he asks, you dragged it out of me."

I straightened, annoyance flickering. "So Derek doesn't want me to know what he is? The same guy who threw *necromancer* in my face and demanded I accept it. If he doesn't want—"

"He does. He will. It's just . . . complicated. If you don't ask, he won't tell you. But if you ask . . ."

His eyes lifted to mine, pleading with me to make this easy.

I sighed. "Fine, I'm asking. What's Derek? One of these half-demon things?"

"No. There's not really a name for what he is. I guess you could call it the superman gene, but that's really cheesy."

"Uh-huh."

"Which is why they don't call it that. Guys like Derek have . . . physical enhancements, you might say. Extra strong, as you saw. Better senses, too. That kind of thing."

I glanced at the math text. "Smarter?"

"Nah, that's just Derek. Or so my dad says."

"Your dad's a . . . sorcerer, too, then, I guess. So he knows others . . . like us?"

"Yeah. Supernaturals have a kind of community. Maybe *network* is a better word. You know others so you can talk to them, get things you can't get from the regular world, whatever. My dad used to be right into it. These days, not so much. Stuff . . . happened."

He went quiet for a moment, plucking at a loose thread on the comforter, then he dropped it and flopped onto his back again. "We'll get into all that later. Huge story. Short answer is, yes, Dad used to be into the whole supernatural network. He worked for this research company, supernatural doctors and scientists trying to make things easier for other supernaturals. Dad's a lawyer, but they needed people like that, too. Anyway, that's how we got Derek."

"*Got* Derek?"

Simon made a face. "That didn't come out right. Sounds like Dad brought home a stray puppy. But that's kind of how it was. See, Derek's type? It's rare. We're all rare, but he's really, really rare. These people, the ones my dad worked for, they were raising him. He'd been orphaned or abandoned or something when he was just a baby, and they wanted to make sure he didn't end up in some human foster home, which would be bad when he hit, like, twelve and started throwing people across the room. Only, my dad's company wasn't really equipped to raise a kid. Derek doesn't talk much about living there, but I think it was like growing up in a hospital. My dad didn't like that, so they let him bring Derek home. It was . . . weird. Like he'd never been out before. Things like school or a shopping mall or even a highway totally freaked him out. He wasn't used to people, all that noise—"

He went still, head turning toward the hall. The pipes clanked as the water shut off.

"Later," he mouthed.

"He just got out. He can't hear—"

"Oh yes, he can."

I remembered what Simon said about Derek's "enhanced senses." Now I understood why Derek always seemed to be able to hear things he shouldn't have been able to. I made a mental note to be more careful.

I cleared my throat, pitching it to normal. "Okay, so we've got sorcerers, witches, half-demons, necromancers, shamans, and other really rare types, like Derek. That's it, right? I'm not going to run into any werewolves or vampires, am I?"

He laughed. "That'd be cool."

Cool, maybe, but I was happy to leave werewolves and vampires to Hollywood. I could believe in magic and ghosts and even spirit travel, but turning into an animal or sucking blood stretched disbelief farther than I cared to.

A dozen questions leaped to my lips. Where was their father? What about the people his dad worked for? Why'd he leave them? What about Simon's mother? But Simon said he'd "get into that later." To demand their personal story now would be prying.

"So there are three of us? In one place? That has to mean something."

"Derek thinks it's because some supernatural powers— like yours and his—can't be explained, so humans chalk them up to mental illness. Some kids in homes could be supernatural. Most aren't. You have to talk to him about that. He explains stuff better."

"Okay, back to me, then. What do these ghosts want?"

He shrugged. "Help, I guess."

"With what? Why me?"

"Because you can hear them," Derek said as he walked in, towel-drying his hair. "Not much sense in talking to someone who can't hear you."

"Well, duh."

"I wasn't going to say it."

I glared at him, but he had his back to me, neatly folding the towel and hanging it on the desk chair.

He continued. "How many necromancers do you think are walking around out there?"

"How would I know?"

"Well, if the answer was 'a whole lot,' don't you think you'd have heard of them?"

"Ease up, bro," Simon murmured.

"We're talking hundreds in the whole country." Derek yanked a comb through his hair. "Have you ever met an albino?"

"No."

"Statistically speaking, you're about three times more likely to bump into an albino than a necromancer. So, imagine you're a ghost. If you see a necro, it's like being stranded on a desert island, then spotting a plane overheard. Are you going to try to get their attention? Of course. As for what they want?" He turned the desk chair around and straddled it. "Who knows? If you were a ghost and you bumped into the one living being who could hear you, I'm sure you'd want *something* from her. To know what they want, you're going to need to ask them."

"Easier said than done," I muttered.

I told them about the ghost in the basement.

"There could still be something back there. Something you didn't find. Something important to him." He idly scratched his cheek, winced, and pulled his hand back. "Maybe a paper or an object he'd like you to pass onto his family."

"Or clues to his murder," Simon said. "Or buried treasure."

Derek fixed him with a look, then shook his head. "Moving right along . . . it's probably something stupid, like a letter he forgot to give to his wife. Meaningless."

That didn't sound stupid to me. Or meaningless. Kind of romantic, really. The ghost lingers for years, wanting to pass along that undelivered letter to his wife, now an old woman in a nursing home . . . Not my kind of movie, but

I wouldn't call it stupid.

"Whatever it is," I said, "the point is moot because as long as I'm on these pills, I can't make contact to ask."

Derek swiped at a drop of blood on his cheek, where he'd scratched a zit. He scowled with annoyance, letting it bubble over into his voice as he snapped, "Then you need to stop taking the pills."

"Love to. If I could. But after what happened last night, they're giving me urine tests now."

"Ugh. That's harsh." Simon went quiet, then snapped his fingers. "Hey, I've got an idea. It's kinda gross, but what if you take the pills, crush them and mix them with your, you know, urine."

Derek stared at him.

"What?"

"You did pass chem last year, didn't you?"

Simon flipped him the finger. "Okay, genius, what's your idea?"

"I'll think about it. We should get her off those meds. I don't really care what that ghost wants, but he could be useful. As long as we have a willing subject, Chloe should take advantage of it, so she can learn. It's not like she's going anywhere soon . . . unless they ship her off."

Simon shot him a look. "Not funny, bro."

Derek raked his fingers through his wet hair. "Not trying to be funny. Seeing ghosts isn't easy to hide. It's not like casting spells. After this morning, with Dr. Davidoff and

Gill, I caught some of their conversation later—" Derek glanced at me. "I was walking by and heard—"

"She knows about your hearing, bro." Derek scowled at Simon, who only shrugged and said, "She figured it out. She's not stupid. Anyway, you overheard . . ."

He stopped, head lifting. "Someone's coming."

"Boys? Chloe?" Mrs. Talbot called from the stairs. "Snack time. Come on down."

Simon called back that we were coming.

"Just a sec," I said. "You heard the doctors talking. What about?"

"You. And whether Lyle House is the right place for you."

twenty-five

WAS DEREK TRYING TO scare me? A few days ago I would have said yes, without hesitation. But now I knew it was only honesty. He'd heard it, so he passed it on, with no attempt to soften the blow because the thought wouldn't cross his mind.

But it did make me all the more determined to get at least one question answered when the nurse popped her head in to announce lights-out.

"Mrs. Talbot?"

"Yes, dear?" she said, peeking back in.

"Can we call Liz yet? I'd really like to talk to her. To explain about that last night."

"There's nothing to explain, dear. Liz is the one who feels horrible about it, frightening you like that. I'm sure you can call her on the weekend."

"This *weekend*?"

She slipped into the room, shutting the door behind her. "The other doctors tell me Liz is having some difficulty adjusting."

Rae popped up from bed. "What's wrong?"

"It's called post-traumatic stress. That last night here was very difficult for her. The doctors in her new hospital don't want her reminded of it."

"What if I don't mention it?"

"Even talking to you will be a reminder, dear. By Sunday, they say she should be fine. Next week at the latest."

Fingers of dread plucked at me.

Not now, dear.

Maybe next weekend.

Maybe next week.

Maybe never.

I glanced at Rae, but pictured Liz instead, perched on the edge of the bed, wriggling her toes, purple and orange giraffes dancing.

Dead Liz.

Ghost Liz.

That was ridiculous, of course. Even if I could dream up a reason why Lyle House would want to kill kids, what about their families? These weren't street kids and runaways. They had parents who would notice if they vanished. Notice and care.

Are you so sure? What about Rae's parents? So attentive,

always calling and coming by to see her? And Simon and Derek's dad? The Invisible Man?

I rolled onto my side and wrapped my pillow around my ears, as if that could stifle the voice.

Then I remembered what Simon had said earlier. Astral projecting. There was a race of supernaturals who could leave their bodies and teleport. Could necromancers see those teleporting spirits, too? I bet they could—that spirit would be the part that left the body, at death or during this astral projecting.

So that's what Liz was. A . . . what did he call it? Shaman. She was astral-projecting here and I was seeing her. That could explain why I could see and hear her, but not the ghosts. It might also explain the poltergeist. Liz was doing that projecting stuff without realizing it, and throwing things around.

That had to be the answer. It *had* to be.

"Here," Derek whispered, pressing an empty Mason jar into my hand. He'd pulled me aside after class and we were now standing at the base of the boy's staircase. "Take this up to your room and hide it."

"It's a . . . jar."

He grunted, exasperated that I was so dense I failed to see the critical importance of hiding an empty Mason jar in my room.

"It's for your urine."

"My what?"

He rolled his eyes, a growl-like sound sliding through

his teeth as he leaned down, closer to my ear. "Urine. Pee. Whatever. For the testing."

I lifted the jar to eye level. "I think they'll give me something smaller."

This time he definitely growled. A quick glance around. Then he reached for my arm before stopping short and waving me onto the steps. He took them two at a time and was on the landing in a flash, then glowered back at me, as if I was dawdling.

"You took your meds today, right?" he whispered.

I nodded.

"Then use this jar to save it."

"Save . . . ?"

"Your urine. If you give them some of today's tomorrow, it'll seem like you're still taking your meds."

"You want me to . . . dole it out? Into specimen jars?"

"Got a better idea?"

"Um, no, but . . ." I lifted the jar and stared into it.

"Oh, for God's sake. Save your piss. Don't save your piss. It's all the same to me."

Simon peeked around the corner, brows lifted. "I was going to ask what you guys were doing, but hearing that, I think I'll pass."

Derek shooed me down the stairs. I tucked the jar into my knapsack. I'd really rather not use it, but if I squirmed at the thought of stockpiling urine, it would only prove I was the flighty girlie girl he expected.

twenty-six

I DID USE THE JAR, as gross as it was. I'd already provided my "sample" for that day, so the next time I had to go, I did it in the upstairs bathroom, in the jar, hiding it behind the cleaning stuff under the sink. Cleaning the bathroom was one of our chores, so I hoped that meant the nurses never went under there.

We didn't do much work in class that day. We tried, but Ms. Wang wasn't cooperating. It was Friday and she saw the weekend looming, so she just set us up with our assignments, then played solitaire on her laptop.

Rae spent most of the morning in therapy, first with Dr. Gill, then in a special session with Dr. Davidoff, while Tori went for hers with Dr. Gill. That meant when Ms. Wang let us out early for lunch, I was left to pass the time with Simon and Derek, which was just fine by me. There was still so much I wanted to know. Asking wasn't nearly so easy, especially since it wasn't stuff we could discuss in the media room.

Going outside would have been the obvious choice, but Miss Van Dop was working in the garden. So Simon offered to help me finish the laundry. Derek said he'd sneak down later.

"So this is where our resident ghost lurks," Simon said, circling the laundry room.

"I think so but—"

He held up a hand, then lowered himself to the floor and started sorting the last basket. "You don't need to tell me there might not be a ghost here, and I'm not going to make you try to contact it. When Derek comes down, he might. Don't let him push you around."

"I don't push her anywhere." Derek's voice preceded him around the corner.

"If I tell someone to do something and they do it?" Derek said, rounding the corner. "That's not my problem. All she has to do is say no. Her tongue works, doesn't it?"

Great. The guy can manage to make me feel stupid even when he's telling me I don't have to let him make me feel stupid.

"So if they decide to transfer you, what are you going to do about it?"

Simon balled up a shirt. "For God's sake, Derek, they're not—"

"They're thinking about it. She needs a plan."

"Does she?" Simon pitched the shirt into the colored pile. "What about you, bro? If word comes down that you're next to go, do you have a plan?"

They exchanged a look. I couldn't see Simon's face, but Derek's jaw set.

I stood and gathered a load for the washer. "If they do, I don't see that I have a lot of options. I can't exactly refuse."

"So you'll just give in? Go along like a good girl?"

"Ease up, bro."

Derek ignored him, scooped up the laundry I'd missed, and dropped it into the washer, moving beside me as he did. "They won't let you talk to Liz, will they?"

"Huh—what?"

"Tori asked this morning. I heard. Talbot told her no and said she'd told you the same thing when you asked last night." He grabbed the soap box from my hands, lifted the measuring cup from the shelf, and waggled it. "This helps."

"They said I can call Liz on the weekend."

"Still, seems a little odd. You barely knew the girl, and you're the first one wanting to call her?"

"It's called being considerate. Maybe you've heard of it?"

He batted my hand from the dials. "Darks, cold. Or you'll end up with the dye bleeding." A glance back at me. "See? I'm considerate."

"Sure, when it's mostly *your* stuff in there."

Behind us, Simon snorted a laugh.

"As for Liz," I continued, "I just wanted to be sure she was okay."

"Why wouldn't she be?"

He'd scoff at my stupidity, thinking Liz was dead, murdered. Oddly enough, that's exactly what I wanted. Reassurance that my head was stuffed too full of movie plots.

I got as far as the part about waking to see Liz on the bed, chattering away.

"So . . ." Derek cut in. "Liz returned from the great beyond to show you her really cool socks?"

I told them about her "dream" and her attic appearance.

When I finished, Simon sat there, staring, a shirt dangling from his hands. "That sure sounds like a ghost."

"Just because she's a ghost doesn't mean she was murdered," Derek said. "She could have had a completely unrelated accident on the way to the hospital. If that happened, they wouldn't want to tell us right away."

"Or maybe she's not dead at all," I said. "Could she be astral projecting? Shamans do that, right? It might also explain how she was moving stuff around. It wasn't a poltergeist spirit—it was *her* spirit or however it works. You said our powers kick in around puberty, right? If we don't know what we are when that happens, this is just the kind of place we'd end up. A home for teens with weird problems."

He shrugged. But he didn't argue.

"Would being a shaman explain what she was doing? Throwing stuff around? Could she have been popping out of her body without knowing it?"

"I . . . don't know." The admission came slowly, reluctantly. "Let me think about it."

We were halfway through dessert when Mrs. Talbot reappeared.

"I know you kids have free time after lunch, and I hate to interfere with that, but I'm going to have to ask you to spend it in this end of the house, and give Victoria and her mother some privacy. Please stay out of the classroom until it's time for classes, and don't play in the media room. You can go outside or in the living room."

Now, last week, if anyone told me to give someone privacy, I'd make sure I stayed away. That was only polite. After a few days at Lyle House, though, when someone said "Don't go there," I didn't say "okay," but "why?" . . . and decided to find out. In this house, knowledge was power, and I was a quick learner.

The question was: How to get close enough to Dr. Gill's office to overhear Tori and her mom, and learn why we had to give them privacy for a friendly mother-daughter chat. I could ask the guy with the supercharged hearing, but didn't want to owe Derek any favors.

Mrs. Talbot said the girls were allowed upstairs, but not

the boys, because getting to their rooms meant passing Dr. Gill's office. That gave me an idea. I went upstairs, crept into Mrs. Talbot's room, through the adjoining door into Miss Van Dop's, then down the boys' hall to the stairs.

My daring move was rewarded the moment I crouched on the stairs.

"I cannot believe you did this to me, Tori. Do you have any idea how much you've embarrassed me? You overheard what the nurses said about Chloe Saunders when I was here Sunday, and you couldn't wait to tell the other kids."

It took me a moment to realize what Tori's mom was talking about. So much had happened this week. Then it hit— Tori telling the others I thought I saw ghosts. Rae had said Tori's mom had some business connection with Lyle House, so when she'd dropped off that new shirt for Tori on Sunday, the nurses must have mentioned the new girl and her "hallucinations." Tori had been eavesdropping.

"If that wasn't enough, they tell me you've been sulking over that girl's transfer."

"Liz," Tori whispered. "Her name is Liz."

"I know her name. What I don't know is why it would send you off the deep end."

"Deep end?"

"Sulking in your room. Bickering with Rachelle. Gloating over that new girl's setback yesterday. Is your medication not working right, Victoria? I told you, if that new prescription doesn't help, you're to let me know—"

"It *is* helping, Mom." Tori's voice was thick, muffled, like she'd been crying.

"Are you still taking them?"

"I always take them. You know that."

"All I know is that if you're taking them, you should be getting better and this week proves you aren't."

"But that doesn't have anything to do with my problem. It's—it's the new girl. She's driving me nuts. Little Miss Goody Two-shoes. Always trying to show me up. Always trying to prove she's better." She switched to a bitter falsetto. "Oh, Chloe's such a good girl. Oh, Chloe's going to be out of here in no time. Oh, Chloe's trying so hard." She switched back to her normal voice. "I'm trying hard. Way harder than her. But Dr. Davidoff already came to visit her."

"Marcel only wants to motivate you kids."

"I *am* motivated. Do you think I like being stuck here with these losers and freaks? But I don't just want to get out—I want to get better. Chloe doesn't care about that. She lied, telling everyone she doesn't think she sees ghosts. Chloe Saunders is a two-faced little bi—" She swallowed the rest of word and said, "—witch."

I'd never been called anything like that, probably not even behind my back.

But I *had* lied. I'd said one thing while believing another. That was the definition of two-faced, wasn't it?

"I understand you don't care for this girl—"

"I *hate* her. She moves in, gets my best friend here

kicked out, shows me up with the nurses and doctors, steals my guy—" She stopped short, then mumbled. "Anyway, she deserved it."

"What's this about a boy?" Her mother's words came sharp, brittle.

"Nothing."

"Are you involved with one of the boys here, Tori?"

"No, Mom, I'm not *involved* with anyone."

"Don't take that tone with me. And blow your nose. I can barely understand you through all that blubbering." A pause. "I'm only going to ask you one more time. What's this about a boy?"

"I just—" Tori inhaled loudly enough for me to hear. "I like one of the guys here, and Chloe knows that, so she's been chasing him to show me up."

Chasing him?

"Which boy is it?" Her mother's voice was so low I had to strain to hear it.

"Oh, Mom, it doesn't matter. It's just—"

"Don't you 'oh, Mom' me. I think I have the right to be concerned—" Her voice dropped another notch. "Don't tell me it's Simon, Tori. Don't you dare tell me it's Simon. I warned you to stay away from that boy—"

"Why? He's fine. He doesn't even take meds. I like him and— Ow! Mom! What are you doing?"

"Getting your attention. I told you to stay away from him and I expect to be obeyed. You already have a boyfriend.

More than one if I recall. Perfectly nice boys who are waiting for you to get out of here."

"Yeah, like that's going to happen anytime soon."

"It will happen when you decide to make it happen. Do you have any idea how embarrassing it is for a member of the board to have her own daughter sent to this place? Well, let me tell you, Miss Victoria, it's nothing compared to the humiliation of having her still here almost two months later."

"You've already told me that. And told me. And told me."

"Not often enough or you'd be doing something about it. Like trying to get better."

"I am trying." Tori's voice rose in a wail of frustration.

"It's your father's fault—he spoils you rotten. You've never fought for anything in your life. Never known what it was to want anything."

"Mom, I'm trying—"

"You don't know what trying is." The venom in her mother's voice made my skin creep. "You're spoiled and lazy and selfish and you don't care how much you're hurting me, making me look like a lousy mother, damaging my professional reputation . . ."

Tori's only answer was a gut-wrenching sob. I hugged my knees, rubbing my arms.

"You don't worry about Chloe Saunders." Her mother's voice lowered to a hiss. "She's not getting out nearly as fast as she thinks she is. You worry about Victoria Enright and about me. Make me proud, Tori. That's all I ask."

"I'm try—" She stopped. "I will."

"Ignore Chloe Saunders and ignore Simon Bae. They aren't worth your attention."

"But Simon—"

"Did you hear me? I don't want you near that boy. He's trouble—him and his brother. If I hear of you two ever being seen together, alone, he's gone. I'll have him transferred."

Life experience. I can talk it up, vow to broaden my horizons, but I'm still limited to the experiences within my life.

How can a person understand an experience that lies completely outside her own? She can see it, feel it, imagine what it would be like to live it, but it's no different from seeing it on a movie screen and saying "Thank God that's not me."

After listening to Tori's mother, I vowed never to badmouth Aunt Lauren again. I was lucky to have a "parent" whose biggest fault was that she cared about me too much. Even when she was disappointed in me, she'd come to my defense. To accuse *me* of embarrassing *her* would never enter my aunt's mind.

Calling me lazy for not trying hard enough? Threatening to send away a boy I liked?

I shivered.

Tori *was* trying to get better. Rae had called her the

queen of meds. Now I could see why. I could only imagine what life was like for Tori, and even my imagination wasn't good enough to stretch that far.

How could a parent blame her child for not overcoming a mental illness? It wasn't like pushing a reluctant student to get a passing grade. It was like blaming one with a learning disorder for not getting As. Whatever Tori's "condition" was, it was like schizophrenia—not her fault and not entirely within her control.

Tori skipped class that afternoon, not surprisingly. The rule about not hiding out in your room apparently didn't apply to her, maybe because of her condition or maybe because of her mother's position. Between periods, I slipped upstairs to find her. She was in her bedroom, her sobs barely muffled by the closed door.

I stood in the hall, listening to her cry, yearning to do something.

In a movie, I'd go in there, comfort her, and maybe even become her friend. I'd seen it on the screen a dozen times. But again, that wasn't the same as experiencing it in real life, something I couldn't really appreciate until I was there, outside the door.

Tori hated me.

The thought made my stomach hurt. I'd never been hated before. I was the kind of kid that, if someone asked others what they thought of me, they'd say "Chloe? She's okay, I guess." They didn't love me, didn't hate me, just didn't think much about me either way.

Whether I'd earned Tori's hate was another matter, but I couldn't argue with her experience of events. To her, I *had* barged in and taken her place. I'd become the "good patient" she desperately needed to be.

If I walked into her room now, she wouldn't see a sympathetic face. She'd see a victor come to gloat, and she'd hate me all the more. So I left her there, crying in her room, alone.

When afternoon break ended, Mrs. Talbot announced classes were over for the day. We were going to make a rare trip into the outside world. We weren't going far—just to an indoor community pool a block away, within walking distance.

A great idea. If only I had a bathing suit.

Mrs. Talbot offered to call Aunt Lauren, but I wasn't about to interrupt my aunt for that, especially after she'd been dragged away for my misbehavior yesterday.

I wasn't the only one being left behind, though. Derek had to go to his session with Dr. Gill. That didn't seem fair, but when I said so to Simon, he said Derek wasn't allowed on the outings. I guess that made sense, considering what he was in here for. The day I arrived, when they'd taken the others to lunch while I settled in, he must have been confined to his room.

* * *

After everyone left, I took advantage of the nurses being gone and hung out in my room, listening to music. I'd been up there only a few minutes when I thought I heard a rap at my door. I pulled out one earbud. Another rap. I was pretty sure ghosts couldn't knock, so I called a greeting.

The door swung open. There stood Tori, looking . . . very un-Tori-like. Her dark hair stood in spikes, as if she'd been running her hands through it. Her shirt was wrinkled, the back untucked from her jeans.

I sat up. "I thought you went swimming."

"I have cramps. That okay with you?" Her words were clipped, with an undertone of her usual snottiness, but forced. "Anyway, I didn't come to borrow your eyeliner. Not like you have any. I just came to say you can have Simon. I've decided . . ." Her gaze slid away. "I'm not interested. He's not my type anyway. Too . . . young." A twist of her lips. "Immature. Anyway. Take him. He's all yours."

I'd have been tempted to shoot back a "Gee, thanks" if it wasn't obvious how much this was hurting her. Simon was wrong. Tori did really like him.

"Anyway"—she cleared her throat—"I've come to declare a truce."

"Truce?"

With an impatient wave, she stepped into the room, closing the door behind her. "This silly feud of ours. You aren't worth my . . ." She trailed off, shoulder slumping. "No more fighting. You want Simon? Take him. You think you see ghosts? That's your problem. All I want is for you to tell Dr. Gill that I apologized for telling everyone you saw ghosts the first day. They were going to let me out Monday, but now they aren't. And it's your fault."

"I didn't—"

"I'm not done." A touch of her old attitude gave the words a snarky lilt. "You'll tell Dr. Gill that I apologized and maybe you blew the whole thing out of proportion. I thought it was cool you saw ghosts and you took it the wrong way, but that I've been nice to you ever since."

"About 'giving' me Simon . . . I'm not—"

"That's part one of the deal. Part two? I'll show you something you want to see."

"What's that?"

"In that—" a flip of her hand "—filthy crawl space. I was going downstairs to see when you were finally going to get my jeans washed, and I heard you and Rae looking for something."

I wiped any expression from my face. "I don't know what—"

"Oh, stuff it. Let me guess. Brady told Rae there was something in there, didn't he?"

I had no idea what she meant but nodded.

"It's a jewelry box full of old stuff." Her lips curled in distaste. "Brady showed me. He thought I might actually be interested in it. It's, like, antiques, he said. Gross." She shivered. "When I wasn't all 'Oh, wow, that's so sweet and romantic. I just love rotting necklaces and filthy crawl spaces,' he must have mentioned it to Rae. If you want, I can show you."

"Sure, I guess. Maybe tonight—"

"You think I'm going to risk getting into more trouble? I'll show you now, when I'll have time to shower after. And don't think you'll find it on your own, because you won't."

I hesitated.

Her mouth tightened. "Fine. You don't want to help me? That's just peachy."

She headed for the door.

I swung my legs over the side of the bed. "Hold up. I'm coming."

Twenty-seven

I CLIMBED ONTO THE LADDER, pushed open the door, and peered inside—into the pitch blackness. I pulled back and looked down at Tori.

"Rae had a flashlight. We need to get it."

An exasperated sigh. "Where is it?"

"I don't know. I thought you'd—"

"Why would I know where they keep flashlights? Do you think I sneak around at night? Read dirty books under the covers? Just go—" She stopped, lips curving in a mocking smile. "Oh, that's right. You're afraid of the dark, aren't you?"

"Where did you hear—"

She plucked at my pant leg. "Get down, little girl. I'll lead the way . . . and fend off all the nasty ghosts."

"No, I've got it. Just give me a sec so my eyes adjust."

Where was Rae and her matches when you needed them? Wait. Matches. She'd thrown them in here. I felt around, but the dark earth floor camouflaged the matchbook.

"Hello?" Tori said. "Petrified with fear already? Move or get out of my way."

I started forward.

"Head left," Tori said as she crawled in behind me. "It's about halfway to the wall."

We'd gone around twenty feet when she said, "Swing right. See that pillar?"

I squinted and could make out a support post.

"It's right behind that."

I crawled to the pillar and started feeling around the base of it.

"*Behind*, not *beside*. Can't you do anything? Here, let me."

She reached for my arm, hand wrapping around my forearm and yanking me off balance.

"Hey!" I said. "That—"

"Hurts?" Her fingers dug in harder. When I tried to wrench back, she kneed me in the stomach, and I doubled over. "Do you know how much trouble you got me in, Chloe? You come here, get Liz sent away, steal Simon, ruin my chance to get out. Well, you're about to get out yourself. A one way ticket to the loony bin. Let's see just how scared of the dark you really are."

She lifted a ragged rectangle. A broken brick? She

swung. Pain exploded in the back of my head and I pitched forward, tasting dirt before everything went black.

Several times I woke, groggy, some deeper part of me screaming, "You have to get up!" before the sleepy, confused part muttered, "It's just the pills again" and I drifted back into unconsciousness.

Finally I remembered I wasn't taking the pills and I did wake. To the sound of labored breathing. I lay there, my brain still fuddled, heart racing, as I tried to call "Who's there?" But my lips wouldn't move.

I rocked wildly, unable to get up, unable to move my arms, scarcely able to breathe. Then, as I struggled to inhale, I realized where the sound of heavy breathing came from. Me.

I forced myself to lay still, to calm down. Something was tight across my cheeks, pulling the skin when I moved. Tape. I had tape over my mouth.

My hands were tied behind my back, and my legs . . . I squinted into the dark, trying to see my feet, but with the door closed and no light coming in, I couldn't see anything. When I moved my legs, I could feel something holding them together near the ankles. Tied.

That crazy bitch!

I never thought I'd call someone that, but with Tori, no other word fit.

She hadn't just lured me into the crawl space and knocked me out. She'd bound and gagged me.

She was nuts. Absolutely nuts.

Well, duh, that's why she's locked up in this place. Mentally disturbed. Read the label, Chloe. You're the idiot who forgot.

Now I was stuck here, gagged and bound in the dark, waiting for someone to find me.

Will anyone find you?

Of course. They wouldn't just leave me here to rot.

You've probably been unconscious for hours. Maybe they've stopped looking. Maybe they think you've run away.

It didn't matter. Once Tori'd had her fun—and her revenge—she'd find a way to let someone know where I was.

Will she? She's crazy, remember. All she cares about is getting rid of you. Maybe she'll decide it's better if you're never found. A few days without water . . .

Stop that.

They'll think someone broke in. Tied poor Chloe up and left her in the crawl space. That would make a good story. Chloe's last story.

Ridiculous. They'd find me. Eventually. But I wasn't going to lie here and wait for rescue.

I flipped onto my back and tried using my hands to push myself up. When I couldn't get a grip, I rolled onto my side, then twisted and squirmed until I was on my knees.

There. At least I could inch forward. If I could make it

to the other side of the crawl space, I could bang on the door, get someone's attention. It would be slow going, but—

"Chloe?"

A man's voice. Dr. Davidoff? I tried to answer, but could only make a muffled "uh-uh" sound.

". . . your name . . . Chloe . . ."

As the voice drew near, and I recognized it, the hairs on my arms went up. The basement ghost.

I braced myself and looked around, knowing even as I did that I couldn't see anything in this blackness.

This complete dark.

". . . relax . . . come for you . . ."

I shifted forward and smacked nose-first into a post. Pain exploded behind my eyes and they filled with tears. When I lowered my head, wincing, I smacked my skull into the post, and toppled sideways.

Get up.

What's the use? I can barely move. I can't see where I'm going. It's so dark.

I lifted my head but, of course, saw nothing. Ghosts could be all around me, everywhere—

Oh, stop that! They're ghosts. They can't do anything to you. They can't "come for you."

". . . summon them . . . you *must* . . ."

I closed my eyes and concentrated on breathing. Nothing but breathing, blocking that voice.

". . . *help* you . . . listen . . . this house . . ."

As terrified as I was, the moment I heard the words "this house" spoken with such urgency, I had to listen.

". . . good . . . relax . . . concentrate . . ."

I struggled against my bonds, trying to push myself up.

"No, relax . . . come for you . . . use the time . . . make contact . . . I can't . . . must get . . . their story . . . urgent . . ."

I strained to pick up more, struggling to understand. Relax and concentrate? Sounded like what Rae suggested. It had worked when I was with her, at least enough for me to see a flash.

I closed my eyes.

". . . good . . . relax . . . summon . . ."

I squeezed my eyes shut and imagined myself making contact with him. Pictured him. Visualized pulling him through. Strained until my temples began to throb.

". . . child . . . not so . . ."

His voice was louder. I balled up my hands, willing myself to pass through the barrier, to contact the dead—

"No!" the ghost said. "Don't—!"

My head jerked up, eyes flying open to blackness.

Are you there? I thought the words, then tried saying them, an "uh-uh-uh" against the gag.

I ticked off two minutes of complete quiet. So much for pulling the ghost through. I must have shoved him farther out of reach.

At least the interlude gave me a moment to calm down. My heart had stopped its scared-rabbit pattering, and even the dark didn't seem so bad. If I could inch toward the door and bang on it . . .

And what direction is the door?

I'd just have to find out.

I started toward a sliver of light that probably came from around the door. The ground trembled, and I pitched forward.

As I straightened, the bindings around my hands moved, loosening. I twisted my arms, pulling my wrists apart. Whatever knot Tori had tied was poorly done, and slipping.

Rich girls, I thought. That's what Rae would say.

I worked my hands free. When I reached for my legs, the tremor came again, stronger now, and I had to brace myself to keep from falling over.

An earthquake?

With my luck, I wouldn't doubt it. I waited it out, then started fumbling with the rope around my feet. It was twisted and knotted in several places, as if it had knots before Tori found it. Finding the right knot, in the dark was—

A *crunch* cut my thought short. It sounded like someone stepping onto the dirt floor. But ghosts didn't make any noise when they moved. I listened. It came again, a shifting, crackling sound, like someone dropping a handful of pebble-filled dirt.

I swallowed and kept working on the knot.

What if there's a real person down here with me?

Someone who could *hurt me?*

A scraping noise behind me. I jumped, wrenching my side. The gag stifled my yelp, and I searched the darkness, heart pounding so loud I swore I could hear it.

Thump-thump-thump.

That's not my heartbeat.

The sound came from my left, too soft to be footsteps. Like someone's hands hitting the dirt. Like someone crawling toward me.

"Stop that!"

I only meant to think the words, but I heard them rip from my raw throat, muffled by the gag. The thumping stopped. A guttural noise, like a growl.

*My God, there isn't some*one *down here, there's some*thing, *some animal.*

A mole. Rae and I had seen a dead mole yesterday.

A mole? Growling? Making a thumping loud enough to be heard across the room?

Just stay still. If you stay still, it can't find you.

That's sharks! You idiot, sharks and dinosaurs can't find you if you stay still. This isn't Jurassic Park!

Hysterical laughter bubbled up in my throat. I swallowed it, twisting the sound into a whimper. The thumping grew louder, closer, underscored now by a new noise. A . . . clicking.

Click-clack-click-clack.

What was that?

Are you going to sit here and find out?

I reached for my gag but I couldn't get a grip on the tape, so I gave up and fumbled for the rope around my feet again, fingertips whizzing along it so fast it cut into my skin. At every knot, I felt for loose ends and, finding none, kept going until—

There it was. A loose end.

I worked at the knot, tugging this bit, then that bit, searching for the one that would yank out an end. I put all my concentration into it, blocking the sounds.

I was trying to get my fingers under a section of knot when something rattled right beside me. A rustle, then a *click-clack*.

A thick musty smell filled my nostrils. Then icy fingertips brushed my bare arm.

Something in me just . . . let go. A small rush of wetness trickled down my leg, but I barely noticed. I sat there, frozen, holding myself so still and tight that my jaw started to ache.

I tracked the thumping, rustling, clicking thing as it seemed to circle me. Another sound rose. A long low whimper. My whimper. I tried to stop it, but couldn't, could only huddle there, so terrified my mind was an absolute blank.

Then it touched me again. Long, dry, cold, fingerlike things tickled across the back of my neck. An indescribable smacking, cracking, rustling sound set my every hair on end. The sound repeated until it became not a sound but a word. A horrible mangled word that couldn't come from any human throat, a single word endlessly repeated.

"Help. Help. Help."

I lunged forward, away from the thing. Ankles still tied, I flopped face-first to the floor, then pushed up on all fours, moving as fast as I could to that distant door.

A hissing, thumping, clicking sound came from my other side.

Another one.

Oh God, what were they? How many were there?

It doesn't matter. Just go!

I dragged myself until I was at the door. My fingertips brushed the wood. I pushed. It didn't budge.

Locked.

I backed up and slammed my fists against it, screaming, banging, calling for help.

Cold fingers wrapped around my bare ankle.

twenty-eight

MY HAND BRUSHED SOMETHING lying in the dirt. The matchbook.

I snatched it up and fumbled with the cover. I pulled out a match, then turned the book over, fingers searching for the strike strip. There.

"Help. Help. Me."

I backpedaled, shimmying and kicking my bound feet to get away, match falling. I stopped, and ran my hand over the dirt, searching for it.

Get another one!

I did. Found the strike strip again. Pinched the match between my fingers and . . . realized that I had no idea how to light it. Why would I? At camp, only counselors started fires. I'd never smoked a cigarette. I didn't share other girls' fascination with candles.

You must have done this before.

Probably, but I didn't remember . . .

Who cares! You've seen it in movies, haven't you? How hard can it be?

I pinched the match again, struck it . . . and it folded on impact. I pulled out another. How many were there? Not many—it was the same pack Rae had used the first day I'd caught her lighting matches.

This time, I held the match lower, near the head. I struck it. Nothing. I struck again and the match head flared, singeing my fingertips, but I didn't let go. The flame burned bright, but gave off very little light. I could see my hand, but beyond that—darkness.

No, there was something to the right, moving on the dirt. I could make out only a dark shape, dragging itself toward me. Big and long. Something reached out. It looked like an arm, splotchy, the hand almost white, long fingers glowing against the earth.

The hands reached forward, clawing the dirt, then pulling the body along. I could see clothes, ripped clothing. The smell of dirt and something dank filled my nostrils.

I lifted the match higher. The thing raised its head. A skull stared at me, strips of blackened flesh and dirty encrusted hair hanging from it. Empty eye sockets turned my way. The jaw opened, teeth clacking as it tried to speak, uttering only that horrible, guttural groan.

"Help. Help me."

I screamed into the gag so loud I thought my head would explode. Anything left in my bladder gave way. I dropped the match. It sputtered on the ground, then went out, but not before I saw a bony hand reaching for my leg and a second corpse slithering up beside the first.

For a second, I just sat there, nearly convulsing with fear, my screams little more than rasps. Then that hand wrapped around my leg, cold bone biting in, scraps of ragged cloth brushing my bare skin. Even if I couldn't see it, I could visualize it, and that image was enough to stop the screams in my throat and jolt me back to life.

I yanked free, kicking, shuddering as my foot made contact, and I heard a dry, snapping sound. As I scuttled away, I heard someone saying my name, telling me to stop.

I tried to pull the gag off, but my shaking fingers still couldn't find an edge. I gave up, crawling as fast as I could, until the thumps and clicks and enraged hisses grew distant.

"Chloe! Stop." A dark shape loomed above me, illuminated by a dim light. "It's—"

I kicked as hard as I could. A sharp hiss of pain and a curse.

"Chloe!"

Fingers clamped down on my arm. I swung. Another hand grabbed that arm, and yanked me off balance.

"Chloe, it's me. Derek."

I don't know what I did next. I think I might have collapsed into his arms, but if I did, I prefer not to remember it that way. I do remember feeling the gag rip away, then hearing that awful *thump-thump* and scrambling up.

"Th-th-there's—"

"Dead people, I know. They must have been buried down here. You accidentally raised them."

"R-r-raised—"

"Later. Right now, you need to—"

The thumping sounded again, and I could see them—in my mind—pulling their limp bodies along. The rustle of their clothing and dried flesh. The clatter and clicks of their bones. Their spirits trapped inside. Trapped in their corpses—

"Chloe, focus!"

Derek grabbed my forearms, holding me still, pulling me close enough to see the white flash of his teeth as he talked. From behind him came that faint light I'd seen earlier. The door had been left open, letting in just enough light to make out shapes.

"They won't hurt you. They aren't brain-eating movie zombies, okay? They're just dead bodies with their spirits returned to them."

Just dead bodies? With their spirits returned to them? I'd sent people—ghosts—back into their corpses? I thought of what that would be like, shoved back into your decomposed body, trapped there—

"I—I—I need to send them back."

"Yeah, that'd be the general idea."

Strain sapped the sarcasm from his words; and when I stopped shaking, I could feel the tension running through him, vibrating through the hands gripping my arms, and I knew he was struggling to stay calm. I rubbed my hands over my face, the stink of dirt filling my nostrils.

"O-okay, so how do I send them back?"

Silence. I looked up.

"Derek?"

"I . . . I don't know." He shook it off, rolling his shoulders, the gruffness returning to his voice. "You summoned them, Chloe. Whatever you did, undo it. Reverse it."

"I didn't do—"

"Just *try*."

I closed my eyes. "Go back. Back to your afterlife. I release you."

I repeated the words, concentrating so hard sweat trickled down my face. But the thumping kept coming. Closer. Closer.

I closed my eyes and made myself a movie, starring a foolish young necromancer who needs to send spirits back to the netherworld. I forced myself to picture the corpses. I saw myself calling to their ghosts, freeing them of their earthly bonds. I imagined their spirits lifting—

"Help. Help."

My throat went dry. The voice was right behind me. I opened my eyes.

Derek let out an oath and his hands tightened around my forearms.

"Keep your eyes closed, Chloe. Just remember, they won't hurt you."

A bony fingertip touched my elbow. I jumped.

"It's okay, Chloe. I'm right here. Keep going."

As I held myself still, the fingertips poked my arm, then slid along it, stroking, testing, feeling, like the blind man with the elephant. Bone scraped over my skin. A rustling clatter as the corpse pulled itself closer. The smell of it—

Visualize.

I am!

Not like that!

I closed my eyes—meaningless since I could see nothing with them open, but it made me feel better. The fingers crept and poked over my back, plucking my shirt, the corpse making *gah-gah-gah* noises as if trying to talk.

I gritted my teeth and blocked it out. Not easy, knowing what was touching me, pressing up against my side—

Enough already!

I concentrated instead on Derek's breathing. Slow, deep breaths through his mouth, as he struggled to stay calm.

Deep breaths. Deep breaths. Find a quiet spot. The creative place.

Slowly the sounds and touches and smells of the real world faded. I squeezed my eyes shut, and let myself free-fall into my imagination. I focused on the bodies, imagining myself tugging out their spirits, setting them free, like caged doves, winging their way into the sunlight.

I repeated the images—freeing the spirits, wishing them well, apologizing as I sent them on their way. Dimly I heard Derek's voice, telling me I was doing fine, but it seemed to float, dreamlike on the edge of consciousness. The real world was here, where I was undoing my mistake, reversing the—

"They're gone, Chloe," he whispered.

I stopped. I could still feel bony fingers, now on my leg, a body resting against mine, but it wasn't moving. When I twisted sideways, the corpse fell, an empty shell, collapsing at my feet.

Derek let out a long, deep breath, running his hands through his hair. After a moment, he asked, as if in afterthought, whether I was okay.

"I'll live."

Another shuddering deep breath. Then he looked at the body.

"Guess we've got some work to do."

twenty-nine

B Y "WORK," HE MEANT cleanup. As in, reburying the bodies. All I'll say about that is that I was glad even with the door open it was still too dark to see those corpses very well.

The graves were shallow, barely more than a few inches of dirt over the bodies, enough for them to claw through when their spirits were slammed back into their corpses. But I didn't want to think about that.

I could tell the bodies had been buried quite a while, probably before Lyle House had become a group home. And they were adults. For now, that was all I needed to know.

As we worked, I asked Derek how he'd found me. He said that when he realized Tori had stayed behind, he knew she was up to something, so he went to check on me. How exactly he found me, he didn't say, only shrugged and mumbled something about checking "the obvious places" when I seemed to be missing.

The question now was: What to do about Tori?

"Nothing," I said, wiping my trembling hands after smoothing over the second grave.

"Huh?"

Nice to hear *him* say that for a change.

"I'm going to act like nothing happened."

He considered it, then nodded. "Yeah. If you blame her, things will only escalate. Better to ignore her and hope she gives up."

"*Pray* she gives up," I muttered as I crawled for the door.

"Is there still clean clothing down here?" Derek asked.

"One load in the dryer. That's it. Why—? Oh, right. Better not to go upstairs covered in dirt." I climbed down the ladder. "Most of what's in the dryer was yours so—"

"Chloe? Derek?" Mrs. Talbot stood in the laundry room. "What are you two doing together? Derek, you know you're not supposed to—" Her gaze traveled over my filthy clothing. "Dear Lord, what happened to you?"

There was no sense denying we'd been in the crawl space, since she caught us stepping from the closet, me caked in dirt. I moved my legs together, hoping it hid the wet mark. The blow to the back of my skull throbbed and I struggled to speak, praying Derek would jump in. He didn't. One rescue a day must have been his limit.

"I was doing laundry, and D-Derek came down, looking for—"

Dr. Gill stepped into the room. My gaze shot to her.

"Go on, Chloe."

"H-he wanted his shirt. I—I asked about stain stuff, because I couldn't find any and I opened the closet to look, and Derek said it was usually l-locked. We f-found the ladder and the crawl sp-space and we were curious."

"Oh, I bet you were curious," Dr. Gill said, crossing her arms. "Kids your age are very curious, aren't they?"

"I—I guess so. We were exploring—"

"I bet you were," Dr. Gill cut in.

I realized what she thought Derek and I had been doing.

Even as I denied it, I saw she'd given us the perfect out. If I just dropped my gaze sheepishly and said "Yep, you caught us," they'd have their explanation, with no reason to go into the crawl space and discover those hastily reburied corpses.

If it had been Simon, I'd have done it in a second. But Derek? I wasn't that good a liar.

It didn't matter. The more I denied it, the more certain they were that we'd been fooling around. Dr. Gill had already made up her mind. If you find a teenage boy and girl in a dark, private place, was there really any question what they'd been up to?

Even Mrs. Talbot seemed convinced, her mouth tight

with disapproval as I blathered.

And Derek? He didn't say a word.

Once we were released, I hurried upstairs to change my jeans before anyone noticed the pee mark. When I checked my head, I had two goose eggs, one from Tori and one from hitting that pillar.

Back downstairs, I showed the smaller one to Dr. Gill, hoping it would support my story that we'd been exploring—see, I even bopped my head. She just took a cursory look, handed me Tylenol, and told me to lie down in the media room. Aunt Lauren was on the way.

"I don't know what to say, Chloe."

Aunt Lauren's voice was barely above a whisper. These were the first words she'd said to me since arriving at Lyle House. I'd heard her arguing with Dr. Gill and the nurses earlier, demanding to know why they weren't making sure Derek stayed away from me, as she'd been promised. But now, with me, that anger had disappeared.

We were alone in Dr. Gill's office. Just like Tori and her mother had been. While I knew this meeting wouldn't end in threats and bruises, I imagined I'd leave feeling no better than Tori had.

Aunt Lauren sat ramrod straight, her hands cupped in her lap, fingers twisting her emerald ring.

"I know you're fifteen. Even if you haven't really dated

yet, you're curious. In a place like this, isolated from your friends and family, living with boys, the temptation to experiment—"

"It wasn't like that. It wasn't *anything* like that." I twisted to face her. "We found the crawl space and Derek wanted to check it out and I thought that'd be cool."

"So you followed him in there? After what he'd done to you?" She'd gone still, the disappointment in her eyes changing to horror. "Oh, Chloe, I can't believe— Did you think harassing and hurting you the other day meant he liked you?"

"What? No, of course not. Derek isn't— He made a mistake. He didn't really hurt me and he didn't mean to do it. It was a misunderstanding."

She reached forward and gripped my hand. "Oh, Chloe. Sweetheart, no. You can't fall for that. You can't make excuses for him."

"Excuses?"

"Maybe this is the first boy who's ever said 'I like you,' and I know that feels good, but this will not be the only boy who likes you, Chloe. He's just the first with the nerve to say so. He's older. He took advantage of the situation. At school, I imagine girls won't look at him twice and here he is, with a pretty girl, young, impressionable, trapped—"

"Aunt Lauren!" I yanked from her grasp. "God, it's not—"

"You can do better, Chloe. Much better."

From the distaste on her face, I knew she wasn't talking about how Derek treated me. I felt an odd surge of outrage. Sure, I couldn't bring myself to pretend that I'd been fooling around with him. But I'd felt bad about thinking that way.

How Derek looked wasn't his fault. He was obviously aware of it—and how others reacted to it—and it certainly wasn't like he tried to be repulsive. An adult should know better. Aunt Lauren should be the one giving me the you-can't-judge-a-book-by-its-cover speech.

Any notion I'd had of confessing the truth to Aunt Lauren evaporated. She looked at Derek and she saw a creep who'd attacked her niece. Nothing I could say would convince her otherwise, because he *seemed* like a creep. And nothing I could say would convince her I was really seeing ghosts, because I *seemed* like a schizophrenic.

"Aren't you going to say anything, Chloe?"

"Why?" I heard the chill in my voice. "I've tried. You've already made up your mind."

She shifted in her seat, inching to the edge, closing the gap between us. "I'd like to hear your side."

"Just because I'm in this place, just because I'm 'sick,' doesn't mean I'm any different than I was a week ago. Back then, you'd know something was wrong with this story. You'd have asked for my explanation *before* accusing me of anything. But now?" I stood. "Now I'm just the crazy girl."

"Chloe, I don't think—"

"I know exactly what you think," I said, and walked out.

Aunt Lauren tried to follow, but I wouldn't listen. I was too angry. Too hurt. To think I'd fool around in a basement crawl space with the first boy who showed an interest in me? That really stung.

God only knew what she thought we'd been doing. I was pretty sure her imagination had taken her way past the sweet first-kiss stage. To think I'd go from "never been on a date" to "rolling around in the dirt with a stranger"? That was insulting. No, more than insulting. It made me furious.

Did Aunt Lauren know the first thing about me? And if *she* didn't, who did?

When it was clear I wasn't going to "calm down" and talk to my aunt, it was time for the next phase. The trial. I was summoned back into the office, with Derek as my code-fendant and Dr. Gill and Dr. Davidoff as judge and jury. It was a closed court. Even Aunt Lauren wasn't allowed in.

I didn't bother to argue about why we'd been in the crawl space. I'd moved well past the "Oh, my God, I don't want anyone to think I'm that kind of girl" stage. If they thought Derek and I had been grappling in the dirt, then at least it meant they wouldn't go into the crawl space and see the signs of disturbance . . . or, if they did, they'd figure they knew what caused it.

Despite what Aunt Lauren believed, I was sure Derek was as horrified by the thought as I was. When Dr. Gill tried to get a confession from him, he only shrugged, and muttered "whatever," arms crossed, big frame slumped in his seat, defiance in the set of his chin. Like me, he'd realized there was no use arguing, but he wasn't about to confess either.

"This isn't the first time you two have . . . tangled," Dr. Gill said finally. "And I have a feeling it won't be the last. We need to nip this in the bud, and the only way we're going to do that is with a transfer. One of you will have to go."

"I will." I heard the words and it took a moment to realize they'd come from me.

Was I crazy? Volunteering to be transferred when I was already worried about what such a transfer meant?

But I didn't take it back. If one of us had to leave, it should be me. As frightened as I was of being shipped out, I wouldn't separate Simon and Derek.

Still, I expected Derek to jump in. I don't know why— certainly not chivalry. But, it seemed only right to at least raise a token protest. The polite thing to do . . . which I supposed should explain why he didn't say a word.

"No one's going anywhere," Dr. Davidoff said softly. "For now, I'm putting you both on notice. But don't give me any reason to revisit this discussion. Is that understood?"

It was.

Thirty

W HEN THE DOCTORS DISMISSED us, Derek and I headed into the hall together. I tried to dawdle, fussing with an imaginary spot on my shirt and giving him time to walk ahead, avoiding any awkwardness. He parked himself in front of me, arms crossed, fingers rapping his biceps with impatience.

I reminded myself of how he'd rescued me. I should be grateful. I was. Right then, though . . . I don't know. My head hurt and I was still smarting over my aunt's rejection, and when I'd offered to be sent away and he didn't argue, it stung. I didn't want it to. But it did.

"What are you wiping at?" he whispered finally.

"A spot."

"There's no spot."

I straightened, tugging my shirt down and adjusting it.

"That's because I fixed it."

I tried to step past him. He didn't budge.

"We need to talk," he whispered.

"Do you really think that's a good idea?"

"Simon'll be there," he said. "Five minutes. Out back."

I really didn't think it was wise for me to be seen hanging out with Derek, even if Simon was there. So five minutes, later, I was in the media room, lying on the love seat, listening to my iPod, trying to lose myself in my music.

When a shadow passed over my head, I jumped up.

Rae stood there, hands out. "Down, girl. It's just me."

I pulled out my earbuds.

She draped her sweatshirt over a chair. "So what happened?"

"Not what everyone thinks."

"Well, duh."

She settled in at the other end, feet pulled up under her, throw pillow on her lap, getting comfortable, waiting for the real story. She'd known me less than a week, and *she* knew I hadn't been fooling around in a crawl space with Derek.

"I'll tell you later," I murmured, "when we're in our room."

"But you *will* tell me, right?"

I nodded.

"Good. So, how'd it go?"

I told her about the meeting with the doctors and about

Aunt Lauren. "It's one thing when strangers think you'd do stuff you wouldn't. They don't know you. But when it's someone who should? Someone you thought *did*?" I shook my head.

"Yeah, I've had my share of that. At school, if I did anything wrong, I got hauled into the counselor, who lectured me on the temptations of the street and the importance of staying in school. It's, like, excuse me? Is there anything in my record that says I've ever been near a gang? Or that I don't think school's important? I get straight Bs, and I never skip class—go lecture someone else."

She hugged the pillow to her chest. "I tell myself that's cool—they don't know me. But I get the same crap from my mom. Every time we get into it, she reminds me about my friend Trina. Ran away at fourteen, got mixed up in a gang, and killed in a drive-by shooting. Hello? What does that have to do with me? There's a reason Trina and I weren't friends anymore. I'm not like that."

"They mean well, I guess. But it stings."

"The worst of it—" Her gaze rose above my head. "What do you want?"

Derek circled in front of me and tapped his watch. "Did I say five minutes?"

"Yes, you did. And I said it wasn't a good idea."

"We need to talk to you."

Rae started to rise. "Should I get the nurses?"

I waved her down, then turned to Derek. "No."

He pushed his hands into his jean pockets, rocked back on his heels, then said, "Simon wants to talk to you."

"Does Simon have feet?" Rae asked. "A mouth? What are you? His faithful Saint Bernard, lumbering around, bearing your master's messages?"

He swiveled, putting his back to Rae. "Chloe?" There was a note of pleading in his voice that made my resolve falter. "Chloe, pl—" He held the *l*, stretching it; and for a second, I thought he was actually going to say "please," and if he had, I'd have given in, despite my reservations about being seen together. But after a second, he snipped the syllable off and stalked out.

"Bye!" Rae called after him. "Always a pleasure chatting with you!" She turned to me. "You *are* going to tell me what all this is about, right?"

"I promise. So how did swimming go?"

"Okay, I guess. Nice to get out, but not much fun. Simon swam laps, I can barely dog-paddle, so we went our separate ways. Nothing new there. They have a cool slide, though, and—"

She looked behind me again and offered a cautious nod.

"Hey," Simon said.

He perched on the love seat arm. I moved over to give him room, but Rae was on the other side, so I couldn't go far, and his hip brushed my shoulder.

"I—" I began.

"Don't want to go outside," he finished for me. "That's

cool. We can both hide out from Derek in here, see how long it takes him to find us."

"I'll leave you two—" Rae began, pushing up from the sofa.

"No, stay," Simon said. "I didn't mean to butt in."

"You didn't. I hear chores calling my name, though, so I'll take off."

When she was gone, I moved over. Simon slid down beside me. I gave him plenty of room, but he stayed close, not touching but almost, and I gazed at the gap between us, that scant inch of bare sofa, staring at it because, well, I didn't know what else to do, to say.

The horror in the crawl space had been hovering over my head, cushioned by the shock and confusion and stress of dealing with the doctors and Aunt Lauren, but now that cushion began to sag, the weight sliding down, the memories returning.

"I feel awful," he said. "About Tori. I knew she was mad about seeing us together, so I tried setting her straight, but I think I only made it worse."

"It's not your fault. She has problems."

A small, sharp laugh. "Yeah, that's one way of putting it." After a minute, he glanced over at me. "You okay?"

I nodded.

He leaned over, his shoulder rubbing mine, breath warm against my ear. "If it was me, I wouldn't be okay. I'd have been scared out of my mind."

I dipped my head, and a strand of my hair fell forward. He reached over with his free hand, as if to brush it back, then stopped. He cleared his throat, but didn't say anything.

"It was pretty interesting," I said after a moment.

"I bet. The kind of thing that's really cool in the movies, but in real life . . ." Our eyes met. "Not so much, huh?"

I nodded. "Not so much."

He twisted, backing into the corner of the couch. "So, what's your favorite zombie movie?"

I sputtered a laugh and as it bubbled up, the weight eased. I felt my thoughts shift, settling into a place where I could make some sense of them. I'd been trying to forget what happened, to push past it, be strong, be tough, be like Derek. Raising the dead? No biggie. Send 'em back, bury the bodies, next problem please.

But I couldn't do it. I kept seeing them, smelling them, feeling their touch. My gut kept seizing up with remembered horror, then thinking about what I'd done to them, *their* horror. The best way for me to handle it right now was to get some distance. Don't forget it—just shift it aside with safe images of celluloid.

So we talked about zombie movies, debating and discussing the merits of films that, according to the ratings board, neither of us should have seen.

"It has the best special effects," Simon said, "hands down."

"Sure, if you make enough things blow up, you can hide

plot holes big enough to drive a truck through."

"Plot? It's a zombie movie."

He was now sprawled on the floor, having moved there to demonstrate a particularly lame zombie "death scene." I lay on the couch, looking down at him.

"Let me guess," he said. "You're going to write the world's first art-house zombie movie to premiere at Sundown."

"Sun*dance*. And, no. If I ever have to direct any art-house film?" I shuddered. "Shoot me now."

He grinned and sat up. "I'll second that. No art flicks for me. Not that I'm going to ever write or direct *any* film. So which is it you want to do? Write or direct?"

"Both if I can. Screenwriting's where the story's at, but if you want to see that story come to life, you've got to direct, because in Hollywood, the director is king. Screenwriters? Barely even register on the radar."

"So the director is at the top of the heap."

"No, that's the studio. The director is king. The studio is God. And they just want something they can sell, something that'll fit their four little quadrants."

"Quadrants?"

"The four main demographic groups. Guys and girls, divided by young and old. Hit all four, and you've got a blockbuster . . . and a very happy studio. That is not, however, going to happen with a zombie movie, however cool it is."

He flipped onto his stomach. "How do you know all this?"

"I might be stuck in Buffalo, but I'm wired. I subscribe to *Variety*, *Creative Screenwriting*, a whack of industry loops, bookmark the blogs . . . If I want to be in this business, I have to know this business. The sooner the better."

"Oh, *man*. I don't even know what I want to be yet."

"I can hire you to do all my fog effects."

He laughed, then looked behind me. "Hey, bro. Get enough fresh air?"

"I wanted to talk to you." Derek swung his glare to include me. "Both of you."

"Then pull up a chair. The current topic of conversation is zombie movies." Simon glanced at me. "Are we still on zombie movies?"

"I think so."

"Zombie movies?" Derek said, slowly, as if he'd misheard. His face darkened and he lowered his voice. "Have you two forgotten what happened today?"

"Nope. That's why we're talking about it." Simon tossed a grin my way. "Kinda."

Derek lowered his voice another notch. "Chloe is in danger. Serious danger. And you're lounging around, yapping about zombie movies?"

"Lounging? Yapping? Good word choices. Very evocative. You making a point? I know perfectly well what happened and what it could mean for Chloe. But the sky isn't going to fall if we don't discuss it this very minute, Chicken Little." He stretched. "Right now, I think we could all use some time to just chill."

"Chill? You do a lot of that, don't you?" Derek walked over to Simon. "In fact, that's pretty much all you do."

I stood. "I—I'd better see if Rae needs help. With her chores."

Simon sat. "Hold up. We're almost done here." He turned to Derek. "Right?"

"Sure. Go ahead. Take it easy. I'm sure Dad will walk in that door any minute and rescue us. And if he's in trouble? If he needs help? Well, too bad, 'cause that would require effort and you're too busy . . . chilling."

Simon sprang to his feet. Derek stood his ground. They faced off for a moment, then Simon nudged me toward the door.

"Let's go."

When I hesitated, he mouthed "please." I nodded and we left.

Thirty-one

A S WE WALKED DOWN THE HALL, I glanced at Simon. His face was hard, expressionless. When he caught me looking, he managed a smile as if to reassure me he wasn't mad at me.

"Mrs. Talbot?" he called. "Can I go out back? Shoot some hoops before dark?"

"Of course, dear."

We waited at the door. She stepped from the kitchen, drying her hands on a towel, and punched in the security code. Only then did she look over and realize Simon wasn't alone.

"Oh, Chloe . . . I'm not sure you two should . . ."

"It's basketball, Mrs. Talbot." He pushed open the screen door and held it for me. "You can watch from the window if you need to."

"Just . . . just don't go anywhere I can't see you."

He slammed the screen door shut behind us and marched into the yard so fast I had to jog to keep up. I glanced over my shoulder. The door was closed, no sign of Mrs. Talbot.

He looked around. "You see the ball?"

"I think it's in the shed. I'll go get—"

He touched my elbow. "No. Unless you really want to play."

I shook my head and he led me toward the stone bench near the central garden. "Talbot can still see us from there." He exhaled. "Derek sure knows how to push my buttons. Worst of it? I *know* he's pushing my buttons, trying to get a rise out of me, and I rise anyway. Stupid, stupid, stupid."

For a moment, he said nothing, gaze moving across the yard.

"Derek wants me to go looking for our dad."

"How? Like, break out? You can't—"

"That's no big deal." He settled back on the bench. "When you're raised like us, as supernaturals, it's . . . different. The rules are different. They have to be. If there's trouble, you have to run."

"But you don't want to go?"

"Oh, I *want* to. I've been chomping at the bit since we got here. My dad's out there—somewhere—maybe in trouble and I'm sitting around in a group home? Going to class? Hanging with Derek? Acting like nothing's wrong? It's *killing* me, Chloe. Derek knows how bad I want out. Like I said, he's pushing my buttons."

"Where is your dad?"

He shook his head. "We don't know. He just— Things went wrong and he disappeared and we ended up here. It's a long story . . ."

"Then it can wait."

"Thanks. Point is, he's gone and I'm sure he didn't leave willingly. So we're stuck here, supposedly waiting to get released, but then what? Where would we go? There's no grandma or great-uncle or family friend waiting to take us. We'd go into foster care and then we'd need to escape from there, so what's the point of waiting?"

"You want out now, but you can't *get* out."

"We *can* get out. Derek's got a plan." A small laugh. "Trust me, the man's always got a plan. But it's an escape plan for one—for me. He won't go. Flat-out refuses."

"*What?* He's making you feel guilty about staying when he won't go himself? Where does he get off?"

"Yeah, I know, and I don't want to sound like I'm defending him, but he has a reason for not wanting to go. It's a stupid reason, but it's a big deal to him and there's no sense trying to change his mind. He just . . . freaks."

"Freaks?"

Simon flexed his hand, staring down at it. "It's complicated. Derek's idea, though, is for me to get out and find Dad. Dad taught me ways to get in touch with him. Spells and stuff. But I can't leave Derek."

"Can't?"

"Won't, I guess. I'm worried about Dad, but he can take care of himself, way better than Derek can."

I must have looked skeptical, because he went on, "I know Derek seems like he can and in most ways he can, but in others . . ." He shook his head. "It's complicated. If I take off and something goes wrong, I'm afraid he'll just . . . let it."

"I don't understand."

"I know." He stared down at his hands. "I know I'm not making any sense, but . . ."

"It's complicated."

"Yeah. But—" He inhaled. "I'm starting to think I need to take that chance. Derek's right. Sitting on my butt isn't getting us anywhere. Now there's you to consider. You really need to get out."

"I do?" The words escaped as a squeak.

"Derek's right. It doesn't matter how hard we work to hide your powers, they aren't like mine. They *can't* be hidden. Not when you're living under a microscope."

"If I get transferred to a hospital, I'll get through it."

"But what if it's *not* a transfer?" He glanced over, worry in his eyes. "What you said about Liz keeps gnawing at me. Maybe she is a shaman. Or if she is dead, maybe it was an accident. Why would they kill kids who don't get better? It sounds nuts, but even Derek's worried."

"Derek? But he said—"

"I know what he said. But when I talked to him later, he wasn't so quick to brush it off. Even raised some questions himself. With Derek, that's as close to agreement as you can get. But you still need help. Say everything goes fine and you get released, what will you do? Who will you talk to? How will you learn how to get back to normal?"

Normal. Such a simple, boring word. Funny how it shone now, like a brass ring on a merry-go-round, bright with promise, just out of reach.

Getting out wouldn't solve my problems. Aunt Lauren would always be watching, misinterpreting every "abnormal" thing I did as a sign that I needed to return to Lyle House . . . or worse.

But to run away?

I knew what Derek would say. I could even picture his expression, that scowl of disdain and frustration. I wasn't Chloe Saunders, sheltered art-school girl anymore. I wasn't even Chloe Saunders, schizophrenic. If Chloe Saunders, necromancer, followed the old rules, she could wind up in a padded cell, ranting about voices no one else could hear.

I wasn't naive. I read the news. I knew what happened to kids who ran away, and it wasn't the wonderful life of freedom they imagined. How long would it take to find Simon's dad? How would we live in the meantime? What would we eat? Where would we sleep? I had some money, but how long would that last? What would happen when our pictures were splashed across the news? When every cop and concerned citizen was looking for us?

I could hole up here, screw my eyes shut, and pray nothing bad happened. Or I could take matters into my own hands. Take action.

Getting help from Simon's missing father wasn't exactly my idea of a firm plan. But if I got out of here, I could track down Liz. That would be easy. There were a limited number of hospitals in Buffalo. And if she wasn't safe in a hospital, what did that mean for the rest of us? Were we in danger? I couldn't keep plugging my fingers in my ears and pretending everything was fine.

"If you're getting out of here, I'll go with you," I said.

"You don't have to. I just meant that *I* need to leave, for me and Derek and, now, for you. When I find Dad, he can help us."

"Who will help *you*? Out there?"

A twist of a smile. "I've got my killer fog spell."

"You need back up. Derek would be a lot better at that, but you're going to be stuck with me. I'm going."

Thirty-two

I WAITED IN THE BOYS' bathroom, tucked in beside the storage tower. With every noise from the hall, my heart thudded, telling me I was about to make the biggest fool of myself yet.

But I wasn't wrong. Like Derek, I could add two plus two and see the answer. I wiped my sweaty palms against my jeans, glanced at my watch, and prayed I'd come to the proper conclusion. And, in some ways, prayed I hadn't.

When my watch hit 8:00, the bathroom door swung open. Derek flipped the light on and shut the door. As he turned toward the mirror, he saw me and he let out a yelp of surprise that would have been very satisfying under any other circumstances.

"Are you nuts?" he hissed. "What are you doing here?"

I walked past him and locked the door.

"If you want to discuss the plan, this really isn't the place," he said.

He pivoted, gaze following me as I crossed to the shower and turned on the cold water, so it would drown out our conversation without steaming up the room.

"Great," he muttered. "Now they're going to think we're showering together. Maybe we can just tell them we were washing off the crawl space dirt and trying to conserve water."

I planted myself in front of him. "You set me up."

He opened his mouth, but, for once, nothing came out and he settled for a token scowl.

"All this time, I've been trying to figure out why you want to help me. Why do you care if I know I'm a necromancer? Why do you care if I get booted out? Why stick your neck out for me, like you did this afternoon?"

"I just want—"

"To help. Sure, you're obnoxious and arrogant, but underneath, there's a decent guy who wants to help a fellow supernatural. Yeah, right. There has to be another reason. Today I found it. Simon."

He crossed his arms. "Yeah, Simon wanted me to be nice to you. Okay? Can I have my shower now? Alone?"

"You want Simon to run away. To find your dad. But he won't go without you. He needs a reason to go right now. So you gave him one. The designated damsel in distress."

"I don't know what you're talking about," he muttered,

but his gaze wouldn't quite meet mine. My remaining doubts vanished in a fresh surge of anger.

"Here I was, a real necromancer, naive and lost. Perfect bait. Just keep pushing us together, make a big deal out of how helpless I am, and eventually he'll pull on his shining armor. Great plan. But it still lacks something. Stakes. In any great thriller, your hero needs three things. Goal, motivation, and stakes. Goal: find your missing dad. Motivation: help the poor necromancer chick. The stakes were missing, though. You needed to put your damsel in actual distress. What if she was about to be transferred to a real mental hospital? Where she'd be out of Simon's reach and beyond help? Or, worse, where she might die, the victim of some evil plan. So you get Tori to—"

"No!" He raised his hands, genuine shock in his eyes. "I did not have anything to do with that. Even if Tori would get close enough to me to carry on a conversation—which you may have noticed, she won't—I wouldn't do that. I did nothing to *make* them transfer you."

"Okay, so you just took advantage of the situation."

I gave him a moment to respond. He didn't, which was all the answer I needed.

"When I first told you about seeing Liz, you brushed it off. But then you realized this could work in your favor, so you changed your tune with Simon. You planted the seeds of doubt, then waited for them to sprout. That's why you didn't argue when I offered to be the one transferred. That's exactly where you wanted me. You manipulated the situation and you lied—"

"I never lied."

I fixed him with a look. "You really heard the doctors talking about transferring me yesterday?"

He shoved his hands in his pockets. "I heard them talking about you and they seemed to be suggesting—"

"Okay, you didn't lie. You exaggerated."

He scowled. "You *are* in danger. The more I think about Liz—"

"Cut the crap, okay, Derek? You got your wish. Simon's going. I'm going with him. You're right. He needs to get out and find his father. Of course, you could have saved us all this trouble by just going with him yourself. But that might be dangerous. And he's not your father so it's not really your problem—"

He shot toward me so fast I stumbled back, but managed to catch myself and stand my ground. It wasn't easy with him looming over me, eyes blazing.

"Is that what I think, Chloe?"

I locked my knees, refusing to break eye contact.

"I don't know what you think, Derek," I said, calmly— or so I hoped. "Simon says there's a reason you won't go. A stupid reason, according to him. So maybe it's an excuse. Maybe you just don't want to bother."

"An excuse?" A bitter laugh. Then he backed away from me slowly, as if forcing himself. "You read my file, right?"

"I—"

"I know you read it that night when you and Rae pretended to be raiding the kitchen."

"Only because of what you did. I had to know—"

"How dangerous I was. I don't blame you. But you got your answer, right? You know *exactly* how dangerous I am."

I swallowed. "I—"

"You know what I did, and you think I should be walking the streets?" His lip curled. "I'm exactly where I belong."

Something in his eyes, in his voice, in his face, made the back of my throat ache. I glanced over at the shower, watching the water dapple the doors as the harsh pounding filled the silence.

After a moment, I looked back at him. "You must have had a reason for doing it."

"Did I?" When I tried looking away again, he sidestepped and snagged my gaze. "Is that what you want, Chloe? To hear my reason? My excuse? That the guy pulled a gun on me and if I hadn't thrown him into a wall, I'd be dead? Well, that's not how it happened. There's a kid out there who'll never walk again and I have no excuse. It's my fault. *All* my fault. Our dad disappearing. Simon being thrown in here. I—"

He snapped his mouth shut, hands going into his pockets as he stared out over my head, the muscles in his jaw working.

After another moment, he said, "So, yeah, I want Simon out, and I'll do anything to get him out, but it's not like I'm putting you in danger. You're getting something out of it. You don't have any reason to complain."

I could only stare, any sense that maybe I understood him evaporating as it always did. I'd glimpse something underneath, and he'd snatch it away so fast it left bruises that called me a fool for hoping for more.

"No danger?" I said slowly. "I'm running away. From the home. From my family. From my *life*."

"You'll be with Simon. Don't pretend that's any big hardship."

"What?"

"You know what I mean. A few days alone with Simon? That'll be tough. And it means a lot to him. A *lot*. Running away to help him find his dad? He'll never forget that."

I widened my eyes. "Oh my God, do you think so? Really? That's so cool. I bet he'll ask me to go steady and everything. We can send love letters between my juvenile detention center and his, and maybe they'll let us meet at the coed dances. . . ."

He glowered down at me.

"You really think I'm an idiot, don't you?" I said, then shot up my hand. "No, don't answer that. *Please*. News flash: getting a boyfriend is not at the top of every girl's priority list. Right now, it ranks about as low on mine as you can get—way below such trivial concerns as getting my life back together."

"All right—"

"After this is over, I wouldn't be surprised if Simon wanted to never see me again. Just put this all behind him. You know what? That's fine. Because I need to find out what happened to Liz. And I want to help Simon because it's the right thing to do, not because I think he's sooo cute. I might not be a genius like you—"

The glower returned. "I'm not—"

"But I'm smart enough to know this isn't going to be some grand romantic adventure. I'm running away. I'll be living on the streets. Even if we find your dad, I'm not sure he's going to be able to fix my life." I thought of Aunt Lauren and felt a pang of grief. "I'm not sure it can be fixed."

"So I'm supposed to be grateful to you for going?"

"I never said—"

He shifted back into looming mode. "You need to get out of here just as much as Simon does, maybe more. You might not see the danger you're in, but I do. And I'm worried."

"Worried? About me?"

He shrugged. "Sure. Concerned. You know." He couldn't even look me in the eye when he said it. "Yeah, we need you, but I *do* want to help a fellow supernatural." He snuck a glance my way. "We gotta stick together."

"Don't you dare."

"What?"

His gaze broke away, started roaming the bathroom.

"You're right," I said. "I do need help. My life is falling apart and maybe someday I'll look back on this as the biggest, stupidest mistake I've ever made, but at this moment, it's the only solution I see. You need me to be your designated damsel in distress? Okay. But don't *ever* say you're doing this for me. This has nothing to do with me. Don't you dare pretend it does."

I turned and walked out.

Thirty-three

I WONDERED WHETHER, AFTER our escape, I'd find time to sleep. Because I certainly hadn't been getting much at Lyle House.

That night I was so exhausted I didn't even have a chance to lie there, raging about Derek or fretting about the step I was about to take. I hit the bed and fell straight into dreams of wailing police sirens and baying tracking dogs. Of a boy trapped in a hospital bed and a boy trapped in a group home and ghosts trapped in rotting corpses. Of zombies screaming for mercy and a girl screaming, "But I didn't mean it," and a boy saying, "I didn't mean it either. Doesn't matter."

The dreams spun and melted together until one slid free. An image buried by the stronger, louder ones, separating and saying, "What about me?"

I bolted awake and sat there, suspended in the dark, reeling in that tangled memory, the questions it raised, the answers it promised.

Then I leaped from bed.

I tapped at the bedroom door.

"Derek?"

Rough snores answered.

I rapped at the door again, raising my voice as loud as I dared.

"Derek?"

My toes curled against the icy hardwood and I rubbed the goose bumps on my arms. I should have grabbed a sweater. And socks.

I shouldn't even be here. I'd told the guy off, made the perfect exit . . . and was now creeping back, begging him to talk to me.

Talk about ruining a scene.

As I lifted my hand to knock, the doorknob clicked. When the door creaked open, I lifted my gaze to eye level, an apology on my lips, and found myself staring at a chest. A bare chest . . . and not a boy's chest. Broad and muscular, a scattering of angry red acne dots the only sign that it *wasn't* attached to a grown man.

Around the house, Derek always wore oversized sweat-shirts and baggy jeans. If I'd pictured what he looked like under them—which I hadn't—I would have guessed stocky, bordering on overweight. All that food he scarfed down had to go somewhere. And, apparently, it did—just not to fat.

My cheeks heated and my gaze dropped from Derek's chest . . . only to see he was wearing nothing but boxers.

"Chloe?"

My gaze shot—gratefully—to his face.

He peered at me. "Chloe? What—?"

"You owe me."

"Huh?" He rubbed his eyes with his thumb and fore-finger, snarled a yawn, and rolled his shoulders. "What time is it?"

"Late. Or early. It doesn't matter. I need your help and you owe me. Get dressed and be downstairs in five min-utes."

I turned on my heel and headed for the stairs.

Would Derek follow me? Probably not, considering I'd ignored his "meet me in five minutes" command that after-noon.

I'd planned to not leave his doorway until he agreed to help me. But I hadn't expected him to be nearly naked dur-ing the conversation. It also reminded me that I was wear-ing only pajama pants and a tank top. When I got downstairs, I found the sweatshirt Rae had shucked in the media room earlier. I was pulling it on as I walked into the hall, and nearly smacked into Derek.

He wore sweatpants and a T-shirt and had stopped in the

middle of the hall, furiously scratching one bare forearm.

"Fleas?" I said.

The joke was an admittedly lame attempt to lighten the mood from earlier, and I didn't think it deserved the glower he gave me.

"Let's just get this over with," he said. "I'm not in a good mood."

I could have asked how that was different from normal, but bit my tongue, motioned him into the media room and closed the door. Then I cocked my head, listening.

"We're fine here," he said. "Just keep it down. Someone comes, I'll hear."

I moved across the room and stopped in a patch of moonlight. When he followed, I got my first good look at him in the light. His face was pale, his cheeks flaming red, and not from the acne. Sweat plastered his hair around his face and his red-rimmed eyes glittered, struggling to focus.

"You've got a fever," I said.

"Maybe." He raked his hair back. "Something I ate, I guess."

"Or some bug you picked up."

He shook his head. "I don't . . ." He hesitated, then pushed on. "I don't get sick. Not often anyway. Part of my . . . condition. This seems to be a reaction." He scratched his arms again. "No big deal. I'm just off. Crankier than usual, Simon would say."

"You should go back to bed. Forget this——"

"No, you're right. I owe you. What do you need?"

I wanted to argue but could tell he'd made up his mind.

"Hold on," I said, and hurried into the hall.

He whispered an exasperated, "Chloe!" after me, followed by a halfhearted string of profanity, as if he couldn't work up the energy to even curse properly.

I returned with a glass of cold water and handed it to him, along with four Tylenol.

"Two for now, two for later, in case you——"

He tossed all four in his mouth and drained half the water.

"Or you could just take them all now."

"I've got a high metabolism," he said. "Another part of my condition."

"I know a lot of girls who wouldn't mind that."

He grunted something unintelligible and drained the glass. "Thanks, but . . ." He met my gaze. "You don't need to be nice to me just because I'm not feeling great. You're mad. You've got a right to be. I used you and I made it worse by pretending I hadn't. If I were you, I wouldn't be bringing water unless it was to dump over my head."

He turned away to set the empty glass on the table, and I'm glad he did, because I was pretty sure my jaw had dropped. Either that fever had gone straight to his brain or I was still asleep, dreaming, because that had sounded suspiciously like an admission of guilt. Maybe even a roundabout apology.

He turned back. "Okay, so you need . . . ?"

I waved him to the love seat. Annoyance flickered across his face—getting comfortable was a distraction he couldn't be bothered with—but when I sat on the opposite chair, he lumbered to the couch. If I couldn't get him to return to bed, at least he could rest while I talked.

"You know something about necromancy, right?" I began.

He shrugged. "I'm no expert."

"But you know more than me, Simon, or anyone else I can talk to at this moment. So how do necromancers contact the dead?"

"You mean like the guy in the basement? If he's there, you should see him. Then you'd just talk, like we are right now."

"I mean contacting a specific person. Can I do that? Or am I restricted to those I just stumble across?"

He went quiet. When he spoke, his voice was uncharacteristically soft. "If you mean your mom, Chloe—"

"No." The word came sharper than I intended. "I haven't even thought— Well, yes, I've considered it, for someday maybe, of course I'd like to, love to—" I heard myself rambling and took a deep breath. "This is connected to our situation."

"You mean Liz?"

"No. I—I should try to contact her, I guess. J-just to be sure. But that's not it. Forget why I want to know."

He leaned back into the sofa pillows. "If I knew why, I could answer a lot easier."

Maybe, but I wasn't telling him until I had enough facts to confidently lay out my theory.

"If I *can* contact a specific person, how would I do it?"

"You can, but it's not easy and it's not guaranteed at your age. Like Simon and his spells, you're at the . . . apprenticeship level."

"Where I can do things by accident, like raising the dead."

"Well, no." He absently scratched his arm, the *skritch-skritch* filling the silence. "From what I heard, raising the dead is the toughest thing to do, and it needs this complicated ritual." He shook his head and stopped scratching. "I must have heard wrong. Like I said, I'm not an expert."

"Back to *how*, then. How do I call up a specific ghost?"

He slouched, head resting on the sofa back, staring at the ceiling before nodding, as if to himself. "If I remember right, there are two ways. You could use a personal effect."

"Like with a tracking dog."

A small noise that sounded like a laugh. "Yeah, I guess so. Or like one of those psychics you see in movies, always asking for something that belonged to the person."

"And the second way?" I tried not to show how much I wanted this answer, how much I hoped I'd already guessed it.

"You need to be at the grave."

My heart hammered, and it was a moment before I could speak. "At the grave. Presuming that's where the body is buried. It's the body that's important, not the grave site."

He waved off my petty distinction, the old Derek sliding back. "Yeah, the body. The ultimate personal effect."

"Then I think I know what that ghost in the basement wanted."

I explained how the ghost had urged me to "make contact" to "summon them" and "get their story."

"He meant the buried bodies. That's why he wanted me to go into the crawl space. So I could get close enough to the bodies to contact those ghosts."

Derek reached back to scratch between his shoulders. "Why?"

"From what he seemed to say, it's about Lyle House. Something they can tell me."

"But those bodies have been down there way longer than Lyle House has been a group home. And if this ghost knows something, why not just tell you himself?"

"I don't know. He said . . ." I strained to remember. "He seemed to be saying he couldn't make contact with them himself."

"Then how would he know they had anything important to tell you?"

Good questions. This was why I'd gone to Derek. Because he'd challenge my assumptions, show me where the holes were and what I had to learn before jumping to any conclusions.

"I don't know," I said finally. "However they got there, I'm pretty sure they didn't die of natural causes. You're probably right, and it's completely unconnected to us, and this ghost is confused, losing track of time. Or maybe he wants me to solve their murder." I stood. "But, whatever he wants me to hear, I'm going to listen. Or at least try."

"Hold up."

He lifted a hand, and I braced for more arguments. It was a waste of time. Dangerous, too, after we'd been caught down there earlier. And, don't forget, last time I tried to contact these ghosts, I'd returned them to their corpses. Do that again, and I'd better not call him for reburial duty.

He pushed to his feet. "We should take a flashlight. I'll grab that. You get our shoes."

Thirty-four

I WASN'T SETTING FOOT—bare, stockinged, or shoed—in that crawl space until I'd talked to the first ghost and asked all the questions Derek had raised.

We went down to the laundry room. Derek took up a position at the side, leaning back against the dryer. I sat cross-legged in the middle of the floor, closed my eyes, and focused.

It didn't take long, as if the ghost had been waiting for me. I still couldn't catch more than phrases and glimpses. I told Derek this, then said, "I stopped taking the meds after you gave me that jar. But they must still be in my system."

". . . not medic . . ." the ghost said. ". . . block . . ."

"What's blocked?"

"Spell . . . ghosts . . . blocking . . ."

"A spell to block ghosts?" I guessed.

That got Derek's attention and he shifted forward, arms uncrossing. "Did he say a spell's blocking him? What kind?"

I was about to translate, but the ghost could obviously hear and answered. "Magic . . . ritual . . . important."

"It's important?"

"Not . . . *not* important," he said emphatically.

I related this to Derek who grumbled about the imperfection of this mode of communication as he furiously scratched his forearm, then said, "Tell him to say one word at a time. Repeat it until you get it and you say it back. It'll be slow, but at least we won't miss—"

He stopped, his gaze following mine to his forearm. His skin was . . . moving. Rippling.

"What the—?" he began, then growled in frustration and gave his arm a fierce shake. "Muscle spasms. I've been getting them a lot lately."

He peered down at the rippling skin again, made a fist, and pumped his arm, trying to work it out. I was about to suggest he see a doctor, then realized that might not be so easy for someone like Derek. I could see now that it *was* his muscles, expanding and contracting on their own. A side effect of his condition, I guess, muscles developing in overdrive. Like the rest of him, slamming through puberty.

"Just as long as you don't rip through your clothing and turn green," I said.

"What?" His face scrunched up, then he got it. "*The*

Incredible Hulk. Ha-ha. *Incredibly Stupid Movie,* more like."
His rubbed his forearm. "Ignore me and get back to your ghost."

The ghost had heard Derek's suggestion about taking it one word at a time, and that's what we did. It worked much better, though it felt a bit like charades, him saying a word over and over, and me excitedly repeating it when I finally understood.

I started with questions about the ghost himself, and learned he was a necromancer. He'd been at the hospital when I'd been admitted. Something about stopping ghosts from harassing the mental patients, which I didn't really understand, but it wasn't important.

Ghosts recognize necromancers, so he'd known that's what I was. Realizing that *I* didn't know what I was, he knew I needed help. But before he could make contact, they moved me. So he'd followed me to Lyle House. Only it was somehow blocked against ghosts. He thought it was a spell, though when Derek challenged that assumption, the ghost admitted that it could be anything from the construction materials to the geographic location. All he knew was that the only places he could make even partial contact with me were the basement and the attic.

As for the bodies in the crawl space, he knew two things. One, they'd been murdered. Two, they were supernaturals. Put those together and he was convinced their stories would be important. He couldn't get them himself because he couldn't contact the dead as easily as he could *before* he became one of them himself.

"But they were just skeletons and dried up flesh," Derek said. "Like mummies. Whatever happened to them wouldn't have anything to do with us, here, now."

"Maybe," was the ghost's only answer.

"Maybe?" Derek threw up his hands and started pacing. He muttered under his breath, but there was no anger in it, just frustration, trying to work through this problem and see a connection when he really should be in bed, nursing a fever.

"Samuel Lyle," the ghost communicated next. "Original owner. Know him?"

I said I didn't and asked Derek.

"How would I know the guy who built this place a hundred years ago?"

"Sixty," the ghost said, and I relayed it.

"Whatever." Derek resumed pacing. "Does he even know what year this is?"

I could have pointed out that if the ghost knew how long ago the house had been built, he obviously knew the current year, but Derek was just grouching, his fever making it hard to concentrate on this puzzle.

"Supernatural," the ghost said. "Lyle. Sorcerer."

That made Derek stop when I relayed it.

"The guy who built this place was a sorcerer?"

"Dark magic. Alchemist. Experimented. On supernaturals."

A chill ran up my arms and I crossed them. "You think that's how those people in the cellar died? This sorcerer, Lyle, experimented on them?"

"How does he know so much about this guy?" Derek said. "He followed you here, didn't he?"

"Everyone knew," the ghost replied. "In Buffalo. All supernaturals. Knew where he lived. And stayed away. Or didn't."

Derek shook his head. "I *still* don't see how any of this is connected to us."

"Maybe," the ghost replied. "Maybe not. Need to ask."

Derek hissed a curse and smacked his hand into the wall hard enough to make me wince. I walked over to him.

"Go to bed. You're probably right. I'm sure it's nothing—"

"I'm not saying that. I'm just saying . . . A sorcerer built this place sixty years ago; there are supernaturals buried in the cellar; and now we're here, three supernatural kids. The group home is named after him. Is that significant? Or is it just named after the guy who built it? It seems too much to be a coincidence, but I'm just not getting the connection."

"I can do this. Go back—"

"No, he's right. We need to ask. I just . . ." He shoved his hand up the back of his shirt, scratching. "I feel like crap and it's making me cranky. But we need to do this."

The ghost followed us into the crawl space.

"How do I avoid what I did earlier?" I asked. "Returning them to their bodies?"

Silence. I counted to sixty, then said, "Hello? Are you still there?"

"Stay calm. Focus. But go easy. Soft. Your power. Too strong."

"My powers are too strong?"

I couldn't suppress a smile. I might not be certain I wanted these powers, but it was kind of cool to hear that I had more than the average necromancer. Like taking an IQ test and finding out you're smarter than you thought.

"Your age. Should never be able to . . ."

Silence. I waited patiently to catch the next word. And waited.

"Hello?"

He started again, word by word. "Too soon. Too much Too . . ."

A longer pause.

"Something's wrong," he said finally.

"Wrong?"

Derek crawled from the shadows, where he'd been silently watching. "What's he saying?"

"Something about my powers. That they're . . . wrong."

"Too strong," the ghost said. "Unnatural."

"Unnatural?" I whispered.

Derek's eyes blazed. "Don't listen to him, Chloe. So you're powerful. Big deal. You're fine. Just take it slow."

The ghost apologized. He gave a few more instructions, then said he'd watch from the "other side," in case his presence had boosted my powers earlier. If I needed him, he'd come back. One last warning against trying too hard, and he was gone.

Thirty-five

DEREK RETURNED TO THE shadows, leaving me alone, sitting cross-legged again, the flashlight lying in front of me. As much as I'd have liked to use it as a candle, pushing back the dark, I'd set it on its side, the beam directed at the spot where the bodies were buried in hopes that, if the ground so much as quivered, Derek would warn me before I raised the dead.

To free the ghosts from their corpses, I'd used visualization, so I did that again. I imagined myself tugging the ghosts from the ether, drawing them out like a magician pulling an endless scarf from his sleeve.

A few times I caught a flicker, only to have it vanish again. I kept working, slowly and steadily, resisting the urge to concentrate harder.

"What do you want?" a woman's voice snapped, so close

and so clear I grabbed the flashlight, certain one of the nurses had discovered us.

Instead, I shone the beam on a woman dressed in a sweater set. Or that's what her top half was wearing. She was standing, her head brushing the low ceiling, meaning she was "buried" to mid-thigh under the dirt floor. She was maybe thirty, with a blond bob. Her sharp features were rigid with annoyance.

"Well, necromancer, what do you want?"

"Tell her to leave us be," a man's voice whined from the darkness.

I shone the beam in his direction but could make out only a faint form by the farthest wall.

"I just w-want to talk to you," I said.

"That much is obvious," the woman snapped. "Calling and pulling and pestering until you drag us out against our will."

"I didn't m-mean—"

"Can't leave well enough alone, can you? It wasn't enough to shove us back into our bodies. Do you know what that's like? Sitting down, enjoying a nice afternoon, and all of a sudden you're back in your corpse, buried, clawing your way to the surface, terrified you've been trapped by some demented necromancer looking for zombie slaves?"

"I didn't mean—"

"Oh, do you hear that, Michael? She didn't *mean* it." The woman moved toward me. "So if I accidentally unleash a storm of hellfire on your head, it'll be all right, as long as I didn't really *mean* it? You have a power, little girl, and you'd better learn to use it properly before someone decides to teach you a lesson. Summon me again and *I'll* do it."

She started to fade.

"Wait! You're—" I struggled to remember what Simon had called a female spellcaster "—a witch, right? What happened to you here?"

"I was murdered, in case that isn't perfectly obvious."

"Was it because you're a witch?"

She surged back so fast I jumped. "You mean, did I bring this on myself?"

"N-no. Samuel Lyle—the man who owned this house— did he kill you? Because you're a witch?"

Her lips curled in an ugly smile. "I'm sure my being a witch added a little extra dash of pleasure for him. I should have known better than to trust a sorcerer, but I was a fool. A desperate fool. Sam Lyle promised us an easier life. That's what we all want, isn't it? Power without price. Sam Lyle was a seller of dreams. A snake oil salesman. Or a madman." That twist of a smile again. "We could never figure out which, could we, Michael?"

"A madman," came the whisper from the back. "The things he did to us . . ."

"Ah, but we were willing subjects. At least, in the beginning. You see, little girl, all scientific advancement requires experimentation, and experimentation requires subjects, and that's what Michael and I were. Lab rats sacrificed to the vision of a madman."

"What about me?"

She sneered. "What about you?"

"Does this have anything to do with me being here? Now? There are more of us. Supernaturals. In a group home."

"Are they experimenting on you? Tying you to beds and prodding you with electrical wires until you bite off your tongue?"

"N-no. N-nothing like that."

"Then you count your blessings, little girl, and stop pestering us. Sam Lyle is dead and—if the Fates are just—rotting in a hell dimension."

She started fading again.

"Wait! I need to know—"

"Then find out!" She surged back again. "If you think you're here because of a dead sorcerer, then you're as mad as he was, but I don't have your answers. I'm a shade, not an oracle. Why are you brats here, where I died? How should I know? Why should I care?"

"Am I in danger?"

Her lip twisted. "You're a supernatural. You're always in danger."

"Mission accomplished, but nothing gained. Except more questions," I said as we brushed off our clothing in the laundry room. "Now you can finally get back to bed."

Derek shook his head. "Doesn't matter. I won't sleep."

"Because of this? I'm sorry. I didn't mean—"

"I wasn't sleeping before you got me up." He tugged off his shoe and dumped a trickle of dirt down the sink. "This fever or whatever. It's making me edgy. Restless." As if on cue, his forearm muscles started twitching. "Part of the problem is I'm not getting enough exercise. Tossing a ball around with Simon just doesn't cut it. I need more . . . space. More activity. I think that's what's causing this." He rubbed harder at the rippling muscles.

"Could you ask for workout equipment? They seem pretty good about stuff like that."

He slanted a look my way. "You've seen my file. You really think they're going to buy me a set of dumbbells and a punching bag?" He looked around the laundry room. "You tired?"

"After that? No."

"How about some fresh air? Get out, go for a walk?"

I laughed. "Sure, if there wasn't the small matter of an alarm system standing in our way."

He raked his hand through his hair, shaking out dirt he'd brushed from the crawl space ceiling. "I know the code."

"What?"

"You think I'm going to push Simon to leave and not know the security code? I can get us out, and we really should do a walk around, check out escape routes, hiding places. I don't get to go on many field trips, so I haven't gotten a look at the neighborhood."

I crossed my arms. "You can walk out anytime? Get that exercise you need? But you never have?"

He shifted his weight. "Never thought of it—"

"Of course you have. But there could be an alert when the alarm is turned off. Or a record of it being disabled. So you've never taken the chance. But now we should. If we get caught, well, everyone already thinks we're fooling around. We'd get in trouble for sneaking off, but not like Simon and I would if we were caught running away."

He scratched his chin. "That's a good idea."

"And it never crossed your mind."

He said nothing. I sighed and headed for the stairs.

"Chloe," he said. "Hold on. I—"

I glanced back. "Coming?"

Thirty-six

FIVE MINUTES LATER, WE were walking down the sidewalk, the lights from Lyle House fading behind us. We circled the block and mapped out all routes from the house. We were in a section of Buffalo I didn't recognize, once filled with old houses on big lots, where you'd expect to find a Mercedes or Cadillac in every drive. But I could see why it didn't—the billowing smokestacks a few blocks to the east.

After two blocks walking west, the light pollution ahead suggested a business district, which Derek confirmed. Like this neighborhood, it was older and decent enough, but not fancy. No pawn- and porn shops, but no bistros and baristas either. On Simon's rare outings, he'd told Derek he'd seen lots of older, ordinary businesses with plenty of alleys and dark corners.

"When you get to that business area," Derek said, "you'll be home free. If you can't go that way?" He waved east, toward the factory. "Go there. It's all industrial. I'm sure you'd find an abandoned warehouse or two, if you needed to hole up for a while." He looked around, scanning the neighborhood, nostrils flaring as he drank in the chill night air, probably a welcome relief from his fever. "Will you remember all that?"

"Can you say it again? Slower? Maybe write it out for me? With pictures?"

He scowled. "I'm just checking, okay? It's important."

"If you're worried we can't handle it, there's an obvious solution. Come with us."

"Don't."

"I'm just saying . . ."

"Well, don't."

He walked faster, leaving me jogging to keep up. I could tell Simon was right—the subject was closed to discussion—but I couldn't help myself.

"Simon's worried about you."

"Yeah?" He stopped, turned, and spread his arms. "Do I look okay to you?"

"No, you look like a guy who should be in bed, nursing a fever, not prowling—"

"I'm not prowling," he snapped, harsher than necessary. "I mean, where am I? On the street, right? Blocks from Lyle House. No cop cars are ripping down the road after me. If anything goes wrong, I can get out. Do you really think Talbot and Van Dop could stop me?"

"The question isn't whether you *can* escape. It's whether you *will*."

He paused. While I was gratified to know he wasn't just going to tell me what I wanted to hear, I didn't like seeing how much thought the answer required. Simon had said he was afraid that if something went wrong, Derek might just let it. He'd already decided he belonged at Lyle House. Would he leave even if he was in danger? Or could he see only the danger he posed . . . or thought he did?

"Derek?"

He shoved his hands in his pockets. "Yeah."

"Yeah what?"

He yanked one hand out and scratched his arm, nails digging in until they left red marks. "If I'm in danger, I'll get away and find you guys. Okay?"

"Okay."

I woke to see a figure on my bed and sat up, Liz's name on my lips. But it was Rae, leaning against the wall, knees up, eyes sparkling with amusement.

"Thought you saw a ghost?" she said.

"N-no. Maybe." I rubbed my eyes and yawned.

"I suppose it's not a good idea to surprise someone who sees spooks, huh?"

I peered around the bedroom, blinking hard. Early

morning light poured in. I glanced at Rae's bed and pictured Liz there, toes wiggling in the sunlight.

"Did Liz leave anything behind?" I asked.

"What?"

I pulled myself up, shoving the covers back. "When you moved in, did you find anything?"

"Just a shirt of Tori's. I didn't bother giving it back yet. Not like Tori's in any rush to return that green hoodie she borrowed from Liz. I saw her wearing it the other day. Why? Did Liz finally call?"

I stretched. "No. I was just . . ." Another yawn. "It's early and half my brain is still in dreamland. Did I miss Mrs. Talbot's knock?"

"No, we have a few minutes yet. I wanted to talk to you before everyone got up."

"Sure, what's—" I jerked upright. "Yesterday! We were supposed to talk. I totally forgot."

"You've been busy." She plucked at the hem of her baby doll nightdress. "So am I going to get an invite?"

"Invite?"

"On the great escape. That's what you were going to talk to me about last night, right? What you and Simon and Derek have been scurrying around planning for the past few days."

I don't want to imagine the look on my face at that moment. Shock, horror, disbelief—I'm sure it was all there, writ large enough to erase her doubts.

"I d-don't—"

"—know what I'm talking about?" She twisted a loose thread between her fingers and ripped it off, gaze fixed on it. "So what were you going to tell me? Make up a story to throw me off the trail?"

"N-no. I was going to tell you what happened in the crawl space. With Derek. I contacted that ghost again."

"Oh."

Her gaze dropped. As fascinating as my zombie story would normally have been, it wasn't what she'd been hoping to hear. She let the thread fall to the bed.

"So I'm not invited, am I?"

"Th-there's no—"

She held up her hands. "I overheard Simon and Derek arguing about escaping once. Now, with all this talk of transferring you or Derek, and you guys suddenly hanging out together . . ."

"It's not—"

"Last night, I woke up and you were gone. I went downstairs just as you and Derek were sneaking in and I caught enough to know you weren't taking a moonlight stroll."

"Derek isn't running away." Which was true, if not exactly what she meant.

She eased back against the wall again, drawing her knees up. "What if I met the club requirement? Would that snag me an invite?"

"What?"

"Your club. The special kids. The ones with super-powers."

I let out a laugh that sounded more like the yip of a startled poodle. "Superp-powers? I wish. My powers aren't winning me a slot on the Cartoon Network anytime soon . . . except as comic relief. *Ghost Whisperer Junior.* Or *Ghost Screamer*, more like. Tune in, every week, as Chloe Saunders runs screaming from yet another ghost looking for her help."

"Okay, *superpower* might be pushing it. But what if you could shove a kid out of your way with a flick of your fingers? Bet that would come in handy."

I swung out of bed and walked to the dresser. "Sure, but that's not what Derek did. He grabbed me. Believe me, I felt physical contact."

"I'm not talking about Derek. A few days before Brady got shipped out, he and Derek got into it. Or Brady was trying to. Derek wasn't having any of it, so Brady kept razzing him, trying to get a rise, and when he got in Derek's face, Simon flicked his fingers and, *wham,* Brady flew into the wall. I was there. Derek and Simon never touched him. That's why I wanted to see Simon's file."

"Well, as you saw, Simon doesn't have a file. He's here because of Derek. Their dad disappeared and Derek was sent here because of his problem, so they put Simon in the same place."

"How'd their dad disappear?"

I shrugged and pulled out a shirt. "They haven't said much about it. I don't want to push."

A thump. When I looked over my shoulder, Rae had thudded back onto the bed.

"You're too nice, girl," she said. "I'd have been all over them for that story."

I shook my head. "I think I hear Mrs. Talbot—"

"You don't. It's Saturday. We can sleep in, and you aren't getting off that easily. I know Simon's got some magic power, like you. And I'm pretty sure Derek does. That's why they're so tight. That's why Simon's dad took Derek in, I bet."

I looked in the mirror and ran the brush through my hair.

"What makes me so sure of all this?" Rae continued. "Remember when I told you about my diagnosis? How it didn't fit? I didn't tell you the whole story. You didn't read *my* file, did you?"

I slowly turned, brush still raised.

She went on. "According to the report, I got into a fight with my mom and burned her with a lighter. Only I wasn't holding a lighter. I just grabbed her arm and gave her first-degree burns."

"Why didn't you—?"

"Tell you?" she cut in. "I was waiting until I knew you

303 ◆

better. Until you'd believe me. But then you figured out you were seeing ghosts and I knew how it would sound. Like a little kid jealous 'cause his friend's going to Disney World—gotta show that he's special, too. And my power isn't like yours. I can't make it happen. It just *does*, when I get mad."

"Like with Tori. You *did* burn her, didn't you?"

She hugged my pillow to her chest. "I think so. But where's the proof? She *felt* like she'd been burned and there was a red mark, but it wasn't like I set her shirt on fire." She grinned. "As fun as *that* might be. So with my mom I lied and said I had been playing with a lighter and, when I went at her, I forgot I was still holding it. No one cared that there *wasn't* a lighter. They see what they want to see. Stick a label on it; medicate it; and, if you're lucky, it'll just go away. Only what we've got doesn't go away."

My brain struggled to take it all in. I knew I should say something, but what? Admit? Deny?

Rae rolled off the bed to her feet, twisted her long curls back, and held out her hand. When I didn't move, she said, "Elastics? Behind you?"

"Right."

I tossed her one. She wrapped it around her ponytail and headed for the door.

"Wait," I said.

She shook her head. "You gotta talk to the guys first."

"I don't—"

She turned to face me. "Yes, you do. You should. Would you want them blabbing your secrets before checking with you? Talk to them. Then get back to me. Not like I'm going anywhere."

Thirty-seven

I ATE BREAKFAST WITH Tori. I'm sure, yesterday, she'd been hoping to see me carried from the house, tied to a stretcher, ranting, driven mad after hours bound and gagged in the dark. Yet this morning, she just sat there and ate, eyes forward, expression empty, like she'd given up.

If I'd told the doctors what she'd done, she'd have been booted out, no matter how important her mom was. Maybe, when I came out of the crawl space and didn't tattle, she'd realized how close she'd been to getting transferred. Maybe she'd realized her stunt could have been fatal.

Maybe she even felt bad about it. That was probably too much to hope for, but from the look on her face this morning, any feud between us was over. She'd gotten it out of her system and seen how close she'd come to making a very big mistake. As hard as it was for me to be near her, thinking of what she'd put me through, I wasn't giving her any satisfaction. So I sat down and struggled to eat like nothing was wrong.

Every mouthful of oatmeal I forced down sank to the pit of my stomach and congealed into a lump of cement. Not only did I have to eat with someone who could have gotten me killed but also now I had to figure out what to do about Rae. How would I tell the guys? Derek would blame me for sure.

I was so wrapped up in my thoughts that it wasn't until I was coming back down after my shower and heard the weekend nurse, Ms. Abdo, talking about a "door" and a "new lock" that I remembered our dry run the night before. Had we been caught?

"Dr. Davidoff wants a deadbolt," Mrs. Talbot replied. "I don't know whether they make them for interior doors, but if you can't find one at the hardware store, we'll call Rob to replace the door. After yesterday, Dr. Davidoff doesn't want the kids getting into that crawl space."

The *basement* door. I breathed a sigh of relief and continued down. I reached the bottom just as Simon peeked from the dining room.

"Thought I heard you. Catch." He tossed me an apple. "I know you like the green ones. Derek's been hoarding them." He beckoned me in. "Sit and eat with us. You'll need your energy. It's Saturday and around here, that means all chores, all the time."

As I passed, he leaned down to whisper. "You okay?"

I nodded. He closed the door. I looked at the empty table.

"How's Derek?" I asked, keeping my voice low.

"He's in the kitchen, loading up. I hear you guys had a little adventure last night."

Derek had insisted on telling Simon that contacting the zombie ghosts had been his idea, so if Simon was put out by being excluded, the blame would fall on him. I thought he'd been trying to grab the glory—pretend *he'd* figured out what my ghost wanted. But Simon's expression told me he felt he *had* missed out on something. So I was kind of glad he didn't think I'd been the one who left him sleeping.

As I settled at the table, Derek came in, glass of milk in one hand, juice in the other. Simon reached out for one, but Derek set them both down at his plate with a grunted, "Get your own." Simon pushed to his feet, slapped Derek's back, and sauntered into the kitchen.

"Are you okay?" I whispered.

Derek's gaze shot to the closing kitchen door. He didn't want Simon knowing he'd been sick. I wasn't sure I liked that, and we locked glares, but the set of his jaw told me it wasn't open for discussion.

"I'm fine," he rumbled after a moment. "Tylenol finally kicked it."

His eyes were underscored with dark circles and were faintly bloodshot, but so were mine. He was pale, his acne redder than normal. Tired, but recovering. There was no fever in his eyes and by the way he attacked his oatmeal, he hadn't lost his appetite.

"Do I pass, Dr. Saunders?" he murmured under his breath.

"I guess so."

A grunt as he spooned more brown sugar into his bowl. "Some kind of reaction, like I said." He ate three heaping spoonfuls of porridge. Then, gaze still on his breakfast, he said, "What's wrong?"

"I didn't say a word."

"Something's up. What is it?"

"Nothing."

His head turned, gaze going to mine. "Yeah?"

"Yes."

A snort and he returned to his bowl as Simon came back.

"Anyone see the chore list for this morning?" he said, handing me a glass of orange juice. He sat down and reached for the sugar bowl. Derek took it from him, paused, then spooned more onto his oatmeal. A look passed between them. Simon gulped his orange juice and said, "We're on leaf-raking duty. Van Dop wants the dead leaves from last fall cleared . . ."

As he talked, Derek's gaze lifted to mine again, studying. I glanced away and bit into my apple.

* * *

Saturday was indeed chore day. Normally, I'd have been groaning at the thought—and wishing for school instead—but today it worked out perfectly. With Dr. Gill, Ms. Wang, and Miss Van Dop gone, Ms. Abdo out running errands, and Mrs. Talbot doing paperwork, we had the run of the house and I had an excuse for getting Simon outside alone, by offering to help him with the raking while Derek was upstairs changing the bedding.

"You're having second thoughts," Simon said when we were far enough from the house to not be overheard.

"What?"

He bent and retied his sneakers, face down. "About running away. You're afraid to tell Derek because he'll give you a hassle, get up in your face."

"That's not—"

"No, that's okay. I was surprised you offered in the first place. Surprised in a good way but— If you've changed your mind, that's totally cool and I don't blame you."

I continued toward the shed. "I am coming . . . unless *you're* having second thoughts about taking me."

He swung open the shed door and motioned for me to stay as he vanished in its dark depths, dirt and dust swirling in his wake. "I should probably say I don't *need* any help. But honestly?" His words were punctuated by rattles and clanks as he hunted for the rakes. "Though I don't expect trouble, a second pair of eyes would really come in handy if I'm on the run."

"I'd rather be that second set of eyes than sit here waiting for rescue," I said as he emerged holding two rakes.

"Like Derek you mean?"

"No, that wasn't a slam." I shut the shed door and fastened the latch. "Last night he told me why he was staying. Because of what he did. Which I already knew about because I kind of—"

"Read his file?"

"I—I was—"

"Checking up on him after he grabbed you in the basement. That's what he figured. Smart move." He motioned for us to start in the farthest corner, where a layer of decomposing leaves from last year blanketed the ground. "Don't let him razz you about it. He read yours."

I shrugged. "Fair is fair, I guess."

"He read yours *before* you read his. Bet he didn't mention that when you confessed."

"No, he didn't."

We started raking. For at least a minute, Simon said nothing, then he glanced over at me. "I bet he didn't mention how it happened either. The fight, that is."

I shook my head. "He just said the guy didn't pull a gun on him. He wouldn't discuss it."

"It happened last fall. We'd moved to some hick town outside Albany. No offense to small towns, I'm sure they're very nice places to live . . . for some people. Hotbeds of multiculturalism, they are not. But my dad hooked a job in Albany and this was the only place he could snag a sublet before the school year started."

He raked his leaves into the pile I'd started. "I was hanging out behind the school, waiting for Derek to finish talking to the math teacher. They were trying to come up with a special curriculum for him. Small school; not used to guys like Derek. Or, like me, as it turned out."

A mouse scampered from under a tree root, and Simon crouched to squint into the hole, making sure there weren't any more coming out before he raked around it. "I was shooting hoops when these three senior guys came strolling over. They're wearing Docs and beaters, and they're sauntering my way and I smell redneck trouble. I'm not going to bolt, but if they want the hoop, I'll get out of their way, you know?"

A blast of wind scattered the top layer of our pile. He sighed, shoulders slumping. I motioned for him to continue while I tidied it up.

"Only they didn't want the court. They wanted me. Seems one guy's mom worked at this 7-Eleven before it was bought by a Vietnamese family who gave her the boot. This was, like, a year before but, naturally, I must be related to them, right? I pointed out that, shockingly, not all Asians are related and we don't all own convenience stores."

He stopped raking. "When I say I'm not Vietnamese, one guy asks what I am. I say American, but eventually I give them what they want, and say my grandfather came from South Korea. Well, wouldn't you know it, one guy's uncle was killed in the Korean War. If this guy ever took a history class, he slept through it. He thought Koreans declared war on Americans. So I set him straight. And, yeah, I was a bit of a smart-ass about it. My dad always says if I can't learn to keep my mouth shut, I'd better work on my defensive spells. And that day—" he resumed raking, voice dropping "—that day, he was right.

"I'm smart-mouthing but keeping it light, you know? Goofing. Next thing I know, one guy pulls a switchblade. It's closed, though, and I'm staring at it like an idiot wondering what it is. Cell phone? MP3 player? Then, flick, out comes the blade. I tried to make a break for it, but it was too late. Another guy kicks out my feet and down I go. The guy with the blade is standing over me, and I'm readying a knock-back spell when Derek comes ripping around the corner. He grabs the guy with the knife, throws him aside, punches a second guy, and the third runs. Second guy gets up—he's fine—runs after his buddy. But the first guy? The one he threw off me?"

"Doesn't get up," I whispered.

Simon speared a leaf on the tines of his rake. "Derek was right. There was no gun. But you know what?" He lifted his gaze to mine. "If a guy came at Derek with a gun, he'd have kept his cool and handled it smart. But *he* wasn't the one in danger. I was. With Derek, that's a whole different thing. It's in his nature, my dad says, the—" He started raking hard, tearing through new grass and dirt. "So that's how it happened. I was a smart-ass and I couldn't back down from a bunch of rednecks and now Derek . . ."

He trailed off, and I knew Derek wasn't the only one who blamed himself for what had happened.

"Anyway," he said after a moment, "you didn't bring me out here to talk about that, and if I keep yapping, Derek will track us down. I get the feeling this isn't something you want to discuss with him."

"It's not."

I told him about Rae. "I didn't know what to say and that only made it worse, but she caught me completely off guard. Now Derek's going to think I let something slip or I was chatting with my girlfriend, telling her my secrets, which I didn't do, I swear—"

"I know. You aren't like that." He leaned on his rake. "Rae's right about Brady. I used a knock-back spell on him. It was careless and stupid, but after what happened with those other guys, I wanted to be quicker on the draw, you know? When I saw Brady was trying to get into it with Derek, I just . . . reacted."

"You wanted to diffuse the situation."

"Yeah. And if Rae caught you guys coming in last night, that's Derek's fault. He should have been on the lookout. He's got the ears and the—" he stopped "—the eyes. He can see pretty good in the dark, better than us. Normally, he'd have noticed Rae, but he must have been busy thinking about the escape."

Not preoccupied—sick and feverish. But I couldn't say that.

Simon went on. "He's been in a mood, too. Crankier than usual. He broke our shower. Did you hear about that?" He shook his head. "Snapped the handle right off, so I had to tell Talbot it had been loose. But as for Rae, we're going to have to tell him."

"Do you think she's one of us? A supernatural?"

"Could be half-demon. If she is, though, what does that mean, for us, being here? Four out of five kids? Maybe Liz, too, if she's a shaman? That's no coincidence. It can't be." He paused, thinking. "We'll worry about that later. For now, I'm more concerned with her knowing about our plan."

"She doesn't just know. She wants to sign up."

He cursed under his breath.

"She'd be useful," I said. "She's way more street smart than me."

"And me. It's just . . ." He shrugged. "I'm sure Rae's cool, but I wouldn't have argued about it just being the two of us."

He glanced over at me. My heart started pounding double time.

"There's a lot I want to talk to you about." He touched the back of my hand, leaning so close I could feel his breath against my hair.

"What's this about Rae?" a voice demanded. We turned to see Derek crossing the lawn.

Simon swore. "Anyone ever tell you your sense of timing really sucks."

"That's why I don't play the drums. Now what's up?"

I told him.

Thirty-eight

SIMON DOUBTED RAE HAD supernatural powers. There were five half-demons, but by fifteen she should have been doing more than leaving marks that barely qualified as first-degree burns. He didn't think she was lying. She was just too eager to believe.

I suspected he was right. Given up at birth, displaced by younger siblings, tossed into Lyle House with strangers and forgotten, it would mean so much to Rae to be special. I'd seen it in her face that morning, glowing with excitement.

The person slowest to dismiss the idea was Derek. He didn't say he believed Rae was a half-demon, but his silence said he was considering the possibility. Last night was still bugging him—and me—our failure to find or dismiss a connection between us, Samuel Lyle, and those supernatural bodies in the cellar. If Rae *was* a half-demon and Liz might be a shaman, then the possibility we were here by chance plummeted.

You could argue that a group home for disturbed teens isn't an unusual place to find teenage supernaturals, especially those who don't know what they are. Our symptoms could be massaged to fit known psychiatric disorders, and, since everyone knew it was impossible to contact the dead or to burn people with your bare hands or toss a kid aside and break his neck—the obvious solution would be that we were mentally ill. Hallucinating, obsessed with fire, uncontrollably violent . . .

But there was nothing paranormal about Tori's mood swings. Peter had apparently been in for some kind of anxiety disorder and that didn't fit the pattern either.

Still, I couldn't shake the feeling I was missing something, that the connection was there and my brain was too distracted by other problems to see it. I suspected Derek felt the same.

Whether Rae was a supernatural or not, we all agreed, she should come with us. To Derek, it wasn't so much a matter of *should we let her come* as *do we dare let her stay.* What if she retaliated by telling the nurses? I couldn't see that, but after we were gone, if they came down hard on her, she'd cave before Derek did.

Derek's only condition was that we'd keep the details about our powers and our plans vague, at least for now.

* * *

I told Rae, and then Derek dropped the bomb none of us expected. We had to leave that night.

Since it was Saturday, we'd have all day to prepare, and chores gave us an excuse for poking around the house, gathering supplies. Tonight Miss Van Dop was off and the weekend nurse was much less likely to realize we were up to something. It was better to go now, before anything else went wrong.

Once I got past the initial "OMG, you mean *tonight*!" panic, I had to agree the sooner we left, the better.

So, while Rae stood guard cleaning the girls bathroom, I packed.

I'd packed for camp many times but, in comparison, this was agonizing. For every item I put in, I had to consider how badly I needed it, how much room and weight it would add, and whether I'd be better off picking it up on the road.

The brush was out, and the comb was in. Deodorant, definitely in. My iPod and lipgloss might not be essential for daily life, but they were tiny enough to keep. Soap, a toothbrush, and toothpaste would need to be bought later because I couldn't afford to have anyone notice them missing from the bathroom now.

Next came clothing. It was still cool, especially at night. Layering would be the key. I packed as Aunt Lauren taught me when we'd spent a week in France. I'd wear a sweatshirt, long-sleeved pullover, and T-shirt with jeans. In the bag, I'd have two more T-shirts, another pullover, and three pairs of socks and underwear.

Would that be enough? How long would we be on the run?

I'd been avoiding that question since I'd first offered to go. Simon and Derek seemed to think we'd find their dad pretty quickly. Simon had spells and just needed to travel around Buffalo, casting them.

It sounded easy. Too easy?

I'd seen the looks in their eyes. Derek's barely concealed worry. Simon's stubborn conviction. When pressed, they'd both admitted that, if they couldn't find their dad, there were other supernaturals they could contact.

If it took longer than a few days, I had a bank card and the money from my dad. Simon and Derek had a bank card, too, with emergency funds their dad had stashed for them, at least a thousand dollars each, they thought. We'd need to withdraw as much as we could immediately, before anyone knew we were gone and started tracking us. Derek would keep his card and cash in case he needed it, but we'd have Simon's money plus mine. That would get us through.

Whatever happened, we'd be fine. Another shirt, though, might not be a bad idea.

Shirt . . . That reminded me . . .

I shoved my backpack under the bed, slipped down to Tori's room. The door was ajar. Through it, I could see that Tori's bed was empty. I gave a gentle push.

"Hello?" She sprang up from Rae's old bed, ripping out

her earbuds. "Knock much?"

"I—I thought you were downstairs."

"Oh, so you were going to take advantage of that, were you? Set your little scheme in motion?"

I opened the door and stepped inside. "What scheme?"

"The one you and your gang have been planning. I've seen you skulking around, plotting against me."

"Huh?"

She wound the earbud wire around her MP3 player, yanking it tight, as if imagining it going around my neck instead. "You think I'm stupid? You're not as sweet and innocent as you seem, Chloe Saunders. First, you seduce my boyfriend."

"Boy— *Seduce?*"

"Then you bat your baby blues at tall, dark, and gruesome, and next thing you know, he's trailing you like a lost puppy."

"*What?*"

"And now, to make sure *everyone* in the house is against me, you pull in Rachelle. Don't think I missed your powwow this morning."

"And you think we're . . . plotting against *you?*" I sputtered a laugh and leaned back against the dresser. "How do you get that ego through the door, Tori? I'm not interested in revenge. I'm not interested in you at all. Get it?"

She slid to the edge of the bed, feet touching down, eyes narrowing. "You think you're clever, don't you?"

I slumped back against the dresser with an exaggerated sigh. "Don't you ever quit? You're like a broken record. Me, me, me. The world revolves around Tori. No wonder even your mom thinks you're a spoiled—"

I stopped myself, but it was too late. For a moment, Tori froze in mid-rise. Then, slowly, she crumpled back onto the bed.

"I didn't mean—"

"What do you want, Chloe?" She tried to put some bite in the words, but they came out quiet, weary.

"Liz's shirt," I said after a moment. "Rae says you borrowed a green hoodie from Liz."

She waved toward the dresser. "It's in there. Middle drawer. Mess it up and you can refold everything."

And that was it. No "Why do you want it?" or even "Did she call asking for it?" Her gaze had already gone distant. Doped up? Or beyond caring?

I found the shirt. An emerald green Gap hoodie. A personal effect.

I shut the drawer and straightened.

"You got what you came for," Tori said. "Now run along and play with your friends."

I walked to the door, grasped the handle, then turned to face her.

"Tori?"

"What?"

I wanted to wish her luck. I wanted to tell her I hoped

she got what she was looking for, what she needed. I wanted to tell her I was sorry.

With everything that went on at Lyle House, and the discovery that at least three of us didn't belong here, it was easy to forget that some kids did. Tori had problems. Expecting her to behave like any normal teenage girl, then shunning and insulting her when she didn't, was like mocking the slow kids at school. She needed help and support and consideration, and she hadn't gotten it from anyone but Liz.

I clutched Liz's shirt in my hands and tried to think of something to say, but anything I did say would come out wrong, condescending.

So I said the only thing I could. "Good-bye."

Thirty-nine

ISTUFFED LIZ'S HOODIE INTO my bag. It took up more room than I could afford, but I needed it. It could answer a question I really needed to answer . . . just as soon as I worked up the courage to ask.

When Derek had announced we'd be leaving that night, my first thought had been *there's not enough time*, but there was too much time. We did homework we'd never submit, helped Mrs. Talbot think up meals we'd never eat, all the while fighting the urge to slip away and plan some more. Both Rae and Tori had noticed my "powwows" with the guys, and if we kept it up, the nurses might suspect it was more than teen hormones at work.

I warned the others about Tori, but no one seemed concerned. It was like I told her—she was totally out of our minds. Insignificant. I wondered whether that hurt her most of all.

We spent the evening watching a movie. For once, I paid so little attention that if I was asked for a log line ten minutes after the credits rolled, I couldn't have given one.

Derek didn't join us. Simon said his brother was wiped from the night before and wanted to rest up so he'd be clear-headed for helping us tonight. I wondered whether his fever was coming back.

When Mrs. Talbot asked after Derek, Simon said he "wasn't feeling great." She tut-tutted and withdrew to play cards with Ms. Abdo, not even going upstairs to check on him. That's how it always was with Derek. The nurses seemed to leave him to his own devices, like his size made them forget he was still a kid. Or maybe, given his file and his diagnosis, they wanted as little contact with him as possible.

Did he notice how they treated him? I'm sure he did. Nothing escaped Derek, and I suspected it only reinforced that he needed to be in here.

As the movie droned on, I fretted about him. He'd been so careful not to let Simon know he'd been sick. If Simon could tell he "wasn't feeling great," that had to mean he was too sick to hide it.

I slipped from the media room, got four Tylenol and a

glass of water, and took it upstairs.

I tapped on the door. No answer. Light shone under it, but he could have fallen asleep reading.

Or be too sick to answer.

I rapped again, a little louder.

"Derek? It's me. I brought water and Tylenol."

Still nothing. I touched the doorknob, cold under my fingertips. He was probably asleep. Or ignoring me.

"I'll leave it here."

As I bent to set the glass on the floor, the door opened, just enough for me to see Derek's bare foot. I straightened. He was in his boxers again, and my gaze shot to the safety of his face, but not before noticing the sheen of sweat on his chest. Sweat plastered his hair around his face, and his eyes were feverish, lips parted, breath coming hard, labored.

"Are y-you—?" I began.

"Be fine."

He ran his tongue over his parched lips and blinked hard, as if struggling to focus. When I held out the glass, he reached for it through the gap and took a long gulp.

"Thanks."

I handed him the Tylenol. "Are you sure you're okay?"

"Good enough."

He braced the door with his foot and reached around his back, scratching.

"Maybe you should take a bath," I said. "A cold bath,

for your fever. Baking soda would help the itching. I could get—"

"Nah, I'm okay."

"If you need anything . . ."

"Just rest. Go on back down before someone notices."

I headed for the stairs.

"Chloe?"

I glanced back. He was leaning out the door.

"Nothing to Simon, okay? About how bad I am?"

"He knows you're not feeling well. You really should tell—"

"I'm fine."

"You're not fine. He's going to figure that out—"

"He won't. I'll take care of it."

He withdrew and the door clicked shut.

That night in bed, Rae couldn't keep quiet. She wanted to talk about her backpack and what she'd packed and whether she'd made the right choices and should she take anything else . . .

I hated to shush her. She was as excited as a kid getting ready for her first overnight camp, which was weird because after what had happened to her friend, Rae should know that life on the street wasn't going to be some fabulous, unchaperoned adventure.

I suppose, to her, this wasn't the same thing. She was

going with Simon and me, and there were few kids less likely to turn Bonnie and Clyde. This wasn't an act of delinquency; it was a mission. And, besides, like Simon and Derek said, old rules didn't apply to us anymore.

" 'Cause we're special." She gave a bubbling laugh. "That sounds so lame. But it's what everyone wants, isn't it? To be special."

Do they? There were a lot of things I wanted to be. Smart, sure. Talented, definitely. Pretty? Okay, I'll admit it. But special?

I'd spent too much of my life being special. The rich girl who lost her mother. The new kid in class. The drama major who didn't want to be an actor. For me, special meant different, and not in a good way. I'd wanted to be normal, and I guess the irony is that, the whole time I was dreaming of a normal life, I already had one . . . or a whole lot closer to it than I'd ever have again.

But now I watched Rae lying on her stomach, matches in hand, struggling to light one with her bare fingertips, the tip of her tongue sticking through her teeth, determination bordering on desperation, and I could see how badly she wanted a supernatural power. I had one, and I cared so little for it that I'd gladly give it to her.

It was like in school, when other girls drooled over designer jeans, counting the babysitting hours until they could buy a pair, and I sat there wearing mine, four other pairs in the closet at home, no more meaningful to me than a pair of no-names. I felt guilty for not appreciating what I had.

But necromancy wasn't a pair of expensive jeans, and I was pretty sure my life would be better without it. Definitely easier. And yet, if I woke tomorrow and couldn't talk to the dead, would I be disappointed?

"I think it's getting warm," she said, pinching the match head between her fingers.

I crawled out of bed. "Let me see."

"No." She pulled it back. "Not yet. Not until I'm sure."

Was Rae half-demon? Derek said they did burn things with their hands. By her age, Rae should have been lighting that match no problem. But then he'd never heard of a necromancer who woke up one morning and suddenly started seeing ghosts everywhere. Usually it was a gradual process.

Wasn't that typical for development in general? A book might say "at twelve, children begin a process of puberty, ending at eighteen," but that's a generalization. You get girls like me and guys like Derek, neither of us fitting the norm.

Maybe Rae's supernatural powers were late blooming, like me and my period. And maybe my powers were like Derek's puberty, the changes hitting all at once.

Apparently half-demons had a human mother and a demon father, who'd taken human form to impregnate her. That fit Rae's history, with a mother who'd given her up at birth, no father in the picture.

"Smoke!" she squealed before slapping a hand over her mouth. She waved the match. "I saw smoke. I swear it. Yes, I know, I need a life, but it was just so cool. Here, watch."

She pulled another match from the book.

Was Rae a half-demon?

I really hoped so.

ᖴᴏʀᴛʏ

RAE'S WATCH ALARM WAS set to go off at three. According to Derek, that was the quietest time of night, when we'd be least likely to be spotted. At 2:45 we shut the alarm off, and by 2:50 we were out of our room, backpacks in hand.

When I eased our door shut, the hall fell to pitch-black. The ticking of the grandfather clock guided us to the stairs.

I swore this time *every* step creaked, but as hard as I strained for sounds of Tori or Mrs. Talbot stirring, I heard only the clock.

At the bottom of the stairs, the moon peeked in around the drawn curtains, lifting the darkness just enough so I could make out chairs and tables before I crashed into them. I was turning into the hall when a dark shape stepped from the shadows. I bit back a yelp and scowled, ready to blast Derek. But it was Simon, and one look at his ashen face killed the words in my throat.

"What's—?" I began.

"Is Derek with you?"

"No, wh—"

"He's gone." He lifted something that glinted and it took a moment for me to recognize it as Derek's watch. "He had the alarm set for 2:45. When it went off, I woke up and found it on my pillow. His bed was empty."

Rae's fingers closed on my arm. "But Derek's not coming, right? Let's just go."

"Did he say anything to you last night?" I whispered.

Simon shook his head. "He was asleep. I didn't wake him."

"Maybe he's in the bathroom," Rae whispered. "Come on, guys, we have to—"

"I checked the bathrooms. And the spare room. And the kitchen. Something's wrong. Something happened to him."

"If it did, would he have left you the watch? Maybe . . . ," I struggled for a reasonable explanation, fighting the rising panic that said there wasn't one. "Maybe he's afraid we'll try to drag him along at the last minute and we'll wake someone up."

"Speaking of which . . ." Rae said with a pointed look at the ceiling.

Simon and I looked at each other and I knew, as logical as my explanation was, Derek would know Simon couldn't leave without making sure he was okay.

"Guys . . ." Rae said.

"You two go," said Simon. "I'll find—"

"No," I said. "I will."

"But—"

I lifted my hand to cut him short. "What good will it do if I get away and you don't? It's your dad. You know how to find him."

Simon's gaze slid to the side.

"What?" Rae turned to me. "Forget Derek, Chloe. He's not coming, remember? He'll be fine. We have to go."

"I'll find him and come after you," I said. "We'll meet behind the factory, okay?"

Simon shook his head. "He's my responsibility—"

"Right now, your *dad* is your responsibility. You can't help Derek—or me—if you can't find him."

Silence.

"Okay?"

His brows knitted, and I could tell that it *wasn't* okay, that he hated to run.

"You have to go," I said.

He took my hand, wrapped his fingers around it, and squeezed. I'm sure I turned as red as if he'd scooped me up in a kiss.

"Be careful?" he said.

"I will. I'll find him, then I'll find you."

"I'll be waiting."

* * *

Simon took my backpack. It'd be a dead giveaway if I was caught carrying it. If I stashed it someplace, I might not get a chance to retrieve it.

We had the security code—Derek had written it out for us, together with instructions and hand-drawn maps. I could take that as proof that he hadn't planned to be here when we left, but I knew it was just Derek being Derek, leaving nothing to chance.

So why take off and risk Simon not going? My last memory of Derek flashed past—standing in his bedroom doorway, bathed in sweat, barely able to focus—and I knew what had happened.

If Simon saw him like that, he'd know how sick Derek was. If Simon knew, Simon would stay. No question. So Derek had done the only thing he could—holed up someplace, left the alarm on, and prayed Simon would go. A slim chance versus no chance.

So where was he? I headed to the basement first. The door was closed, light off, but he wouldn't leave any sign if he was hiding. The laundry room was empty. The door to the closet was locked.

Last night, when we'd gone on our walk, he'd gulped down the cold air. When we'd returned, his fever seemed gone and I'd chalked it up to the Tylenol kicking in, but maybe the cold air had been enough. If he was desperate for a quick fix, he'd go outside, in hopes of cooling down enough to see Simon off.

I stepped onto the back porch. The quarter moon had slid behind clouds and it was as dark as the upstairs hall. I could make out the glimmer of lights at a neighbor's, but the towering trees blocked all but that faint glow.

My gaze swept the black yard, seeing only the pale box that I knew was the shed. It was colder than the night before, and my breath hung in the air. The only sound was the creak of branches, as steady and monotonous as the ticking of the grandfather clock.

I took three tentative strides across the deck. By the time I climbed down the steps to the concrete pad, I could make out more pale shapes in the yard—the bench, a lawn chair, the garden angel, and a soccer-ball-sized blob near the shed.

An engine revved and I froze, but it was only a car passing. Another two slow steps. I glanced over my shoulder and considered dashing back in for a flashlight, but Simon had taken the only one I knew about.

I peered around. My lips parted to whisper Derek's name, then closed. Would he answer? Or hide?

When I drew closer to the presumed ball, I saw it was a big white sneaker. Derek's. I scooped it up, looking about wildly now.

A blast of wind struck me, so cold it made my eyes water. I rubbed the icy tip of my nose as the wind moaned through the trees. Then the wind died down . . . and the moaning continued, a long, low sound that made the back of my neck prickle.

I turned slowly. The sound stopped. Then came a stifled cough, and as I wheeled toward it, I saw a white sock peeking from behind the shed.

I dashed over. Derek was there, deep in the shadows, on all fours, his head and upper body barely visible. The stink of sweat rolled off him, and the breeze brought a sharp, bitter smell that made the back of my throat constrict, reflexively gagging.

His body tensed as he retched, a dry, ragged heave.

"Derek?" I whispered. "It's Chloe."

He went rigid. "Go away." The words were a guttural growl, barely intelligible.

I stepped closer, dropping my voice another notch. "Simon's gone. I convinced him to go on ahead while I found you."

His back arched, arms stretched out, pale fingers digging into the soil. A low moan, cut short by a grunt.

"You found me. Now go."

"Do you really think I'd leave you like this?" I took another step forward. The stink of vomit made me clap my hand to my nose. I switched to breathing through my mouth. "If you're throwing up, that's more than a fever. You need—"

"Go!" The word was a snarl and I staggered back.

His head dropped. Another moan, this one ending in a

high-pitched sound, almost like a whimper. He wore a T-shirt, bare muscles bunching as he gripped the ground again. His arms darkened, as if a shadow passed over them, then reappeared, pale against the surrounding shadow.

"Derek, I—"

His back arched, stretching so high I could see the rigid line of his spine, T-shirt pulled tight, muscles writhing and rippling. Then he sagged, his panting breaths as ragged as the rustling leaves.

"Please. Go." The words were a deep mumble, like he wasn't opening his mouth.

"You need help—"

"No!"

"Simon, then. I'm getting Simon. I'll be right—"

"No!"

He twisted and I caught a glimpse of his face, contorted, misshapen . . . wrong. He whipped his head down before I could process what I'd seen.

He gagged, the sound horrible and raw, like he was coughing up his insides. His back shot up again, limbs stretching to the very limits, bones crackling. His arms went dark, then lightened, the muscles and tendons rippling. The moon chose that moment to peek from the cloud and when his arms darkened, I could see it was hair sprouting, just enough to break the surface, then sliding back under his skin. And his hands . . . His fingers were long and twisted like talons, digging into the earth as his back arched.

In my mind, I heard Simon again. "Guys like Derek have . . . physical enhancements, you might say. Extra strong, as you saw. Better senses, too. That kind of thing."

That kind of thing.

Then my own voice asking lightly, "I'm not going to run into any werewolves or vampires, am I?"

And Simon's answer, coupled with a laugh. "That'd be cool."

Not an answer at all. Avoiding a reply he couldn't give.

Derek convulsed, his head flying back, jaw clenched, an awful moaning howl hissing through his teeth. Then his head whipped down and he gagged, strings of saliva dripping.

"Derek?"

He retched, his whole body racked with heaves. When they subsided, I inched forward. He tilted his head away.

"Is there anything I can do?"

A voice inside my head said, "Sure. Run for your life!" But it was a small warning, not even serious, really, because there was no question of running. This wasn't a matinee monster. Even now, with hair sprouting on his arms, fingers twisted into claws, when he looked away and growled at me to leave, I knew that whatever was happening, he was still Derek.

"Is there anything I can do?"

A ridiculous question. I could imagine the response he'd make any other time—the curl of his lip, the roll of his eyes.

But after one halfhearted "go away," he crouched there, head turned, body trembling, each breath a rasp ending in a quaver.

"Don't." His fingers dug into the ground, arms stiffening, then relaxing. "Go."

"I can't leave you here. If there's anything I can do . . ."

"Don't." A sharp intake of breath, then he expelled the words. "Don't go."

His head lifted my way, just enough for me to see one green eye, wide with terror.

His arms and legs went rigid, back shooting up as he heaved. Vomit sprayed the grass, a fresh wave with every spasm. The sickly smell filled the air.

And I sat there, doing nothing, because there was nothing I could do. My brain raced through ideas, discarding each as fast as it came. I inched over and put my hand on his arm, feeling the coarse hair push through red-hot skin that writhed and pulsed. That was all I could do—stay and tell him I was there.

Finally, with one last heave, one last spray of vomit dappling the fence three feet away, it stopped. Just stopped.

The muscles under my hand went still, the coarse hair receded. Slowly, he relaxed, his back dropping, hands releasing their grip on the earth. He crouched there, panting, hair hanging around his face.

Then he slumped onto his side, hands going over his

face, fingers still long, misshapen, the nails thick, like claws. He curled up on his side, knees drawn in, and moaned.

"Should I—? Simon. Should I get Simon? Will he know what to—?"

"No." The word was hoarse, guttural, as if his vocal cords weren't quite human.

"It's over," he said after a minute. "I think. Pretty sure." He rubbed his face, still shielded behind his hands. "Shouldn't have happened. Not yet. Not for years."

In other words, he knew perfectly well what he was, he just hadn't expected the . . . transformation until he was older. I felt a spark of anger that he'd misled me, made Simon lie to me, but I couldn't sustain it, not after what I'd seen, not sitting there, watching him, shirt soaked with sweat as he struggled to breathe, his body shaking with exhaustion and pain.

"Go," he whispered. "I'll be fine now."

"I'm not—"

"*Chloe*," he snapped, the old Derek back in his voice. "Go. Help Simon. Tell him I'm fine."

"No."

"Chloe . . ." He drew my name out in a low growl.

"Five minutes. I want to make sure you're okay."

He grunted, but settled into silence, relaxing onto the grass.

"See you *did* rip out of your clothes," I said, trying to

keep my tone light. "Hope you didn't like that shirt, 'cause it's toast."

It was a weak joke, but he said, "Least I didn't turn green."

"No, just . . ." I was going to say "hairy," but I couldn't get the word out, couldn't wrap my head around what I'd seen.

The back door banged. Derek shot up, his hands falling from his face. His nose looked crushed, wide and flat, cheekbones jutting as if rising to meet it, his brows thick and heavy. Not monstrous, more like an artist's reconstruction of Neanderthal man.

I tore my gaze away and crawled toward the corner of the shed. He caught my leg.

"I'll be careful," I whispered. "I'm just getting a look."

I slid on my belly, creeping to the corner and peeking around it. A flashlight beam swept the yard.

"A woman," I whispered, as low as I could. "I think it's Rae—no, too skinny. Ms. Abdo, maybe?"

He tugged my ankle. My jeans had hiked up, and his hand was wrapped around bare skin above my sock. I could feel his palm, rough, like the pads on a dog's feet.

"Go," he whispered. "I'll boost you over the fence. Climb the next one and—"

The flashlight beam cut a swath across the back of the yard.

"Who's out there?" The voice was high, sharp, with a faint accent.

"Dr. Gill," I whispered to Derek. "What's she—?"

"Never mind. Go!"

"I know someone's out here," she said. "I heard you."

I glanced at Derek, his face still deformed. Dr. Gill couldn't find him like this.

I grabbed the shoe of his that I'd dropped, and kicked off one of my own, and that confused him enough for me to wrench from his grasp and dart to the side fence, squeezing between it and the shed. At the last second, he scrambled up and lunged at me, but I was wedged in too far to reach, and he couldn't follow.

"Chloe! Get back here! Don't you dare—"

I kept going.

forty-one

I SQUEEZED THROUGH THE gap between the fence and shed, with Derek's shoe clutched in one hand, while the other tugged the shirt from my jeans, and mussed my hair. When I reached the end of the shed, I peeked out. Dr. Gill had her back to me, her flashlight scanning the other side of the yard.

I darted behind the shrubs and continued along the fence until I reached the porch. Then I crouched in the bushes there, daubed dirt on my cheek, and stumbled out, twigs crackling.

"D-Dr. Gill." I fumbled to shove my shirt back into my jeans. "I—I was just out g-getting some air."

I hopped on one foot, trying to put on Derek's shoe.

"I don't think that's yours, Chloe," she said as she approached, flashlight in my eyes.

I shielded my face from the light and lifted the shoe, squinting at it. Then I let out a nervous laugh. "Whoops. Guess I grabbed the wrong one when I came outside."

"Where is he?"

"Who?" I squeaked.

She pointed at the shoe. "Derek."

"Derek? Is this his?" I cast a surreptitious glance over my shoulder, into the bushes, drawing her attention there. "I—I haven't seen Derek since dinner. Is h-he out here, too?"

"Oh, I'm sure he is. Long gone, I suppose, with Simon and Rae. Making their escape while you stand guard and provide a diversion."

"Wh-what?" That time the stammer wasn't faked. "E-escape? N-no. Derek and I were . . ." I gestured at the bushes. "He knew the code so we came outside to be alone and . . . you know."

She stepped closer, beam right in my eyes. "Pick up where you left off Friday afternoon?"

"Right." I tugged down my shirt and tried to look embarrassed.

"Do you really think I'm going to buy that, Chloe? Girls like you wouldn't give boys like Derek Souza the time of day, much less roll around in bushes and crawl spaces with them."

My head shot up. "B-but you caught us. Friday. You're the one who said—"

"I know what I said, Chloe. And I know what you were really doing in that crawl space. I found your new friends."

I stood, feet rooted, unable to believe what I was hearing.

"What did they tell you?" Her fingers went around my arm. "They were his, weren't they? Samuel Lyle's subjects." She leaned toward me, eyes glittering, as feverish as Derek's but with a glimmer of madness behind them. "Did they tell you his secrets? His discoveries? I'll make sure no one knows you ran away. I'll say I found you asleep in the TV room. Just tell me everything those ghosts said."

"I—I can't talk to ghosts."

I tried to pull away, but her fingers clamped down tighter. I went limp, as if giving in, then threw myself in the other direction. Her hand fell from my arm, but I'd pulled too hard and stumbled, off balance. She plunged toward me. I dove, hitting the ground. As I clambered out of her way, a dark shape vaulted over the deck railing.

Dr. Gill only had time to see a shadow passing over her. She turned, mouth opening. Derek landed right in front of her. Her arms flew up, and she let out a shriek, falling back, but she was still in mid-turn and tripped over her own feet. As she went down, she fumbled for something in her pocket. Derek dove and pinned her arm as she pulled out a two-way radio. It flew onto the grass. Her skull smacked into the cement pad.

I ran forward. Derek was already crouching at her

side, checking her pulse.

"She's fine," he said, exhaling with relief. "Just unconscious. Come on. Before she wakes up."

His fingers closed around my arm. Dirty, but very human fingers, his face and hands back to normal, the ripped and sweaty shirt the only sign of his ordeal. I brushed him off, jogged over to his shoe and picked it up, then turned to see him holding the sneaker I'd discarded.

"Trade?"

We pulled our shoes on.

"Simon's waiting at the factory," I said. "We have to warn him. They know about the escape."

He pushed me toward the side fence. "The road won't be safe. Cut through the yards."

I glanced over my shoulder.

"I'm right behind you," he said. "Now *go!*"

At the first fence, I started climbing, but I was too slow for Derek, who grabbed me and swung me over, then vaulted like it was a hurdle. Two doors down, the wail of a siren sent us diving behind a child's playhouse.

"Police?" I whispered.

"Can't tell."

After a moment, I said, "Dr. Gill knows about the bodies. When I raised them, she must not have been holed up in her office like we thought. She knows I can contact the dead, and about Samuel Lyle, and—"

"Later."

He was right. I squeezed the thought from my head and concentrated on the siren. It whipped past, heading back the way we came, then disappeared.

"Did it stop at the house?" I asked.

He shook his head. "I can still hear it. Now go."

According to Derek, there were seven backyards between Lyle House and the end of the block. Trust him to have counted. We were racing through the fifth when his hand shot out like a railway guard and I plowed into it. When I turned, he had his head cocked, listening. Ten seconds passed. I plucked at his shirt, but he ignored me for another ten. Then he lowered his head and whispered, "I hear a car idling. Someone's out there."

"Where?"

An impatient wave. *"There.* On the street we need to cross." He held up a finger. "Footsteps. Someone's talking. A woman. She's whispering. I can't make it out."

"Do you recognize the voice?"

He shook his head. "Stay here. I'll get closer, see if that helps."

He loped closer to the house, stopping behind a cluster of bushes.

I looked around. I was standing in the middle of the yard, exposed to anyone who heard a noise and glanced out the window. His spot looked a whole lot safer. When I approached, he whirled, pinning me with a glare.

"Sorry," I whispered, and moved slower, quieter.

He waved me back. When I didn't stop, he glared again, then turned away. I crept up behind him and went still. His head moved slowly, tracking the voices, I presumed. But when his head swiveled my way, I noticed the lift of his chin, the flare of his nostrils, and realized he was sniffing the air.

When he noticed me watching, I got a full-blown scowl.

"Can you recognize the, uh . . . ?"

"Scents." He spat the word. "Yes, I can track scents. Like a dog."

"I didn't mean—"

"Whatever."

He looked away again, scanning the fence line. "I suppose you figured out what I am."

"A werewolf."

I tried to say it casually, but I wasn't sure I succeeded. I didn't want to sound freaked out because that was exactly what he expected—why he hadn't told me the truth. I told myself it was no different than being a necromancer or a sorcerer or a half-demon. But it was.

As the silence stretched, I knew I should say something. If he'd told me he was a half-demon, I'd be peppering him with questions, and when I didn't now, my silence damned him as something different than us, something less natural, something . . . worse.

"So what . . . happened back there? You were, uh . . ."

"Changing." He stepped to the right, leaning out for a better listen, then pulled back. "It's not supposed to start until I'm at least eighteen. That's what Dad thought. Last night, the itching, the fever, the muscle spasms—that must have been a warning. I should have figured it out."

His head tilted as a breeze fluttered past. He took a deep breath, then shook his head. "No one I recognize." He pointed to the back of the yard. "We'll climb the back fence, go through that way, and loop around. Hopefully, they'll have driven off by then."

We dashed over the rear fence, and through the next yard to the drive. Derek scanned the street, looking and listening and, I guess, sniffing, then waved me across the street. We slipped into the first yard and continued heading east, cutting through yards.

When we reached the road, I saw the car he'd been talking about. It was a silver SUV, a block down. The headlights were off, but someone stood at the driver's window, leaning in, as if talking.

"We'll have to make a run for it," Derek said. "Hope they don't notice us."

"You think they're looking for us?"

"No, but—"

"Then if we run, it'll look suspicious."

"It's three-thirty in the morning. We're going to look suspicious anyway." He looked at the car for a moment. "Fine. But any sign of trouble? Follow my lead."

"Yes, sir."

forty-two

WE CLIMBED THE FENCE under a weeping willow, letting its branches and shadows hide us. Then Derek positioned me on his left, away from the car. From this distance, they'd only see what looked like a grown man and maybe a woman beside him.

"We're going to walk and talk, okay? Normal couple, late night walk. Not hiding anything."

I nodded, and his hand closed around mine. We moved quickly to the sidewalk, then slowed as we cut to the curb.

"Okay, talk," he murmured.

"So when you . . . change . . ."

A short laugh, this obviously not being what he'd had in mind. But I was keeping my voice low, and if I couldn't hear them talking, they wouldn't hear more than the murmur of my voice.

"You change into . . ." I struggled to think of the right word for the image that came to mind—a Hollywood werewolf, half human, half beast.

"A wolf." He steered us to the left, away from the car.

"Wolf?"

"You know. Large wild canine. Commonly seen in zoos."

"You change into . . . ? But that's not—" I stopped myself.

"Physically possible?" Another short laugh. "Yeah, my body was screaming the same thing. No idea how it works. I guess I'll find out later. Much later, if I'm lucky. We're heading for the street to the left. The factory is just up—"

He stopped short, turning sharply at the same moment that the headlights from the idling car flicked on. His hand tightened around mine and he broke into a run, dragging me along.

"They spotted us," he said.

"But they aren't looking for us."

"Yes, they are."

He yanked my arm, propelling me toward the next yard. As we neared the fence, he grabbed me around the waist and threw me over. I hit the ground on all fours, leaped up, and ran for the nearest cover—a metal shed.

Derek dove in behind me and, for a moment, I just stood there, leaning my blazing cheek against the cool metal, gulping the icy air. Then I straightened.

"How—?"

"I heard them say 'It's them' and 'Call Marcel.'"

"Marcel? Isn't that Dr. Davidoff's name?"

"Yeah, and something tells me it's not common enough to be a coincidence."

"But how—"

He clamped his hand over my mouth and I tasted dirt. He leaned down to my ear. "They're circling the block. I hear voices. They must have the windows down, listening for us."

But who were they? Where had they come from? Simon and Rae hadn't been gone more than forty minutes. How had they gotten here so fast?

"Tori," I whispered.

"What?"

"Tori found out about our escape. That's why she was so quiet. She didn't give up; she was—"

"Doesn't matter. They're heading down that road," Derek said, pointing. "Come on."

He prodded me in the opposite direction.

"The factory is at the end. We just need to make it that far. Run on the grass—it's quieter."

We raced along the strip between the sidewalk and the road, our shoes slapping the driveway pavement, then silent on the grass between. We were three houses from the end, the factory looming, when Derek let out a curse. Within three strides, I knew why: there was an eight-foot-high chain-link fence around the factory parking lot, and the gate was padlocked.

"Up," he said.

I grabbed the links and started to climb. He tried to boost me, but I waved for him to forget that and follow. I was almost to the top when the side of the factory lit up in two circles of light. I glanced over my shoulder. The SUV's engine roared as it accelerated.

"Go, go, go!" Derek whispered.

The car slammed to a halt, brakes squealing. I flipped over the top and started scrambling down. Beside me, Derek crouched on the fence top, then jumped. He landed square on his feet and wheeled as the car door was flung open.

"Jump! I've got you."

I was already halfway down, but I let go. He caught me and spun me around onto my feet with a push toward the factory.

"Derek! Chloe!"

It was a woman's voice. I kept running, but had to glance back, hearing my name. A small gray-haired woman gripped the links. A stranger.

A man hurried around the front of the car. He carried a long, dark object, and as he lifted it, my heart stuttered.

"Gun!" I shouted, still running.

Derek glanced over at me, eyes wide.

"They have a—"

He tackled me just as something whooshed past. We

slid into a pile of wooden pallets. They clattered down around us, bouncing hard off my back and shoulders. I scrambled up and dove behind the next stack, then ran, hunched over, until we reached the factory wall.

We raced along the north side and ducked into a delivery dock bay. Derek pulled me behind a rusted metal bin.

"Th-they sh-shot at us," I whispered, barely able to get the words out. "No. I m-must have— A radio maybe. Or a cell phone. I made a mistake."

"You didn't." He twisted, reaching around his back.

"B-but they *sh-shot* at us. They tried to kill us. Th-that doesn't make any sense."

He plucked something from the bottom folds of his T-shirt. A long narrow metal tube with a pointed end.

"It caught in my shirt. It nicked me, but it shouldn't matter. It'd take a lot to knock me out."

"Knock you out?" I stared at it. "It's a tranquilizer dart?"

"I think so. Never seen one outside a nature show."

But we weren't animals. People didn't hunt kids with tranquilizer guns.

"I d-don't understand."

"Neither do I. Point is, they want us back. *Bad*. All the more reason to keep going." He dropped the dart and moved past me to the edge of the bin and inhaled, making no effort to hide it now. "Simon's here. He's not close, but he's been past recently."

"You can find him?"

"Yeah. Right now, though, I'm going to trust he can look after himself and worry about us. He'll lie low until he sees you. We should find a place to do the same until they move on."

He strode to the delivery doors, but they were locked and solid, the handles on the inside. I crept along the bin and scanned the factory yard.

"It looks like a warehouse back there. You mentioned something about that Friday? That it'd make a good place to hide?"

He glanced over my shoulder. "That one's too near the factory to be abandoned." He studied it. "But it'll do for now. I should be able to break in."

He surveyed the yard, then he hustled me along the dark wall, and we dashed across to the warehouse. A sharp wrench on the door and we were inside.

Derek was right: it wasn't abandoned. It was packed with rolls of steel, giving us lots of hiding places. I had to move slowly, feeling my way and following in Derek's tracks, testing each footstep for noise.

When we'd gone about twenty paces, he found a crevice and wedged us inside. We barely got in when a voice outside boomed.

"Derek? I know you're here. It's Dr. Davidoff."

I glanced at Derek, but he had his head turned toward the voice.

"Derek? I know you don't want to do this. You want to get better. You can't do that by running away."

The voice was moving, as the doctor walked through the factory yard. Derek cocked his head, listening, then whispered, "Four—no, five sets of footsteps. All separate. Searching."

Hoping we'd give ourselves away.

"Derek? You know you shouldn't be out here. It's not safe. We've talked about this, remember? You don't want to hurt anyone. I know that, and you know you need our help to get better."

I looked up. Derek's jaw worked, his gaze distant.

"I could go," he whispered. "Create a distraction so you can escape. Simon's around. You just need to find—"

"You're going *back*? After they shot at you?"

"Just tranquilizers."

"Just? *Just*?" My voice rose and I fought to keep it down. "They're hunting us, Derek. Dr. Gill knows what I am."

"*She* knew. That doesn't mean *they* do."

"Are you sure?"

He hesitated, his gaze lifting toward the voice.

"Derek?" Dr. Davidoff continued. "Please. I want to make this easy for you, but you need to make it easy for us. Come out now and we'll talk. That's it. Just talk. No disciplinary action will be taken and we won't transfer you."

Derek shifted against me. Considering.

"You can't—" I began.

"If you don't come out, Derek, we will find you, and you *will* be transferred . . . to a juvenile detention center for kidnapping Chloe."

"Kid—" I squawked.

He clapped his hand over my mouth until I motioned I'd be quiet.

Dr. Davidoff continued. "You already have a documented history of inappropriate behavior toward her. When the police see that, and hear our corroborating statements, you will be in a lot of trouble, Derek, and I know you don't want that. Even if she defends you, it won't matter to the police. You're a sixteen-year-old boy running away with a fourteen-year-old girl." He paused. "You do realize she's only fourteen, don't you, Derek?"

I shook my head vehemently and whispered, "He's lying. I turned fifteen last month."

Dr. Davidoff said, "To the police, it will be a clear case of kidnapping and interference, possibly even sexual assault."

"Sexual—!" I squeaked.

Derek's glare shut me up as effectively as his hand had.

"It's your choice, Derek. Make this hard, and you'll only hurt yourself."

Derek snorted and with that, Dr. Davidoff lost him. Prey on Derek's fears of hurting others, and he might be convinced to surrender. But threaten Derek himself? Like

Simon said, it was a whole different matter.

"Stay here," he whispered. "I'm going to find a way out."

I wanted to argue, insist on helping, but I didn't have his night vision. If I started stumbling around looking for an exit, I'd bring Dr. Davidoff and the others running.

I stayed put.

forty-three

AFTER A FEW MINUTES, Derek returned and wordlessly led me to the back wall, where a window had been broken. It must have been boarded over, but the board was now resting on the floor.

"Hold on."

He swept the broken glass from the lower sill, then laced his fingers into a step for me. As I crawled through, my sleeve snagged on a leftover shard.

A nearby door banged.

"Chloe? Derek? I know you're in here. The door was broken."

I yanked my sleeve free, feeling a sharp sting. The shard tinkled to the pavement below as I scrambled through.

I tumbled to the ground, recovered, and broke into a run, aiming for the nearest cover—a tarp over a lumber pile.

I dropped and crawled under it, Derek shoving me in farther. I found a spot where the tarp tented and stretched out on my stomach. The moment I caught my breath, my upper arm started to throb, telling me the glass had done more than scrape my skin.

"You're hurt," Derek whispered as if reading my mind.

"Just a scratch."

"No, it's not."

He grabbed my arm and pulled it straight. A stab of pain. I stifled a gasp. It was too dark to see, but the sleeve felt wet against my skin. Blood. He'd smelled it.

He gingerly rolled up my sleeve and swore.

"Bad?" I whispered.

"Deep. Gotta stop the bleeding. We need a bandage."

He released my arm. A flash of white, and I realized he was pulling off his T-shirt.

"Hold on," I said. "That's all you've got. I'm layered up."

He turned his head away. I stripped off all three shirts, gritting my teeth as the fabric brushed my wound. I reminded myself that I'd barely felt it before he told me it was bad.

I put the top two shirts back on and handed him my tee. He ripped it, the sound echoing. I must have looked alarmed, because he said, "No one's around. I can hear them searching the warehouse."

He wound the strips around my arm. Then his head lifted, tracking something, and I caught the faint sound of a voice calling, then an answer.

"They're all in the warehouse now," he whispered. "Time to move. I'll try picking up Simon's scent. Follow my lead."

Derek zigged and zagged through the obstacle course of debris, never slowing. Luckily, I was behind him, where he couldn't see how many times I rapped my knees or elbows swerving past some obstacle.

Finally, he slowed. "Got him," he whispered, and jabbed a finger at the south side of the factory. We steered that way. When we neared the corner, a figure leaned from a recessed doorway, then retreated fast. Simon. A moment later, Rae stepped out and waved wildly before being yanked back, presumably by Simon.

We raced over and found them in a deep narrow alcove that reeked of cigarette smoke and looked like a main entrance.

"What are you doing here?" Rae whispered, staring at Derek as if in alarm. "You're supposed to be—"

"Change of plans."

"Good to see you, bro," Simon said, slapping Derek's back. "I was worried Chloe'd never find us. There's a whole bunch of people looking for us."

"I know."

Simon moved to the edge, looked out, then walked over to me, handing me my backpack. "You okay?"

I nodded, keeping my injured arm out of sight. "They have guns."

"What?" Rae's eyes rounded. "No way. They'd never—"

"Tranq guns," Derek corrected.

"Oh." She nodded, as if tranquilizer guns were standard issue for tracking runaway kids.

"Who've you seen?" Derek asked Simon.

"Van Dop, Davidoff, and, I think, Talbot, but I'm not sure. No sign of Gill."

"She's back at the house," I said. "But there are two more we didn't recognize. A man and a woman." I looked at Derek. "Undercover cops, you think?"

"No idea. We'll worry about that later. Right now, we're sitting ducks. We need to get out of here."

As Derek moved to look out, Simon leaned down to my ear. "Thanks. For finding him. Was everything okay?"

"Later," Derek said. "There's another warehouse farther back, with broken windows. It's probably abandoned. If we can get to that—"

"Chloe?" Rae said, staring down at my arm. "What's all over your sleeve? It looks like . . ." She touched the fabric. "Oh, my God. You're bleeding. You're *really* bleeding."

Simon ducked around to my other side. "It's soaked. What—?"

"Just a cut," I said.

"It's deep," Derek said. "She needs stitches."

"I don't—"

"She needs stitches," he repeated. "I'll figure something out. For now—" He swore and jumped back from the opening. "They're coming." He looked around, scowling. "This is the lousiest hiding place . . ."

"I know," Simon said. "I wanted to find a better one, but . . ." A pointed look at Rae said she'd refused to leave.

"What's wrong with here?" she said. She backed up against the wall. "It's completely dark. They won't see me."

"Until they shine a flashlight on you."

"Oh."

Derek strode to the door, grabbed the handle, and gave it a test pull. Then he braced his feet, took the handle in both hands, and heaved until the tendons in his neck bulged. The door quivered, then flew open with a crack as loud as a gunshot.

He frantically waved us inside. "Find cover!" he whispered as I hurried past.

We raced through into a wide hall flanked with doors, some open, some closed. Rae headed for the first. Derek shoved her past.

"Keep going!" he whispered.

He loped by her and led us to a second hall. Then, he motioned for silence as he listened, but even without super senses, I heard the whoosh of the door and the clamor of footsteps.

"It's open!" a man yelled. "They came through here."

"We've got to get out," Derek whispered. "Split up. Find an exit. Any exit. Then whistle, but softly. I'll hear you."

forty-four

AROUND THE NEXT CORNER, we split up to search for an exit.

The first door I tried opened into a long, narrow room filled with worktables. No sign of a way out.

Back in the hall, I could hear voices, but distant, searching the rooms nearest the entrance, presuming we'd ducked into the first one we saw.

Hurrying toward the next door, I spotted a figure in the room across the hall. I stopped short, but too late. I was already standing in plain sight.

As I pulled my heart from my throat, I realized the man had his back to me. Dressed in jeans and a plaid shirt, he was the same size as the man with the gun, and had the same dark hair. I didn't remember the plaid shirt, but he'd been wearing a jacket.

He stood on a raised platform, gripping the railing, looking down at a big industrial saw. He seemed intent on whatever had caught his attention.

I took one careful step forward. When the man shifted, I froze, but he only seemed to be readjusting his grip on the railing. I lifted my foot. The man did the same—stepping onto the lower bar of the barrier.

He climbed onto the railing and crouched there, hands gripping the bar. Something moved below him and my gaze shot to the saw. The blades were turning—spinning so fast that the glint of a distant emergency light bounced off like a strobe. But there was no sound, not even the motor's hum.

The man tested his grip on the railing. Then, suddenly, he pitched forward. I saw him hit the blades, saw the first spray of blood, and I fell back against the wall, my hand flying to cover my mouth but not before the first note of a shriek escaped.

Something—some part of him—flew from the saw, landing in the doorway with a splat. I ripped my gaze away before I could see what it was, staggering back as running footsteps sounded behind me.

Arms grabbed me. I heard Simon's voice at my ear. "Chloe?"

"Th-there was a man. He—" I balled my hands into fists, pushing the image back. "A ghost. A man. He j-jumped onto a saw."

Simon pulled me against him, his hand going to the

back of my head, burying my face against his chest. He smelled of vanilla fabric softener with a trace of perspiration, oddly comforting. I lingered, catching my breath.

Derek wheeled around the corner. "What happened?"

"A ghost," I said, pulling away from Simon. "I'm sorry."

"Someone heard. We gotta go."

As I was turning, I saw the ghost again, standing on the platform. Derek followed my gaze. The ghost stood in exactly the same position, gripping the railing. Then he stepped up.

"It's r-repeating. Like a film loop." I shook it off. "Never mind. We—"

"Have to *go*," Derek said, pushing me. "Move!"

As we started down the hall, Rae let out a piercing whistle.

"Did I say softly?" Derek hissed under his breath.

We veered into Rae's hall to see her standing at a door marked EXIT. She reached for the handle.

"Don't!" Derek strode past her and cracked the door open, listening and sniffing before pushing it wide. "See that warehouse?"

"The one, like, a mile back there?" Rae said.

"Quarter mile, tops. Now go. We're right behind—" His head whipped up, tracking a sound. "They're coming. They heard the whistle. You guys go. I'll distract them, then follow."

"Uh-uh," Simon said. "I've got your back. Chloe, take Rae and run."

Derek opened his mouth to argue.

Simon cut him off. "You want distractions?" He whispered a spell and waved his hand, fog rising. "I'm your guy." He turned to me. "Go. We'll catch up."

I wanted to argue but, again, there was nothing I could offer. My powers had already proved more hindrance than help.

Rae was already twenty feet across the lot, dancing in place like a boxer, waving for me to hurry up.

As I turned to go, Derek shouldered past Simon. "Get in the warehouse and don't leave. For one hour, don't even peek out. If we don't come, find a place to hole up. We'll be back."

Simon nodded. "Count on it."

"Don't stay in the warehouse if it's dangerous, but that'll be our rendezvous point. Keep checking in. If you can't stay, find a way to leave a note. We *will* meet you there. Got it?"

I nodded.

"They must be back here," someone called. "Search every room."

Derek shoved me through the doorway.

Simon leaned out, mouthing "I'll see you soon," with a thumbs-up, then he turned to Derek. "Show time."

I started to run.

forty-five

WE WAITED IN THE WAREHOUSE for one hour and forty minutes.

"They caught them," I whispered.

Rae shrugged. "Maybe not. Maybe they saw their chance to get away and they took it."

A protest rose to my lips, but I swallowed it. She was right. If they had the opportunity to escape and no easy way of alerting us, I'd want them to take it.

I lifted my numb rear off the ice-cold cement. "We'll wait here a bit longer, then we'll go. If they got away, they'll hook up with us later."

Rae shook her head. "I wouldn't count on it, Chloe. It's like I said, the way they act, the way they behave, it's always us against them, and 'us' means the two of them. No one else, except maybe that missing dad of theirs." She shifted into a crouch. "Did they even give you any idea where they think he is? Or why he hasn't come for them?"

"No, but—"

"I'm not arguing, I'm just saying . . ." She crawled to the opening and peeked out. "It's like last year, when I went out with this guy. He was part of a clique at school. The 'cool kids.'" She added the quotes with her fingers. "And, sure, I kinda liked getting to hang with them. I thought it'd make me one of them. Only it didn't. They were nice enough, but they'd been friends since, like, third grade. Just because I had an in didn't mean I'd ever be one of them. You've got these superpowers. That gives you cred with Simon and Derek. But . . ." She turned my way. "You've only known them for a week. When push comes to shove . . ."

"Their first priority is each other. I know that. And I'm not saying you're wrong, just—"

"Simon's nice to you and all, sure. I see that. But—" She nibbled her lip, then slowly lifted her gaze to mine. "When you were back there, looking for Derek, it wasn't you Simon was worrying about. He didn't even mention you. It was all about Derek."

Of course he was worried about Derek. Derek was his brother; I was some girl he met a week ago. But it still stung a little that he hadn't mentioned me at *all*.

I'd been about to tell Rae about the part of the plan she missed, to make this our permanent rendezvous point, and keep checking back. But now it would sound like I was trying to prove the guys hadn't turned their backs on me. How pathetic was that?

I still thought they'd come back after things died down. It had nothing to do with whether Simon liked me or not. They'd come back because it was the right thing to do. Because they said they would. And maybe that makes me a silly girl who's watched too many movies where the good guy always comes back to save the day. But it's what I believed.

That did not, however, mean I was sitting here like an action-flick girlfriend, twiddling her thumbs waiting for rescue. I might be naive, but I wasn't stupid. We'd set a rendezvous point, so there was no need to stick around any longer.

I crawled from our cubbyhole, looked, and listened. I waved Rae out.

"First thing I need to do is get money," I said. "I've got my dad's but we might need more. There's a daily withdrawal limit, and that's probably all I'll get, so I have to act fast, before they put a trace on it or freeze the account. Derek said the nearest ATM was—"

"What are you doing?" Rae asked.

"What?"

She took hold of my arm and pointed at the blood. "You don't need money; you need a doctor."

I shook my head. "I can't go to a hospital. Even if they haven't put out an APB on me yet, I'm too young. They'd call my Aunt Lauren—"

"I *meant* your Aunt Lauren. She's a doctor, isn't she?"

"N-no. I can't. She'd just take us back—"

"After they shot at us? I know you're mad at her right now, but you've told me how she's always worrying about you, always looking out for you, defending you. If you show up at her front door and say that Davidoff and his buds *shot* at you, even with tranquilizers, do you really think she'll march you back to Lyle House?"

"That depends on whether she believes me. A week ago, yes. But now?" I shook my head. "When she was talking to me about Derek, it was like I wasn't even Chloe anymore. I'm a schizophrenic. I'm paranoid and I'm delusional. She won't believe me."

"Then tell me exactly what the gun and the dart looked like, and I'll say I saw it, too. No, wait! The dart. Derek pulled one out of his shirt, right? Do you know where it is?"

"I—I think so." I thought back, pictured him dropping it in the delivery bay. "Yes, I know exactly where it is."

"Then let's go get it."

It wasn't that easy. For all we knew, the factory yard was swarming with cops searching for two teen runaways. But when we looked out, the only people we saw were a half-dozen factory workers, heading in to work Sunday overtime, laughing and talking, lunch pails swinging, takeout coffees steaming.

I took off my blood-soaked sweatshirt and swapped it for

Liz's hoodie. Then we crept out, moving from cover to cover. No sign of anyone looking for us. That made sense. How many teenagers run away in Buffalo every day? Even escaping from a home for disturbed kids wouldn't warrant a full-out manhunt.

Last night, it had probably been only Lyle House employees chasing us. Maybe board members, like Tori's mother, more worried about the home's reputation than our safety. If they wanted to keep our escape quiet, they'd be gone before any factory employees arrived. By now they were probably in a meeting, deciding what to do and when to notify our parents—and the police.

I found the dart easily, and put it into my backpack. Then we headed for the business district, looping three blocks past Lyle House and keeping our eyes open. Nothing happened. We found a pay phone, I called for a cab, and gave the driver Aunt Lauren's address.

Aunt Lauren lived in a duplex near the university. When we walked up her steps, the *Buffalo News* was still there. I picked it up and rang the bell.

After a minute, a shadow passed behind the curtain. Locks clanked and the door flew open. Aunt Lauren stood there in a short bathrobe, hair wet.

"Chloe? Oh my God. Where—" She pulled the door open. "What are you doing here? Are you okay? Is everything all right?"

She tugged me inside by my injured arm and I tried not to wince. Her gaze shot to Rae.

"Aunt Lauren, this is Rae. From Lyle House. We need to talk to you."

As we went inside, I did a proper introduction. Then I told her the whole story. Well, the edited version. Very edited, with no mention of zombies, magic, or werewolves. The boys had been planning to run away and they'd invited us. We'd gone along just for fun—to get out, goof off, then go back later. Knowing Aunt Lauren didn't care for Dr. Gill, I included the part about her attacking me in the yard with her wild accusations. Then I told her about the gun.

She stared down at the dart, lying on her coffee table, on top of a stack of *New Yorker* magazines. She picked it up, gingerly, as if it might detonate, and turned it over in her hands.

"It's a tranquilizer dart," she said, voice barely above a whisper.

"That's what we thought."

"But— They shot this at you? At *you*?"

"At us."

She slumped back, leather squeaking under her.

"I was there, Dr. Fellows," Rae said. "Chloe's telling the truth."

"No, I—" She lifted her gaze to mine. "I believe you, hon. I just can't believe— This is so completely . . ." She shook her head.

"Where did you find Lyle House?" I asked.

She blinked. "Find?"

"How did you find it for me? In the yellow pages? Through a recommendation?"

"It came highly recommended, Chloe. *Very* highly. Someone at the hospital told me about it and I did all my research. Their recovery rate is excellent and they had glowing reports from patients and their families. I can't believe this happened."

So I hadn't randomly arrived at Lyle House. It'd been recommended. Did that mean anything? I fingered Liz's hoodie and thought about us—all of us. No ordinary group home would track runaways with tranquilizer guns. The ghost had been right. There was a reason we'd been at Lyle House and now, withholding the truth from Aunt Lauren, I could be putting her into danger.

"About the ghosts . . ." I began.

"You mean what that Gill woman said?" Aunt Lauren slapped the dart back onto the magazines with such force that the pile fell, magazines sliding across the glass table-top. "The woman is obviously in need of mental help herself. Thinking you can communicate with ghosts? One whiff of that to a review board and her license will be revoked. She'll be lucky if she isn't committed. No sane person believes people can speak to the dead."

Okay, forget the confession . . .

Aunt Lauren rose. "I'm going to start by calling your

father, then my lawyer, and *he* can contact Lyle House."

"Dr. Fellows?"

Aunt Lauren turned to Rae.

"Before you do that, you'd better take a look at Chloe's arm."

forty-six

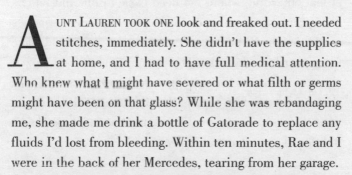

AUNT LAUREN TOOK ONE look and freaked out. I needed stitches, immediately. She didn't have the supplies at home, and I had to have full medical attention. Who knew what I might have severed or what filth or germs might have been on that glass? While she was rebandaging me, she made me drink a bottle of Gatorade to replace any fluids I'd lost from bleeding. Within ten minutes, Rae and I were in the back of her Mercedes, tearing from her garage.

I dozed off before we reached the first traffic light. I supposed all those sleepless nights had something to do with that. Being in Aunt Lauren's car helped, with its familiar smell of berry air freshener and its soft beige leather seats and the faded blue spot where I'd spilled a slushie three years ago. Back home. Back to normal.

I knew it wasn't that simple. I wasn't back to normal.

And Derek and Simon were still out there and I was worried about them. But even that worry seemed to fade as the car bumped along, like I was leaving it behind in another life. A dream life. Part nightmare, part . . . not.

Raising the dead, escaping from the clutches of an evil doctor, tearing through abandoned warehouses with people shooting at me. It all seemed so unreal in this familiar car, the radio station tuned to WJYE, my aunt laughing at something Rae said about her choice of music, saying I complained, too. So familiar. So normal. So comforting.

And, yet, even as I drifted off, I clung to the memories of that other life, where the dead came to life and fathers disappeared and sorcerers conducted horrific experiments and buried the bodies under the house and boys could make fog appear from their fingertips or turn into wolves. Now it was over and it was like waking up to discover I couldn't see ghosts anymore. The feeling that I'd missed out on something that would make my life tougher but might also make it different. An adventure. Special.

I woke to Aunt Lauren shaking me.

"I know you're tired, hon. Just come on inside and you can go back to sleep."

I stumbled out of the car. She caught me, Rae diving in to help.

"Is she okay?" Rae asked my aunt. "She lost a lot of blood."

"She's exhausted. You both must be."

When the cold air hit, I yawned and gave my head a sharp shake. I could make out a building in front of me. I blinked hard and it came into focus. A yellow brick rectangle with a single, unmarked door.

"Is this the hospital?"

"No, it's a walk-in clinic. I called Buffalo General and Mercy and their emergencies are packed. A typical Sunday morning. Between the Saturday night gunshot wounds and the drunk drivers, it's a zoo. I know a doctor here and we'll get you straight in."

She looked up as a small, gray-haired woman rounded the corner. "Oh, there's Sue. She's a nurse here. Rae, Sue's going to take you over to the waiting room, get you some breakfast, and check you over."

I peered at the woman as I struggled to focus. She looked familiar. When she stopped to talk to my aunt, I realized she must be her friend. But even after she walked away, it niggled at the back of my foggy brain, some connection I wasn't getting.

It wasn't until we were inside that I remembered where I'd seen her. Just last night, clutching the chain-link fence, calling my name.

I wheeled on Aunt Lauren. "That woman—"

"Sue, yes. She's a nurse here. She'll take good care of—"

"No! I saw her last night with the man who shot at us."

Aunt Lauren's face crumpled and she put her arm

around me. "No, honey, that's not the same woman. You've been through a lot and you're confused—"

I pushed her away. "I'm not. I saw her. Is she the one who recommended Lyle House? We need to get out of here."

I ducked out of her grasp and raced back to the door. I grabbed the handle, but she caught up, holding it shut.

"Chloe, listen to me. You need to—"

"I need to get out." I pulled on the door with both hands, but she held it fast. "Please, Aunt Lauren, you don't understand. We have to get out of here."

"Would someone please help Dr. Fellows?" a voice echoed down the hall. I turned to see Dr. Davidoff striding toward us.

A man hurried past him, coming at me with a syringe.

"That won't be necessary, Marcel," Aunt Lauren snapped. "I've already given her something."

"And I can see it's working very well. Bruce, sedate Chloe, please."

I looked up at Aunt Lauren. "Y-you drugged me?"

Her arms went around me. "You'll be okay, hon. I promise."

I lashed out, hitting her so hard she stumbled back. Then she turned on Dr. Davidoff.

"I told you this wasn't the way to handle it. I told you to leave it to me."

"Leave what to you?" I said, taking a slow step back and hitting the door.

She reached for me, but my hands flew up, warding her off. "Leave what to you?"

The man with the syringe caught my arm. I tried to yank away, but the needle went in. Aunt Lauren stepped toward me, mouth opening. Then a woman hurried down the hall, calling to Dr. Davidoff.

"The team just called in a report, sir. There's no sign of the boys."

"Surprise, surprise," Aunt Lauren said, turning to Dr. Davidoff. "Kit taught them well. Once they're gone, they'll keep running. I warned you."

"We'll find them."

"You'd better, and when you do, I expect that brute to be handled the way he should have been handled years ago. Put down like a rabid dog. Wait until you see what he did to Chloe's arm."

"D-Derek?" I struggled against the pull of the sedative. "Derek didn't do this. I cut myself—"

Aunt Lauren caught me as I slid down the wall. I tried to push her away, but my arms wouldn't respond. She shouted for them to hurry with the stretcher, then leaned over me, holding me steady.

"You don't need to cover for him, Chloe," she whispered. "We know what he is." A glare back at Dr. Davidoff. "A monster. One that didn't belong in the . . ."

I didn't catch her next few words. The hall flickered, fading.

When I focused, I saw her face over mine. "But we won't let him hurt Simon, Chloe. I promise you that. When you wake up, you're going to help us find Simon and bring him home. I know he's important to you. He's important to all of us. You all are. You and Rachelle and Simon and Victoria. Very special. You're—"

Everything went dark.

forty-seven

I LAY AWAKE, STARING AT the wall. I couldn't bring myself to roll over and look around. Couldn't even bother lifting my head from the pillow. I could feel the pull of the sedative, luring me back into sleep, but I kept my eyes open, gaze fixed on the green painted wall.

Aunt Lauren had betrayed me.

When she'd thought I'd been fooling around with Derek, I'd felt betrayed. Now I looked back on how furious I'd been and my throat tightened as I prayed I could go back there, to where that was the worst thing I could ever imagine her doing.

It was all a lie.

She was a lie. Our relationship was a lie.

Even when I was a child seeing bogeymen in the basement, she'd known perfectly well I was seeing ghosts. My mother knew it—that's why she'd insisted we move.

I fingered my necklace. Was this more than a silly talisman to convince me I was safe? Did my mother really think it would protect me? Is that why Aunt Lauren had insisted I wear it at Lyle House? Simon said necromancy was hereditary. If both my mother and my aunt had known about the ghosts, it must run in their blood.

Did my father know? Was that why he stayed away from me? Because I was a freak?

I thought about my mother. About the accident. The hit-and-run driver had never been found. Had it really been an accident? Or had someone killed—?

No. I squeezed the thought from my brain as I clutched the pillow tighter. I couldn't let my mind start running away like that or I'd go crazy.

Crazy.

Aunt Lauren knew I wasn't crazy, and she let me think I was. Shipped me off to a group home.

A group home filled with other supernatural kids.

When Aunt Lauren said we were special, she'd included Rae. So she must really be one of those half-demons. What about Tori? What was she? Did her mother know? If her mother worked for them, she must know, and if she did, and blamed Tori for not getting better . . .

What kind of parent would do that?

But hadn't my aunt done the same thing? Only she sweetened it with smiles and hugs and maybe that was worse. Right now, it felt worse.

Was Lyle House where they sent us when things went wrong? Put us there and medicated us and tried to tell us we had a mental illness? But why? Wouldn't the truth be easier? Why not tell us when we were young and prepare us, and teach us how to control it?

From what Simon said, that's the way it was supposed to work. You told your kids and you trained them how to use and hide their powers *before* they lost control.

What was Lyle House?

I remembered what Simon said about his dad.

He worked for this research company, supernatural doctors and scientists trying to make things easier for other supernaturals.

Then I heard the ghost of the witch buried in the basement.

Sam Lyle promised us an easier life. That's what we all want, isn't it? Power without price . . . You see, little girl, all scientific advancement requires experimentation, and experimentation requires subjects, and that's what Michael and I were. Lab rats sacrificed to the vision of a madman.

I leaped up, heart thudding so hard I couldn't breathe.

Aunt Lauren said we were special. All of us. Rae and Simon and Tori and me.

But not Derek.

I expect that brute to be handled the way he should have been handled years ago. Put down like a rabid dog.

I had to find Derek before they did.

I turned around, seeing my surroundings. A double bed with big pillows and a thick comforter. Carpet on the floor. A desk. An armchair. A private bathroom through a half-open door. Like a fancy hotel room.

Across the room was a door, painted white. It looked like any interior door, but when I walked over and put my hands against it, it was cold steel. A thick steel door with no window, not even a peephole.

And no doorknob.

Wherever I was, it wasn't a fake group home where I had the run of the house and yard, had chores, classes, and field trips. I was in this room, and I wasn't getting out.

I backed up to the bed.

I was trapped. I'd never escape, never—

Oh, that's great. You've been awake five minutes, taken a quick look around, and given up. Why don't you just lie back and wait for them to come and strap you to a table? What did that witch say? Something about being prodded with electrical wires until she bit off her tongue?

I let out a whimper.

And what about Derek? He got you out of Lyle House and now you aren't even going to try to warn him? Just let them catch him? Kill him?

Derek wouldn't get caught. He was too smart for that. He got out of Lyle House—

He got you *out of Lyle House? He didn't plan to go. That was a total fluke. Remember when Dr. Davidoff tried to call him back? He almost went. What happens if they do that again? Maybe he'll have had second thoughts, decide he really is better off locked away.*

Not as long as he has to protect Simon.

Ah, Simon. Derek will never turn in Simon. But what about distracting them so Simon can escape, like he did for you and Rae? If he thinks turning himself in will let Simon escape, he'll do it. You know he will.

I had to warn him. But to warn him, I had to get out of here. This time, I couldn't just sit back and let someone else make the plans. I had to do it myself.

Maybe I was locked in here for now, but I'd be let out eventually. I wasn't exactly a high-risk prisoner. They'd take me out—for exercise, to eat, to experiment on me . . .

I tried not to think about the last.

Point was, I'd get out, and when I did, I needed to be ready to escape. First, though, I had to get a good look around and plan. But how was I going to do that locked in this room? Pray for a convenient blueprint stuffed under the mattress? Astral-project out the door and look around?

I stopped and slowly looked down at the sweater I wore. Liz's green hoodie.

If she was dead, maybe I could summon her, get her to scout the building and—

If she's dead? So you're hoping she's dead now?

I clenched the comforter and took a deep breath. For

days now, I'd refused to believe Liz had died. No matter how much proof I had, I couldn't believe it because the very idea was insane.

But now, sitting here, locked in this room, betrayed by my aunt, waiting for them to track down and kill Derek like some kind of animal . . .

Liz was dead.

They'd killed her.

She'd been a supernatural of some kind, and her powers were out of control, so they executed her. They must have or they would have included her in that list. And what about Peter? Had his parents pretended to pick him up only to let these people kill him? Or maybe because he got better, he got out. Liz didn't get better . . . so she didn't get out.

Some tiny part of me still clung to the hope that I was wrong about Liz. But I knew I wasn't.

I pulled off the hoodie. I saw my arm, rebandaged. Stitched up, while I'd been unconscious. If they were fixing me, at least that meant they didn't plan to kill me yet.

I stared at the hoodie, thinking of Liz and of dying. Of what it would be like to be dead at sixteen, the rest of your life gone—?

I squeezed my eyes shut. No time for that.

I searched my room for cameras. I didn't find any, but that didn't mean there wasn't one. If they saw me talking to myself, they'd figure out what I was doing, maybe decide my powers were out of control, like Liz's.

Either I did this or I didn't. My choice.

I sat cross-legged on the bed, holding Liz's hoodie, and called her as I'd done the other ghosts. I didn't need to worry about overdoing it and raising the dead. There were no corpses here. Or so I hoped. But I had no idea what was outside my door, maybe a laboratory, maybe the bodies of other failures, like Liz—

No time for that.

The ghost necromancer had said Lyle House was protected by a spell blocking ghosts. That meant this place probably was, too, which meant I needed all that extra power he said I had.

I concentrated so hard my temples hurt, but nothing happened.

I closed my eyes to visualize better, but I kept peeking and breaking my focus. Finally I shut them and kept them shut, putting everything I had into imagining myself pulling Liz out of the ether and—

"Whoa. Where am I?"

I opened my eyes and there she was, still wearing her Minnie Mouse nightshirt and giraffe socks.

Liz.

No, Liz's ghost.

"Hello?" She waved a hand in front of my eyes. "What's wrong, Chloe? There's nothing to be scared of. I know, Lyle House isn't exactly Disneyland but—" She looked around, brow furrowing. "This isn't Lyle House, is it? Where—? Oh my God. We're in the hospital. They put you in here, too. When?"

She blinked hard, shaking her head. "They have some funky meds here. I keep sleeping and having these dreams, and when I wake up, I'm totally confused. Did they give you those, too?"

So where had Liz been all this time? Stuck in limbo? One thing was for sure. She didn't know she was dead. And now I had to tell her.

Tell her? No way. She was happy. If she didn't know, that was better.

And how long do you think it'll be before she figures it out? Shouldn't you be the one to tell her?

I didn't want to. I really, really didn't want to. But I needed her to help me escape and rescue Rae and warn Simon and Derek. It was all on me this time, and to help them, I needed to do something awful.

Fingers trembling, I clutched her hoodie and took a deep breath.

"Liz? There's something I need to tell you."

the DARKEST POWERS series
will continue . . .

I SQUEEZED MY EYES SHUT and imagined myself pulling Liz through the ether. Just one big, quick yank and—

A throaty laugh sent me scrambling to my feet. I spun, but still saw only the empty room.

"Y-you're not Liz."

The laugh circled me, spinning faster and faster until it seemed to stream from every corner of the room.

"Who are you?"

The laughter broke off in a chuckle. Warm air slid along my unbandaged forearm.

I yanked my sleeve down. "*What* are you?"

"A better question."

That warm air tickled my cheek. I rubbed at it, backing up until I hit the wall.

"What are *you*, child? That is the question. When you called to your friend, the spirits of a thousand dead answered, winging their way back to their rotted shells, screaming for mercy. Do you know where those shells are?"

"N-no."

"In a cemetery. Two miles away. A thousand corpses ready to become a thousand zombies. A vast army of the dead for you to control."

"I didn't—"

"No, you didn't. Not yet. Your powers need time to mature. And then?" That throaty laugh filled the room. "Dear Dr. Lyle must be dancing in Hell today, his agonies borne away on the thrill of his triumph."

"Samuel Lyle?"

"Is there another? Dearly departed, scarcely lamented, deeply demented Dr. Samuel Lyle," the voice sang, sailing past me on a current of warm air. "Creator of the prettiest, sweetest abomination I have ever seen."

"Wh-what?"

"A bit of this, a bit of that," she sang. "A twist here, a tweak there. And look what we have. One perfect ball of energy, waiting to explode." The voice came closer, breeze ruffling my hair. "Are there more of you, child? There must be. Little magic makers and monsters, bursting with energy. Have your creators realized their mistake yet?"